THE #VANLIFE MURDERS

A NOVEL

TAYLOR CLUSTER

The #Vanlife Murders

Copyright © 2020 by Taylor Cluster

All rights reserved. No part of this book may be reproduced in any manner whatsoever without written permission except in the case of brief quotations embodied in articles and reviews. For more information, email info@giantsaguaromedia.com.

Printed by Amazon KDP, in The United States of America.
First printing edition 2020

Cover Art by Nick Blair
Chapter Icon Art by Mite Cholakov

ISBN 978-1-7352594-0-6 (pbk)
ISBN 978-1-7352594-1-3 (ebook)

Library of Congress Control Number 2020943096

www.vanlifemurders.com

Dedicated to all the full-time travellers out there, whether living unconventional lives out of vans, RV's, or whatever your means may be; you have inspired me and without you, I'd probably be working behind a nine-to-five desk dreaming of what life would be like on the open road.

"Twenty years from now you will be more disappointed by the things you didn't do than by the ones you did do.

So throw off the bowlines, sail away from the safe harbor. Catch the trade winds in your sails.

Explore. Dream. Discover."

—Mark Twain

THE #VANLIFE MURDERS

Prologue

Hannah took another gasp of the freezing mountain air as she ran through the dark moonlit forest.

"Charlie! Charlie!" she cried out, but he was surely gone by now. The only thing she could hear was the pounding of adrenaline-filled blood rushing through her veins, so loud in her ears that she could barely hear her own panicked thoughts of how she might survive in this moment.

Where the hell was Charlie?? How could her loyal companion just run off into the night without hesitation? He never strayed from the campsite, but when she finally had her ideal scene put together, he was nowhere to be found.

It was early spring, but the frigid chill of winter was still lingering in Yosemite National Park. She had come here with the intention to take the perfect picture for her Instagram feed to announce and thank all of her followers for their love and support in contributing to her goal of five-hundred thousand followers. It was scenes like this that would be liked and commented on by thousands of the app's users who helped her officially rise to her status as a "super influencer."

It was everything she hoped it would be. With her Aztec blanket laid out just right, topped with decorative pillows, a small wooden table that held a mug of steaming hot chocolate, and a plate of strategically placed marshmallows, graham crackers, and Ghiardelli chocolate squares, she had created a delectable scene. The twinkle lights were draped from a white beadboard ceiling—a ceiling that had been added to insulate the space but really served as a way to add charm to an otherwise drab VW Bus ceiling. The rear door to the van was positioned wide open, welcoming the world inside her tiny, yet glamorous, vanlife on the road.

Before she hit the timer on her camera to capture the picture-perfect moment, she needed to add everyone's favorite prop in her photographs: her best friend, Charlie. Charlie was a six-and-a-half-pound Maltese that deserved the credit for most of her followers because who didn't love to see a cute dog camping at a delicately crafted campsite? A campsite that no doubt had been upgraded to a 'glampsite' once she added all the bells and whistles to create the most dynamic camping scene for her Instagram post that her followers craved to see.

But as she looked around, Charlie was nowhere to be seen. She assumed he had run off to sniff the bushes and trees around the campsite, his typical routine when they arrived somewhere new, taking a survey of the area and all the new smells of other animals that had crossed the same path. Yet when she called his name, he didn't come trotting back. She listened intently for the tags of his collar to clap together while he happily scampered back to her, but the clicking of his tags never came. The forest was silent. Her stomach began to knot as goose bumps ran up her back. Something was wrong.

She reached into the side shelf that was at the end of the kitchenette inside of the van and grabbed her spotlight. Holding it out in front of her, she scanned the surrounding woods for any signs of Charlie. Her body felt stiff, and her hands began to shake as she gazed deep into the dark woods for any signs of movement, but the only movements she saw were the shadows that jumped between the trees as she slowly shined her light across each tall, thick trunk.

A branch snapped behind her in the darkness. "Char-lie?" Her whisper cracked as she pivoted towards the sound.

Out of the darkness, a shadowy figure rushed towards her. Having no time to think, her flight instinct kicked in, and she began sprinting through the wilderness as fast as her legs could take her. Pine needles whipped across her face as she stumbled across the bumpy forest floor blanketed with tree roots and clumps of velvet grass.

She ran with no particular safe haven in mind. Not knowing who or what was out there, she couldn't be sure whether she was running towards safety or back to the faceless figure. Tears began to roll down her cheeks as she realized that Charlie may have already been captured, and she was next.

A crack echoed through the wilderness as another twig broke, this time only a few feet away. Hannah froze. She squinted her eyes as she tried to see beyond the snow covered branches, beyond the darkness that filled the space around her. Her body quivered involuntarily as the cold air swept across the sweat droplets that formed at the nape of her neck. She tried to remain quiet and steady her breathing as she listened for any indication of where the figure stood. As the silence persisted, she could feel her heart expanding with fear.

All of a sudden, cold hands wrapped around her neck. One final, desperate, terrified scream escaped her lungs, piercing the silence of the night, before a strong grasp crushed down on her windpipe. Hannah struggled beneath the clutch until the moonlit sky faded to black.

Chapter 1

Hailey set the second bedside lamp down on the faded, white, pop-up table. As she stepped back and looked at the items set up on the driveway, she couldn't help but feel lost. Books, coasters, vases, and un-used kitchenware, which used to represent the happy unification of two people, now only held broken promises, lay strewn out on tables.

Three months. That's all it took. Three months for her perfect life plan to fall apart.

A month before graduation from USC in Los Angeles, Hailey had managed to land a public relations position with a Fortune 500 company in San Diego. It wasn't her dream job, but it was a step towards her passion of becoming an investigative reporter. A baby step to say the least, but she knew she was lucky to land a spot at such a well-ranked company. While she was busy getting ready to start her new position in San Diego, Jeremy found them a quaint little place just outside of the city. They had been dating since their sophomore year of college and decided after graduation that it would be the perfect time to take the plunge and move in together.

Everything seemed to be aligning according to plan, but just as quickly as her life seemed to be falling into place, it began to crumble.

A mere couple of weeks into her new position, for reasons she had yet to understand or justify, Hailey was let go. She now felt more defeated than she could ever remember. The mornings she used to spend quickly consuming her coffee and watching the news before work, she now spent curled up on the couch in her pajamas as she mindlessly scrolled through multiple job boards. Her full-time job had turned into searching for a full-time job. As she spent her days writing cover letters and sending in job applications, Jeremy spent his going to his sales job in the city.

The stress of searching for a job day in and day out was building more and more with every click of the mouse. It wasn't long before Hailey no longer wanted to attend happy hours or nights out with Jeremy and his co-workers. As Hailey spent her nights sitting at home feeling discouraged and rejected, Jeremy spent his out on the town without her. Each week he would leave home earlier and stumble home later and later. Soon he stopped returning home after work, and the chair at the table would remain empty across from her as she would eat another dinner alone.

Naturally, Hailey grew distant as his behavior persisted. Instead of trying to lift her confidence and support her during the tough transition, Jeremy had told her that she was becoming too depressing to be around. He started to go out on the weekends without her, stumbling home after the bars had closed. She convinced herself that things would get better, that they were just hitting a rough patch as they transitioned into life after college, until one Friday evening, Jeremy never came home.

Hailey had stared up at the ceiling as she lay awake in bed, ritually listening for him to fumble with his keys as he tried to find the keyhole just past two a.m., just like all the previous nights. But something didn't feel right this time. She looked at the clock; three-thirty and still no sign of Jeremy. She chalked it up to him missing his Uber, or getting a late night bite with his buddies after the bars had closed, but when she looked at the clock at a quarter past four and hadn't received any calls or texts from him, she knew, it was over.

The following weekend, she watched, fighting back tears, as Jeremy packed up his clothes and family heirlooms into cardboard boxes. She stood in the archway of the kitchen as he walked out their front door for the last time. When the door slammed shut, Hailey realized she had been holding her breath. Holding back her pain.

As she stood in front of her seemingly bright and beautiful home, she saw nothing but the ending to a chapter in her life. She looked at her belongings, knowing she was making the right decision. It was time for a new start, and what better way to start fresh than to get rid of every material item she had that reminded her of her past?

After Jeremy left, when she wasn't spending countless hours online flipping through job boards, she was mindlessly scrolling through Instagram. It wasn't hard to get lost down a rabbit hole scrolling through the pages of complete strangers and feeling envious of the adventurous and jovial lives they appeared to lead.

One night, as she curled up on the couch with a bowl of pasta and a glass of wine, she found herself spiraling deep into the accounts and feeds of travel influencers. While scrolling through the pages of a couple who had over four hundred thousand followers, she decided to click the link in their bio that rerouted her to their travel blog. It wasn't the type of travel blog she had seen before. Instead of flying to different destinations around the world, the couple was traveling across different countries in an RV. Hailey became immersed in their journey. Before she knew it, it became a ritual each night to scroll through Instagram and find as many people as she could that had RV and van-conversion travel blogs that she would read until her eyes grew heavy.

This was just the inspiration she needed. She had wanted to try something new, something that would be different from the conventional life she had been living so far—something that would put her outside of her comfort zone. This was it! Instead of searching for her next job, she decided it was time to start her next adventure of searching for a van.

For the first time in weeks, she felt a flicker of hope as she nestled down at the makeshift card table desk she positioned in the back corner of the driveway early on a Saturday morning. After writing in giant letters "Garage Sale" with a giant arrow on a piece of neon pink poster board, she walked to the end of the street and taped the board to a large cardboard box that Jeremy hadn't used. She was ready to get rid of the pieces of her old life to open up space for new memories to be made.

It was the middle of June, hot in most places, but being in Southern California, it was a pleasant seventy-seven degrees outside. Hailey remained sitting at the table most of the morning but would occasionally get up and take a lap around her makeshift thrift store, rearranging and consolidating displays where items had been bought, leaving gaps behind. She thought it was odd the "FREE" table was the least popular of all, but at least there was a Goodwill nearby where she could drop off her items that didn't sell.

After walking through the maze of tables and chairs she had created on the driveway, she decided to stop and rearrange the CD's to keep herself busy. As she began flipping through the discs, she couldn't stop the memories of Jeremy from resurfacing in her mind. She picked up a Sublime disc and turned it over to read the titles, as if she didn't already know what they were. It felt like just yesterday she was riding shotgun in Jeremy's car, volume on high, as they sat in LA traffic and sang along to every song together. By the time she read the last title, she could feel her chest getting tight as she tried to suppress her emotions. Now was not the time to have an emotional breakdown.

Her flashback was interrupted by a man's voice. "I didn't think kids your age even bought these things anymore," he chuckled.

Recognizing her neighbor's voice, she turned around with a somber smile. "Somehow I ended up with the only car that doesn't have an auxiliary port, so this was the only way I could listen to my music." Her eyes fell back to the discs as she continued, "But these CDs hold too many memories that I don't care to be reminded of, so I'm hoping this garage sale will take some of them off my hands."

His eyes were soft as he picked up an Offspring disc. "I'm sorry to hear about you and Jeremy." He paused and looked up to her for a reaction, but she didn't have one to offer. His gaze fell as he shuffled through the discs. "My wife mentioned that she saw him pack his things up in his truck."

Hailey merely nodded, confirming his assumption.

His lips cracked a side-smile. "We thought you were too good for him anyway."

Hailey smirked as she looked up at him with genuine eyes. "Thank you, John. You and Ilene have always been so kind to me."

He nodded in response as he changed the subject. "Do you mind if I take a look around to see what other treasures I may fill my garage with that Ilene will inevitably say I don't need?"

Hailey laughed at his remark. "Not at all. Please, take your time." She took this opportunity to walk back over to her table and added, "Let me know if you have any questions."

As she slid into her chair, she felt a wave of exhaustion wash over her. She was also suddenly aware of how sore her body was from spending the previous night moving all the items she wanted to sell into her garage, including a giant reclining chair. Grateful the sale wasn't too busy at the moment, Hailey took a deep breath and allowed herself to relax.

John casually perused the items laid out on the tables, picking one up from time to time to get a closer look. "So, what's your plan now?" He asked, while facing away from her inspecting a giant Ninja blender that Jeremy had bought during his crazy workout phase, when he decided every meal needed to be a protein shake. Hailey watched him fumble with the cords of the blender as she bit her bottom lip, thinking of how to answer his inquiry.

"I've been thinking about maybe taking a road trip across the country. Seems like the right time for a new adventure," she responded.

He began coiling the cord around the base of the blender as he tilted his head towards her with a questioning look. Before he could make a judgment on the matter, Hailey began defending her plan, unsure whether she was trying to convince John or herself that it was a good one.

"I don't have anything holding me here, you know?" Hailey stood up and winced as her tired thighs rebelled against her movements. "I don't have a job, no boyfriend anymore, and no pets or kids. So really, what do I have holding me back?" John listened with an unphased expression, sensing the hesitation in her voice.

She looked up at him, searching his eyes for signs of judgment or disapproval. To her surprise, his face softened as he responded, "You know, my wife and I have an old Ford conversion van in the side yard. It hasn't seen adventure in years, and Ilene has been pushing me to get rid of it. We got it back when the kids were little. It was perfect then and had so much space. It even had a TV." She could see him getting lost in the memories as he recounted the details. "The back seat lays out into a bed, and there is plenty of storage. The kids loved it, but they're all out of the house now and we haven't been able to get rid of it. I'd like to say it's because of all the memories, but in reality, we've used it more as a storage unit for random things since getting the new cars. Now it just sits collecting cobwebs in our side yard. " He shrugged his shoulders. "Could be the perfect adventure van for you."

Hailey was caught off guard by his offer. Her mind began swirling, searching for the right response. *Do I actually want to do this? How can I say no when this opportunity has been placed into my lap?*

It seemed like a hypothetical fairytale she cooked up to escape the suffocation of the memories and pain she recently endured. Just as she composed a response, she felt a tug on the back of her shirt. She turned around to see the bright blonde, blue-eyed boy from a couple houses down holding an L.A. Lakers hat that Jeremy had left behind.

"Excuse me, Ms. Hailey, how much is this hat?" he asked.

She couldn't help but smile at his excitement and was impressed by his manners. She realized she had forgotten to put a price tag on the item as she held it in her hands to take a look.

She knelt down to meet his eyes with a smile. "For you? Five dollars."

He rummaged in his front jean pocket, and his hand returned with several wadded up dollar bills. "Is this five dollars?"

Hailey smiled. "Let's see, one...two...three...four...hmm, looks like you are short one dollar."

"Aw man," the boy sighed.

"But you know what? For you, I will sell it for four dollars."

"Really?" His face lit up. "Thanks Ms. Hailey!" He pushed the cap over his curls and took off back down the street, no doubt to tell his parents what a great deal he just got.

As Hailey stood back up and waved goodbye to the boy, she caught John placing a $100 on her cash box, holding the $50 Ninja blender in his hands. He gave her a wink. "We have no use for it anymore, so if you're serious about this adventure and need a van, you know where to find us."

Hailey smiled, and for the first time in weeks, she felt a flicker of excitement kindle in her core.

Chapter 2

It wasn't perfect, but she was proud of her work. After countless hours spent watching YouTube videos of various van remodels and scrolling through Pinterest looking for inspiration that would fit her style, Hailey was ready to pack up her tools and classify her van remodel as complete.

It had taken three weeks of painstaking work. It felt cliché to say, but Hailey couldn't deny that it took three weeks of blood, sweat, tears, and long nights for her to get her new mobile home ready to live in full-time. She had pulled out the backseat's captain chairs to create space for a kitchenette, which she built out of some lightweight Ikea cabinets, using a piece of butcher block for the counter top. After putting in a small sink with a lidded bucket as a catch reservoir and another six-gallon tank as her fresh water supply with a hand pump to bring water to the faucet, she was impressed with her own work. She put in a small fridge that would run off the van's DC adapter and would keep some food cold, but she wasn't sure how the van's battery would handle the extra draw. She had recalled how many "vanlifers" installed solar panels to the top of their vans, but that solution would have to wait for now. Between the renovation and being out of a job for several weeks, she was nearly broke.

Hailey sat on the far backseat bed and looked around the space. She was about to live in a sixty square-foot van full-time, something she never would have imagined doing. After selling her car and moving out of the house, it was hard to believe that she was about to live in a space that would not only be her home but serve as her vehicle as well. It all seemed like a crazy dream, but now that the first stage of her plan was complete, she felt excited and nervous to start her journey.

The renovation was challenging, but it was time to face an even bigger challenge: telling her parents about her plan to travel solo across the country. Her father had an adventurous soul, and frankly never really cared for Jeremy, so she knew he wouldn't take much convincing. He had always supported her when she had her mind set on something, mainly because he knew she took after him, and when her mind was made up, there wasn't much that could be said to change it. Her mother, on the other hand, was going to take some serious convincing.

Growing up, Hailey couldn't do anything without her mother worrying or asking a million questions about every move she made. Knowing her mother would take this news even harder, since her parents lived all the way back in Chicago and wouldn't be there to send her off, Hailey took what she was going to say to them into great consideration.

Hailey held her breath as she pulled out her phone and tapped 'Home' in her contacts. It was time to bite the bullet and hope they would both support her decision.

"Here it goes," she whispered as she held the phone to her ear.

Her mother's reaction was full of distress, just as she predicted. "Wait, you're doing what? That does not sound like a safe plan!"

"But Mom, I can't think of a better time in my life for me to do something like this," Hailey continued, hoping to take back control of the conversation. "A lot of people are traveling full-time from their vans, and there's even Facebook groups and blogs that I can follow along with and join to connect with other solo travelers. So it's not like I'll be totally alone out there."

"But there's also murderers and rapists, and drug addicts, and..." Her mother's panic accelerated with every word, until her father eventually cut in to ease the downward spiral.

"Tracey, darling, Hailey isn't naive. She's made it this far in life with a good head on her shoulders. She's not going to place herself in danger. Isn't that right, Hails?"

Hailey could picture her father's face, stretched with a giant smile, as he gave his stamp of approval. She knew he would be on board with her plan since he, too, had done something similar when he was younger. Maybe that was why she found this opportunity so appealing. She could remember all the stories he would tell her of the people he had met on the road. She loved hearing the tales of all the incredible experiences he had while traveling and how they had changed his life for the better. She felt destined to follow in his footsteps.

"But still," her mother continued, refusing to be dismissed, "she'll be all alone...In the woods, or God knows where."

"Mom, I promise I'll be safe and take all the precautions when traveling. I'll stay within cell phone range, and if there's ever a time I feel unsafe or my surroundings seem dodgy, I'll simply move on to a different location. After all, I'll be self-contained in my van."

"Uh huh. Okay." Her mother wasn't convinced. "So tell me more about this van. How do you know it's even safe? How old is it? Has a mechanic looked it over?"

"Mom, it's fine. I promise." Hailey was irritated, but she knew her mom was only doing her job as a mother, making sure her child was safe. "My neighbor and I looked everything over before he gave it to me. It starts up smooth every time and doesn't leak oil or anything weird like that. I even put a fresh battery in it." She wanted to say more but wasn't sure what else she could say that wouldn't give away the fact this thing hadn't seen much action in the last couple decades, apart from being used as a makeshift storage unit. "Sure, it isn't pretty on the outside, which I'm sure makes you think it is in bad shape, but I've got it how I want it on the inside, and I trust it to get me to where I'm going safely." Hailey paused for a moment, but when she didn't get a response, she continued, "I've worked really hard on it, and I wouldn't travel in it if it wasn't safe."

"Come on, Tracey, you know she's going to do this whether you give her your blessing or not. She's already got her van all tricked out and ready to go. The best you can do from here is ask that she makes sure she is safe and calls her mother every day to check in."

Even though it was two against one, she knew that she, herself, would want to stay in touch and update them on her travels, so calling home every day wasn't really a huge concession in exchange for a blessing. Hailey had always been close with her parents, but even more so since she had moved away for college across the country, only making it back home for the holidays. She knew that life on the road could get lonely, and being able to share all her experiences with her parents along the way would be inevitable.

"Yes, exactly! Mom, I'll call you whenever I get the chance!"

Her mother let out a long sigh. "Okay, I guess I approve. But you better keep your word and call us regularly to let us know that you're okay. Or I'm sending your father to come get you." Hailey knew her mother wasn't kidding about that. "But please, don't do anything crazy. And be sure to bring pepper spray with you everywhere. And bear spray when you hike. And—"

"Dad, will you tell her I'll be fine?" Hailey cut in, not wanting to find out how long it would take for her mother to go through her whole list of concerns.

"Don't worry," he replied. "We know you will make safe decisions. We love you and look forward to hearing all about your journey. But remember, if you do need anything, at any time, you know how to reach us."

"Yes, I do. I love you guys, too. I will keep you updated on where I am and when I am moving locations."

"And be sure to call your mother...each and every day, so I don't have to come looking for you." Hailey knew he was smiling, but she also knew he was serious.

As they exchanged goodbyes, she let out a sigh of relief. *Well, I don't think that went too bad after all.*

It took Hailey a week to pack up all of her clothes and supplies she wanted to take along with her on her journey, setting the rest aside to be put into storage. She was actually impressed with herself for being able to narrow down her clothes to only a couple of bins that would fit beneath the bed in the van. A flood of emotions hit her as she packed the last bin of kitchen utensils into the van. This was it; in two days she would be hitting the road. She couldn't tell if she was more excited or nervous, but either way, she knew she was eager for the adventure to begin.

After she closed and locked up the van for the night, she walked back through her front door, lined with the rest of her stacked up cardboard boxes that needed to go into storage, and put a kettle on the stove for a cup of tea. She stood at her counter looking at the empty room before her. It wasn't long ago that she and Jeremy were deciding which way to layout the furniture in that very room. Little did they know, it wasn't going to matter. As the whistle began to sing from the kettle, Hailey turned off the stove and poured the steaming water into her mug. As she watched the water fade into a deep tan color, she remembered she had picked up maps earlier that day from the local travel shop, and it was the perfect time to start planning out her route. Hailey sat down at the table with excitement and opened up the map labeled 'California.'

The rest of her evening was spent researching the destinations on Google that she wanted to stop at along her journey. She began writing each of the locations down on vibrant sticky notes, using multi-colored pens that lay strewn across the table, until the map was covered with colorful squares. As Hailey took the last sip of her tea that had gone cold hours ago, she leaned back into her chair, pleased by her work. She smiled at the sight and whispered, "Joshua Tree, here I come."

Chapter 3

Hailey pulled the knob with brute force, making sure the door was shut so she could lock it for the last time. The front door never quite fit in the frame properly, just one more reminder that, apart from her neighbors, she wasn't going to miss that place. She placed the house key under the rock in the planter for the landlord to retrieve later that day. That was the moment Hailey realized, her life with Jeremey had officially come to an end. She walked over to her new home on wheels with a feeling of rejuvenation. The day had come that she was officially entering her next adventure.

A rush of adrenaline shot through her chest as she climbed into the driver's seat. She was unsure if she was feeling jittery from the two cups of coffee she had already consumed before her five a.m. departure, or the shock of starting her new life of living in a van.

She was thankful she had filled the fuel and water tanks the night before so she didn't have to worry about them at such an early time in the morning. She pulled out of her driveway and took one last look at the place she used to call home. *Time to leave the past behind.*

As she pulled out of the neighborhood and out towards the highway, she began to question what items she inevitably forgot to pack into the van. With it being her first solo vanlife excursion, it could be easy to miss something important. Confident enough that she grabbed most of the supplies and mementos she wanted to take along for the journey, and that the items she may have forgotten could be purchased at a store along the way, she flipped on the morning radio before she would be too far out of town to receive a signal.

It was a beautiful, clear morning as she watched the road change colors with the rising sun. Hailey was looking forward to seeing Joshua Tree for the first time. As much as she loved to hike and camp, it was hard to believe that she had lived in Southern California for five years and never made it out to the national park. No doubt, Jeremy's lack of adventure and camping skills had something to do with it.

Looking out at the rolling hills as her van cruised through Anza-Borrego Desert State Park, she felt her anger towards Jeremy rise in her chest. There were plenty of camping opportunities not too far out of the city, but she had been blind to them, or rather distracted from seeing them because she was so caught up with trying to please her boyfriend who just wanted to go out and party every weekend. As the sun began to climb higher into the sky, she could feel its warmth beaming through the window against her cheek. It was only eight a.m., but the summer heat engulfed the dusty landscape. Hailey rolled down her window, inviting in the desert air. She pushed the negative thoughts of her past out of her mind as the wind rushed through her free-falling hair.

As she turned onto Box Canyon Road, her stomach grumbled, the only thing she had consumed all morning was two cups of coffee. Remembering that she had placed a bag behind her seat with the last remnants of food from her pantry at the house. With one hand on the wheel, she contorted her arm to stretch behind her seat and rummaged through the bag that was just barely in reach. She pulled out a couple items and dropped them onto her lap: A bag of Goldfish and a Nutrigrain Bar.

"Of course, things I need two hands to open," Hailey commented with a roll of her eyes. She grabbed one corner of the Nutrigrain Bar in one hand and brought the other to her mouth. She clenched her teeth over the wrapper and gave it a swift pull, tearing the corner of the plastic. As the wrapper broke open, the van simultaneously jolted causing her to drop the bar onto the ground.

"Dammit." The van began thumping against the pavement as strong vibrations shot up from the van chassis. Her knuckles were turning white as she clenched the wheel and checked the mirrors for cars behind her. The road was clear. She steadied her hands on the wheel and was able to coast over to the shoulder of the road, coming to a halt. With the combination of the sound and the vibration, she already knew it was a blow out.

"Ugh, I haven't even gone that far!" Agitated, she turned off the ignition and walked to the back of the van to retrieve the spare tire. She rolled the tire along the side of the van until she came to the blown out tire remains. Glancing up and down the shoulder, she noticed it was littered with chunks of rubber and treads from previous blow outs. It made her feel a little better knowing that she wasn't the first to suffer this fate.

As she started loosening the lug nuts, she began to get lost in her thoughts. The last time she had changed a tire was with Jeremy. They had been coming back from a date when a screw in the road punctured the tire. Instead of coming to the rescue and helping her change it, he made the choice to derided her for not having AAA instead.

"What the hell do I need AAA for if I know how to change my own tire?" she'd shouted at him. It was rare for Hailey to raise her voice, but between the flat tire and Jeremy's lack of assistance, she couldn't hold back her frustration. As the fight replayed in her mind, her face began to burn with anger. Clearly, the wound still hadn't healed.

As she loosened the last lug nut, she recalled the first time she had learned to change a tire. It was at the same time Hailey was learning how to drive, and her father had made it a requirement to learn how to change a tire before she was able to get her license. She was less than excited about his requirement, but now she was thankful for it—especially since the skill had now come in handy more than once.

She slid the scissor jack into place and started turning the crank, which proved to be much harder on this van since it had substantially more weight than her old car. Although it was tough, she was enjoying pushing out some of her pent up anger with every crank she made. Just as she made the final crank, a vehicle approached, crunching gravel on the road behind her. She could hear the vehicle slow as it came to a stop in line with her van.

"Hey, do you need help?" a man's voice shouted from the window.

Holding the crank in place, she turned around to see a maroon van stopped in the road behind her with the passenger side window rolled down. Kneeling on the ground, she could only see the top of his forehead and dark hair, which she couldn't decipher whether it was pushed back or pulled into a manbun.

"No thanks, I got this," she answered dismissively as the crank slipped out of its place in the jack, clanged into the chassis, and created a ringing in her ears.

She heard the van roll across the asphalt and let out a sigh, feeling a little guilty for letting her frustration get the best of her and responding in an unwelcoming tone to the stranger. After all, he was only trying to help.

Out of the corner of her eye, she could see his van pulling off the road and parking in front of her. She looked up just as he stepped out of the driver's side door and began walking towards her.

"Looks like you could use a hand," his words pushed through a smile as he approached her van.

"That's nice of you to stop, but I know how to change a tire." She wasn't afraid to flaunt her skills.

"Oh, I don't doubt that. It's just nice to have an extra hand. Or maybe, some extra muscle," he said with a corner of a smile. "I'm not saying you can't do it, but I'm happy to lend a hand."

He reached out for the jack crank, and she caved into his offer. Noticing the strength in his biceps as he stretched his arm out in front of her, she decided he had more than enough muscle to spare.

"Well, thank you." She glanced up at him with a shy smile.

He went to work jacking up the van high enough to get the tattered wheel off and the new one in place. She had already picked up the tire iron, making it apparent that she was going to finish off the job.

As kind as he was to help her, she couldn't fight her instinct to keep her guard up. After all, he was a strange guy she just met while stranded in the middle of the desert—not exactly an ideal location to meet a strong stranger alone. She clenched the tire iron tighter. It was best to be prepared in case he tried anything weird.

After removing the first of five lug nuts, he held his hand out palm up. "You don't want to get this sandy dirt in the threads." Hailey obliged to the gesture and dropped the nut in his hand. Soon enough, the old wheel was off and replaced with the spare.

"Alright, it's all set." She popped back up on to her feet, swiping her hands together to wipe away the dirt and grime. "Thank you for your assistance," she said, hesitant to use the word "help" because her pride of self sufficiency might be lessened.

Lifting her face, she met his eyes. She guessed he was a few years older than her. His dark hair was tousled, medium length and there was part of her that was happy to see it wasn't a man bun after all, as if it really made a difference either way, it was too early to be sizing up this stranger.

"No problem at all," he said, brushing his hands against his shorts. "Happy to be of service." He paused, then reached out his hand. "I'm Luke."

She cautiously stretched out her hand, meeting his in the middle. "Hailey."

A tight smile gripped her lips as their hands clasped together. Hailey felt a hint of embarrassment that she had been so dismissive towards him when he initially pulled up. He probably didn't deserve the tone he received upon offering help. It was not the start to her road trip she was anticipating, and she realized she had let her emotions speak for her.

"Heading into Joshua Tree?" He tilted his head back to look over her shoulder and gesture towards her van.

"That's the plan," she stated. Hailey didn't want to give away too many details to someone she just met, but she also wanted to be cordial, as he did just help her change her tire in the baking sun.

Sensing the ambivalent tone in her voice, Luke took a step back, placing his hands into the pockets of his cargo shorts. "It's a beautiful place, you'll love it."

Hailey smiled and nodded in response as the silence grew awkward between them. "Well, I better get back on the road." She glanced back over her shoulder at the van as she spoke.

"Oh yes, of course," he replied.

They each gave a farewell smile as Luke pivoted and began walking back towards his van. With his door ajar, he stepped one foot into his van before looking back at her. "Hopefully the next time I see you, you won't be stranded on the side of the road." He winked and closed the door, not waiting for a reply.

Hailey stood at her door with her hand wrapped around the handle as a smile touched her lips in response to his cheeky remark. She climbed into the driver's seat and lowered the window. "Thanks again, Luke," she raised her voice in response, unsure if he had heard it or not.

He threw his arm out the window and waved as he slowly pulled away from the shoulder and back onto the road, sending a plume of dust into the dry desert air.

Chapter 4

Two hours behind schedule. She looked down at her watch as she pulled into the Cottonwood Visitor Center at Joshua Tree National Park.

Having done her research, Hailey knew that some of the campgrounds in the park were closed during the summer months, while others transitioned to a first-come basis, which was the main reason she wanted to get a head start on the day. Since her flat tire had set her back, she decided to head into the visitor's center to see if the ranger could give her some insight on which campgrounds would be the best to choose from.

The cool air of the visitor center greeted her as she walked through the glass doors of the small beige building. The inside of the visitor's center looked just as she had imagined it. She could feel dirt scraping between her shoes as she stepped across the outdated, dark beige tile flooring that stretched across the small space, contrasting against the plain cream walls. There were racks of tacky sun hats, postcards, and tourist souvenirs, like gemstones and key chains, positioned next to an information kiosk that held an aged map of all the trails around the park.

"Welcome to Joshua Tree, my name is Martin. What can I help you with today?" A slender man with a welcoming smile stood at the front desk. Judging by his receding grey hairline and crow's feet that splintered from his eyes as he smiled, Hailey assumed he had to be no younger than sixty.

Hailey approached the counter and pulled out her map. She set it down on the counter between them, along with her sunglasses, as she returned his smile.

"I know most of your campgrounds are first-come first-serve this time of year, but I was hoping you could maybe direct me to one that has the greatest chance of having spots available," she said as she looked up at him with hopeful eyes.

"I certainly can." He pulled out a pen from the front left pocket of his dark grey button down shirt.

"This one here is Jumbo Rocks Campground," he said, circling the spot on the map as he spoke. "It's only ten bucks a night and is surrounded by beautiful boulder formations." Hailey could smell the hints of morning coffee still on his breath as he continued. "It's also the largest campground in the park, so it could be your best bet for finding several vacant spots."

He shifted his arm on the map and circled another spot. "But this here is my favorite campground." Tapping his pen over the spot, he added, "Hidden Valley is the most centrally-located campground in the park and is surrounded by beautiful scenery. It would definitely be my top choice."

Hailey looked at his markings and smiled at the man. "Those sound like great options. I will definitely go check them out, thank you so much."

She folded up the map and slid it back into her bag before turning to leave. Just before she was about to walk out the door, Hailey stopped and began to dig in her bag.

"Miss?" Martin called out from behind. Hailey turned around to see him holding up her sunglasses she had left on the counter. "I think you might be needing these."

"I was just looking for those! Thank you." She walked back over and grabbed her sunglasses from the man. "I wouldn't want to walk out into the blazing sun without these!"

"Certainly not," he agreed with a grin. Hailey thanked the man again and headed back towards the exit. Just as she slid her sunglasses onto her face and was about to push open the door, something caught her eye. It was a bright white piece of paper that had been thumbtacked to the old cork bulletin board that hung just beside the exit.

Printed on the paper was a photo of an attractive young girl with blonde hair and perfect white teeth, smiling at the camera. Above her picture, printed in all capital letters, was the ominous word: 'MISSING.' Beneath the image was the girl's name, followed by the date and location that she had last been seen. Hailey lifted her sunglasses onto her head, pushing her hair back to gain a better look at the poster.

"Do you know her?" Hailey looked back over her shoulder to see Martin placing the pen back into his front pocket as he asked the question, as if all young girls in their twenties knew each other.

"No, I don't," Hailey replied, turning back towards the flyer. She scanned the page reading all the other details that were provided. "This is recent." She paused for a moment, taking in the information. "She only went missing a couple of months ago."

"Yes. That's right. You know, it's dangerous traveling alone as a young woman," he said matter-of-factly. "You better be careful out there, young lady."

'Young-lady.' If it wasn't his grey hair and wrinkles that confirmed her estimation of his age, that phrase certainly did.

"Do you know if they have any leads?" She kept her eyes fixed on the photo as she spoke.

"Ahh...I think that they suspect it could be someone she knows, maybe an angry ex-boyfriend or stalker of some sort." He shrugged his shoulders as he shook his head at the assumption. "You know how it goes."

Hailey nodded her head, acknowledging his statement, but her mind continued to fill with more questions.

"The girl came through here actually," he added. Hailey pivoted to look at him; now he had her attention. He looked up at the ceiling as he began recounting the day. "I remember her because she didn't look dressed for the desert. She looked like she was getting ready to walk the runway." He chuckled at the memory. "I told her she should invest in some better shoes if she was planning to go hiking around here."

"How long ago was that?" Her investigative reporter instincts were beginning to surface.

He had both hands resting on the counter now as he leaned forward. "I'd say about four months ago or so." She could tell he was happy to engage in a conversation that wasn't purely focused on camping for once.

Just as Hailey opened her mouth to ask another question, a family of four walked through the doors. A young boy, who looked to be about four years old, was clinging to his mother's leg with one arm and holding a box of apple juice in the other. His older sister walked straight to the stand of sunglasses and began to try each one of them on, checking out each different look in the tiny mirror. The father, tall and wide, stepped up to the counter and began to rattle off his questions. Martin gave Hailey an apologetic look as he retrieved the pen from his front pocket.

It was clear their conversation had come to an end. Hailey waved goodbye and thanked him with a nod before slipping out the door into the desert heat. Throwing her backpack in the passenger seat, she jumped into the van and headed down the road, wondering who else, other than Martin, Hannah Chambers may have encountered during her journey.

Chapter 5

The summer air was warm against her arm as it rested on the bottom of the open window. Her body swayed and bumped with every motion of the road as she cruised through the park. With the map sprawled across her lap, Hailey tried to stay focused on the road to get to the Hidden Valley Campground, but she couldn't get the image of the missing girl out of her mind.

How could a girl just go missing without a trace? It just doesn't make any sense. Then again, if she was traveling alone in the woods, maybe it wouldn't be that hard after all.

Not too far down the road, a sign came into view that read "Hidden Valley Campground" with a smaller sign hanging below it with the word vacancy written in white capital letters. The tires spun beneath the van as she lost some traction turning onto the loose gravel road from the asphalt. It felt good to be off the pavement. It was as if the dirt road was where the adventure was officially beginning. As she drove down the road, she noticed there were only two other campers in the campground, leaving plenty of vacant spots to choose from.

"I guess starting this journey on a Tuesday morning was a great choice after all," she commented to herself as she scanned the area.

After passing several vacant spots, Hailey found a site that she thought looked fairly flat and would give her enough space to turn around, since she certainly wasn't confident in her reversing skills in her new vehicle yet.

The engine fell silent as she removed the key from the ignition. She pulled on her hat and hopped out of the van to check out the surroundings. The spot was far enough away from the other campers that she wouldn't feel as if she were intruding on their space, but also close enough that she wouldn't feel completely alone in the desert on her first night. Glancing down at the spare tire, she shook her head in annoyance. "Of course that would happen to me the first day I get on the road."

It was just past two in the afternoon and the sun was beating down, scorching the dry land. Not a single cloud crossed the sky for relief from the blaze. The campground was even more beautiful than she had imagined. Before she embarked on her journey, she had looked up images of the park, but they certainly didn't do the place justice. Enormous boulders dusted in various shades of red and brown surrounded the campground, creating splotches of shade across the land. Tucked between several tall Joshua trees, the location of the site provided some privacy but mainly created the perfect amount of shade to relax and unwind in after her long drive.

The desert was silent. No wind. No birds. No people. It was the peace Hailey had been craving for months. Just as euphoria was setting in, her pocket began to vibrate, startling her back to reality.

Glancing at the screen she braced herself for the conversation. "Hi Mom."

"You haven't called us all day! Where are you?" No surprise, her mother was already frantic and it was still early in the afternoon.

"I just pulled into a campsite in Joshua Tree." Her tone was light and casual, hoping to put her mother at ease.

Hailey knew things had been difficult for her mother ever since her older brother, Daniel, was hit by a drunk driver several years ago. The incident was tough on the whole family, but her mother took it the hardest. Even though several years had passed, the heartbreak of losing him still weighed down on her every day. Not being there to protect her child was the worst feeling any mother could endure, so Hailey couldn't blame her mom for becoming even more protective of her after the incident. She also knew spending long days on the open road alone wasn't exactly the prescription to ease an apprehensive mother's nerves.

"Why didn't you call us when you left this morning?" her mother asked.

"I had to make sure I packed everything I needed and wanted to get on the road as soon as possible."

"I understand, just please be sure to keep us updated with your traveling. We just want to know you are safe."

Hailey let out a sigh. "I know." She knew she couldn't argue against that.

"Is Dad there?" Knowing her mother would surely be sent into a panic if she told her about the flat tire, she decided it would be best to mention it to her father first.

A ruffled noise shot through the phone as her mother wrapped her palm around the microphone, attempting to muffle the sound of her calling out into the house. After a short pause, his voice chimed in through the phone. "Hey, honey, how's it going?" His warm tone poured through the phone like molasses, and Hailey felt at ease.

"So far it's been pretty good," she said honestly. "Except I got a flat tire on my way out today." Before he had a chance to respond, she quickly added, "Please don't tell Mom. You know how she is. And I don't want her to worry."

"A flat tire? Well that's quite the way to start your journey," he teased.

"But don't tell Mom, okay?"

"Don't worry," he consoled her, "I won't tell your mother."

"Thanks, Dad."

"So I take it you swapped it with the spare, since it sounds like you have made it to the campground?" he asked.

"Yes. I'll have to go get the tire fixed when I'm in the city, but it's fine for now."

"I know you can take care of yourself out there, but stay safe; don't trust anyone you don't know and always be aware of your surroundings."

"I know the drill, Dad," she said, rolling her eyes.

With her father being a retired FBI agent, Hailey was well aware of all of the horrible things that could happen to someone. Growing up, Hailey had loved hearing all the stories and details about the cases her father worked. He made sure to teach her and her brother about all the awful people that were out there, so they would always be on high alert and never talk to strangers since they used to walk to and from school together each day. Luckily for Hailey, despite his need to serve and protect, especially his family, he still had an adventurous side. He had always encouraged her to explore what the world had to offer and left the bulk of worrying to her mother.

"Just have to be sure, kiddo," he replied.

"Yeah, yeah, I know. Hey, can you tell Mom bye for me? I still have a lot of setting up to do." Her mother would likely hop back on the phone with a million questions, and she didn't have the energy, or patience, for it after the morning she had.

"Sure thing, but you better make sure you call her tomorrow."

"Of course."

After saying goodbye, she slipped her phone back into her pocket and walked over to the van, not realizing how far she had wandered. She hadn't been standing in the sun for long, but she could feel the beads of sweat forming on her lower back and her skin beginning to burn. She couldn't even remember the last time she felt the warmth of the sun beat down against her skin like this.

As she pulled the side door open, she was confronted with all of the boxes that had yet to be unpacked and organized into the small drawers and cabinets. It was too hot to go exploring, but she wasn't motivated to empty the boxes either. Glancing around the van, she spotted her camping chair and decided she would find a spot in the shade to relax. Pushing two boxes and a pair of hiking boots aside, she reached down to pull out her fold-up camping chair and a bottle of lukewarm water.

Temperatures were unforgiving this time of year, but she loved the heat. She positioned the chair beneath one of the uniquely shaped Joshua trees that stood along the perimeter of her site. The twisted, spiky-leafed arms sprawled out just enough to provide a spot of sufficient shade for her chair to be protected from the sun.

After listening to an entire playlist on Spotify beneath the tree and doing some research on tire shops on her route, Hailey decided it was time to get her new home organized. As she stepped into the van, she nestled herself between the boxes and began to peer inside each one, debating which one would be the most efficient to start with.

Two hours passed, and she could see the sun creeping down towards the horizon. The summer days in the desert were long, making it easy to lose track of time. Placing the last coffee mug onto the hook that hung above her tiny sink, a wave of hunger washed over her. Not in the mood to make a real meal, she pulled a jar of crunchy peanut butter from the cabinet along with some strawberry preserves and made a sandwich.

She could hear Jeremy's voice chime in the back of her mind intruding on her dinner: *"That's not a real meal."* She smiled as she smashed the pieces of bread together, grateful she had no one but herself to please for once. After pouring herself a glass of almond milk to pair with her "right-sized" meal, she sat down on the bed and started up her laptop.

After connecting her laptop to the hotspot through her phone, she clicked open the browser. Google popped up on the homepage, and she began typing into the search bar: *Hannah Chambers missing.*

The page took a while to process the results since she was barely within cell phone range, which created time for anxiety and anticipation to build with every rotation the circle made as it loaded, painfully slow. Hailey wasn't quite sure why she felt compelled to research the missing girl, or why she felt the anxiety grow within her as she did, but it was something she felt the need to do. Maybe after talking to her father, she felt inspired by his work. She always thought she would become an agent and follow in his footsteps, but with a passion for writing, she decided to work towards a journalism degree instead. Now after losing her most recent job working in public relations, she regretted not sticking with her first plan to major in criminal justice.

When the search results finally finished processing, Hailey began scanning through each article as she scrolled down the page. Halfway down, a link caught her eye by Channel 2 news in Sacramento as she pushed the last bite of sandwich into her mouth.

"Sacramento Girl Gone Missing In One of California's Busiest National Parks."

Hailey clicked on the link, and unsurprisingly, the article was just about as informative as the missing poster she had seen on the bulletin board earlier that day. It did, however, provide several more details on the approximate location of where the girl had gone missing. It also provided some quotes from the girl's family and close friends. As in most cases, each quote mentioned what a smart, outgoing, and kind girl she was and how shocked they all were that she would go missing.

Unimpressed with each news article that she opened, since they appeared to all have the same generic story to report, she began to dig deeper into the web. It wasn't long before she stumbled across a link that connected to Hannah's Instagram account.

Jackpot. Now she was getting somewhere.

Chapter 6

Screen light illuminated the inside of the van as Hailey sat on the bed with her eyes glued to her laptop. Before she knew it, day had turned into night as the sun had fallen beneath the desert's edge and darkness blanketed the land. She wasn't sure how long she had been looking at Hannah's Instagram and Facebook pages, but judging by the darkness of the sky, it had been awhile. It was easy to become lost in the mindless motion of scrolling through someone's online presence, especially someone who had gone missing. Glancing outside her window, she could only see the orange flicker against the face of the giant boulders as other campers enjoyed a fire. Even though they were strangers, it gave her a sense of comfort knowing there were other people nearby in such a dark, secluded place.

Hailey scrolled back to the top of Hannah's account. Five hundred thirty-nine thousand followers and six hundred fifty-four posts. This girl certainly stayed on top of her Instagram game and, seeing that it was public, it was clear that she wasn't trying to run or hide from anyone. She also didn't appear to think she was in any danger, either; she was leaving the door into her personal life wide open.

Scrolling slowly through the grid of colorful thumbnails, it didn't take her long to discover that Hannah's full-time job was posing and posting on Instagram as a vanlife influencer. Each photo looked like it belonged in a magazine, from the string lights that hung over the van's bed, to the matching plates and mugs that sat gracefully on a floating shelf above the sink. Hailey wondered what she did with them when she drove, since they would, without question, come crashing down at the first bump in the road. Each photo was staged, edited, and filtered to perfection. Not only were the items in her pictures flawlessly placed, but even her bright white dog lay with attentive ears, camera ready. Hailey couldn't help but feel a glimmer of jealousy.

Wait a minute. One of the thumbnails with the dog caught her attention. Hailey clicked on the image to get a closer look. The photograph was of the dog lying in the center of a large blue, orange, and yellow blanket sprinkled with a geometric pattern that stretched across the small bed. Hailey wondered how long it took her to get the dog to sit just right for the photograph. But the main question on her mind was: if Hannah had a dog with her when she went missing, then where was that dog now?

The thought sparked curiosity and confusion. There was no question that this dog was her travel companion. Every other photo had the dog running, sitting, or lying somewhere in or around the van, all the way up to her most recent post.

Did the dog go missing too? Is he with her now? Are they both still alive? Or in trouble? The questions darted across her thoughts, unsure which one should take priority.

Hailey rubbed her eyes as they began to sting from staring so intently at the screen for an unknown amount of time. Looking down at the clock, she realized it was way past the time she normally went to sleep; no wonder her eyes felt so dry and heavy. She had been up since the early morning, drove through the desert all day with the windows down, and just spent hours researching the life of a girl, who she didn't even know, on both her phone and computer.

It was time to call it a night. Hailey closed the laptop and swung her legs over the side of the bed to meet the warm vinyl wood plank flooring. She surveyed her new home and naturally started to compare it to Hannah's van remodel. Not only was the interior of Hannah's van decorative and inviting, but her vanlife in general looked so glamorous compared to what Hailey imagined vanlife would be like.

Feeling inspired by Hannah's glamorous shots, Hailey stepped off from her bed and decided she should take a picture to document her first night in her new home on wheels. Grabbing a mug from the hook that read *"I'm A Happy Camper"* painted in pink cursive lettering, Hailey was ready to put her staging skills to the test.

Placing her turquoise kettle on the stove to boil some water, she changed into her pajama shorts and a loose tank top. Even though the sun had been down for hours, the heat of the day still lingered in the mass of the vehicle. Surveying the room, she searched for picturesque items that she could stage on the bed and kitchenette counter to make the place look cozy and inviting.

"Perfect!" Hailey stepped back smiling at her work as she positioned the last item into place. She caught a glimpse of her reflection in the mirror and cringed at what she saw. Her hair was pulled back into a low messy knot, with strands that had broken loose from the hold and fallen beside her cheeks. Dark circles were beginning to appear beneath her eyes, revealing the absence of sleep from the previous night. If her lack of confidence wasn't enough to keep her out of photos, her current untamed look certainly was.

Picking up her Canon DSLR camera, purchased off Craigslist a while back, she situated herself between the front two seats, attempting to get as much of the interior of the van in her shot as she could. After taking several shots from different angles, she decided she had one that was worthy enough to post.

Curling up onto the bed with her camera in one hand and iPhone in the other, she transferred over all the photographs to her phone. As she waited for the pictures to load, she slowly sipped her tea, being reminded of home as the sweet peach steam tickled the tip of her nose. Hailey started making herself a cup of peach tea with a splash of lemon juice and honey each night after she had moved away from home. It was her mother's recipe that she used to make for her and her brother each night as they were growing up. A recipe she still loved to this day.

As the warm concoction cascaded down her throat, and she peered at her surroundings, she realized that she was still trying to wrap her head around the fact that she was now living in a van. It all seemed so surreal. She wondered how long it would take before she no longer felt like she was living in a dream.

After editing her favorite images, she was finally ready to put a post together. She thought long and hard, rereading over her caption one last time, as it had to be admirable. Hailey had only told close family and friends about her journey, so making it public to all her peers from college and her ex-coworkers was a little nerve racking. Pleased with her images and caption, she added one last detail at the end, confirming her step into her new life: *#Vanlife*.

Chapter 7

A bead of sweat slid down her temple, stirring Hailey from a deep sleep. Rubbing her eyes, she kicked the sheet away from her steaming legs. It was early morning, but the sun was already up and fiercely beating down through the windows, heating up the van like a greenhouse. Groggy from sleep, she worked up the strength to slide out of bed and open a window to let in the minute amount of breeze that was swirling through the desert. She slipped her arms through the sleeves of her silk robe and stepped down from her bed into her miniature kitchen to fix up a cup of coffee.

It was only her third day on the road, and the reality of not having regular electricity was beginning to set in as she pulled down her pour over coffee maker from the shelf. At home, she relied on her convenient single-serve Keurig each morning before work, but this time she didn't have a Keurig. But she didn't have work to get ready for either, so there was that perk to be had.

Opening a fresh bag of coffee, she relished in the moment. After placing the kettle on the stove to boil, she scooped the grounds of morning roast from the bag and poured them into the coffee filter. She could already tell it was going to be a two cups of coffee type of day.

As she waited for the water to boil, she grabbed her phone from the small woven basket next to her bed and sat cross-legged on top of the mangled sheets. Out of habit, Hailey tapped the Instagram icon on her homepage to see what the world was up to this morning. As the app filled the screen, she waited in anticipation to see how many people had liked her post from a couple nights earlier. Forgetting how slow the connection was, she tapped her foot impatiently, watching the wheel spin in rapid rotations. The first two days, it appeared that the usual suspects had liked and commented on her photo—mainly family and close friends. So, she was shocked when she saw the latest activity.

"Whoa," she gasped in disbelief. As the red bar popped up above the heart icon, indicating how many notifications she had, she was stunned. Fifteen new followers, six comments, and three hundred likes—and the number was still climbing.

Hailey was behind the times when it came to social media. Unlike most women in their twenties, she rarely posted to Facebook, Instagram, or Snapchat, but that didn't stop her from checking them habitually. After she responded to all the new comments on her post, checked out each new follower's page, and finished her first cup of coffee, Hailey decided it was time to get ready for the day.

Changing into shorts and a t-shirt, she pulled the door open, and the day welcomed her with a rush of hot air against her face that felt like opening up the door to a blazing hot oven. It was her last day in Joshua Tree, and she wanted to make sure she got all the pictures she wanted of the park before she left. After receiving so much attention on her latest post, she decided it was time to start putting some true effort into her photographs and Instagram page.

She picked up her camera from inside its case and jumped out onto the gravel. The sun was hitting her campsite from the perfect angle to highlight the entire side of the van, along with the Joshua trees and boulders that towered just behind. It was a picture-perfect backdrop.

Hailey had seen scenes exactly like this in several old Hollywood movies, especially ones where the bad guys needed a remote place to bury a body. Since those old movie days, the popularity of Joshua Tree reemerged with a new generation as the campfire lit backgrounds showed up in the images of thousands of fashionista's Instagrams. At least her post would be different: A true, sober camping experience with nothing to show but her van and the silence of the desert.

As she began snapping photographs from different angles, the idea emerged to put a journal together. She may not be employed to write anymore, but that didn't mean the passion wasn't still there. Not only would she use photographs to capture the moments during her adventure, but she would write about them, as well.

Finally satisfied with several of her shots, she pulled her phone out from her back pocket and walked over to her camping chair, readjusting it beneath the tree, allowing her head to be in the shade while her legs stretched out in the sun.

Wondering if there was any new information about Hannah, she pulled up Google News and typed in the search bar: *Missing Girl in Yosemite.* "Yikes," she muttered to herself. There were more results of missing girls in Yosemite over the years than she was expecting. She was going to have to be more specific. Deleting her first search, she retyped her search criteria: *Missing Girl, Hannah Chambers, Yosemite National Park* and set the search filter to only scan the last month.

"Damn," she cursed, displeased with the results. The only results that popped up were old news reports being repeated as new. She closed the news app and tapped open Instagram to pull up Hannah's page. Even though the girl was still missing, there was a part of her that anticipated a new post. But the page remained unchanged.

Hailey browsed through the thumbnails and selected an image. The post was a picture of Hannah sitting next to a campfire with a glass of red wine in one hand and a bamboo skewer with a marshmallow stuck to it in the other. Her van was parked behind her with the door open, with twinkle lights dangling from one side of the opening to the other. Her dog was captured in motion trotting towards her from behind. The caption on the post read:

Just another campfire, enjoying the vagabond life.

After reading the caption, Hailey naturally noticed the amount of likes and comments the post had received: 1,384 likes and 170 comments. Out of curiosity, Hailey clicked the comments section to select *'View all 170 comments.'* She began to scroll through all of the envious followers that had made their comments. Most of the comments consisted of emojis, since it was the easiest form of communication on social media. Line after line was filled with smiley faces and hearts that showed their simple admiration. Hailey scanned through the worded comments, mostly containing comments such as:

Gorgeous girl!

Or, *I love your van set up, so cute!*

It was safe to say the majority of the population making comments were either young women who were part of the vanlife or were wishing they were. Then all of a sudden, there was a comment that didn't seem to follow the same trend as the others, causing Hailey to stop and re-read it.

your so fake, go back to beverly hills where u belong

"Geez," Hailey muttered in shock at the harshness of the comment. *Nothing says internet troll like harsh words, bad grammar, and spelling errors.*

Leaning back into her chair, she looked up through the pointy leaves just in time to see a bird fly into her view. She pondered the rude comment for a moment. Could Hailey handle internet trolls? She had completely forgotten about all the cruel people in the world who used the internet as their unfiltered voice; people who felt bulletproof while sitting on the other side of an anonymous computer screen and had no problems tearing others down, likely out of nothing more than sub-conscience jealousy. Before answering her own thought, she brought her phone back into view.

Intrigued to see if there were any other negative comments left on Hannah's other posts, Hailey began shuffling through the comments on her other highly-liked photographs. As she was scanning through all of the comments and screen names, the same name, *@camping_merkins57,* popped up again, leaving another surly comment.

city girls like you shouldnt be allowed in our forests

Hailey wondered why someone would waste their time throwing shade at a stranger online, but unfortunately that seemed to be rampant on social media, especially on influencers' pages. Now her eyes were searching for that same callous person making other comments on her page, and sure enough, there he was again.

ho pretends she's a nature lover for the attention, but probably spends her nights spreading her legs at the marriott for a bug-free place to sleep

The comment made her cringe. There was definitely one nasty person sitting behind that account. Hailey couldn't resist; she clicked on the name to pull up the profile.

"Damn it," she cursed. The profile was set to private. "Of course," she exhaled. He had no problem berating strangers with public profiles, but he didn't want to give any strangers the opportunity to offer up their opinions on his life.

The sweat from her lower back was beginning to seep through her shirt. As much as she loved the warm weather, 100 degrees was pushing her limit. It looked like her stalking was going to have to be put on hold. As the day dipped later into the afternoon, Hailey knew if she didn't call home soon, she would be receiving another panicked call from her mother.

She had enjoyed her brief visit in Joshua Tree, but now that she had captured the photographs she wanted and the desert heat was only getting warmer, it was time to pack up her van and start heading north.

Hailey decided it would be more productive to call her mom from the road and slid her phone back into her pocket. She scooped up her camping chair and tossed it into the van before hopping in herself to make sure everything was 'mobile ready.' Since she was traveling alone, Hailey knew that if one item was out of place in the van and went crashing to the floor, there wouldn't be anyone there to catch it, and cleanup would have to wait until she arrived at her destination.

After taking one last lap around her campsite to be sure she didn't forget anything, she opened up the door and jumped into the driver's seat. The engine roared to life as she turned the key in the ignition. Looking out her window, she took in the emptiness of the landscape and felt a slight sense of loneliness. Maybe it was time to join some of those Facebook groups she had mentioned to her parents. It could be a good idea to connect with some other solo vanlifers to get some tips and tricks on how to travel alone on the road. It could also provide a sense of friendship, even if it was purely virtual.

As Hailey drove out of the campground down the dirt road, she stared out her window into the open desert that stretched beyond where her eyes could see. She thought back to those old Hollywood movies again, the ones where the bad guys would travel to the desert to bury a body. As she gazed out into the scorching land, she wondered how many bodies lay beneath the heat of the desert. How many real life bad guys had used this place to bury their sinful secrets? One thing she did know was that Hannah at least made it out of the desert. She had been last seen in Yosemite National Park, which happened to be one of the next stops on Hailey's list of destinations. But first, she'd need to get her tire replaced.

Pulling back out onto the main road, she wiggled her phone out from her pocket and placed it on the dash.

"Hey Siri, call Mom."

Chapter 8

"The young woman's body was found this morning at approximately 6:30 a.m. in Stanislaus National Forest near Cow Creek."

Hailey stopped in her tracks at the sound of the anchor woman's voice as she relayed the news. She turned around and peered up at the old tube-style TV that hung above the cashier's counter in the gas station convenience store.

"Can you turn it up?" Hailey asked from the aisle as her hand froze on a bag of pretzels, grasping a Gatorade in the other, while her eyes remained fixated on the screen.

"Sure," he muttered with a shrug.

The screen showed a video of water flowing through Cow Creek as a woman's voice overplayed the scene.

"No names have been released at this time, but officers do believe this could be the missing girl from Sacramento, Hannah Chambers."

The same image of Hannah that had been placed on the missing posters filled the screen as the reporter continued, *"We are following this case closely and will keep the public updated as we gain more details."* The screen cut back to the two news anchors as they sat at their desk with somber faces.

Hailey was surprised how upset she felt. It was awful anytime someone went missing and turned up dead, but this time it felt different. More personal, which was strange considering Hailey had never met the girl.

That was the odd thing about social media; it created a sense of connection between complete strangers, even if some of those connections were merely one-sided.

"Will that be all, Miss?" Hailey flinched as the man's voice startled her attention away from the screen. She had been so engrossed by the news cast that she hadn't realized she had made her way up to the check-out counter. Hailey placed her Gatorade on the counter and swiped a bag of Hot Cheetos from the impulse goods shelf, as she had forgotten about the pretzels when the television captured her attention.

"And forty dollars on pump five, please," she replied to the man.

A million thoughts were coursing through her mind as she inserted her credit card into the reader. *Could she really be dead? Was it a simple hiking accident, or was there foul play?* There had to be more details. There had to be more to the story.

The machine began beeping, indicating it was time to remove her card, startling Hailey again out of her thoughts. "Thank you." She flashed the cashier a tight smile as she removed her card and swiped her items from the counter.

It was only about fifty more minutes until she would be in Sequoia National Forest. Hailey was initially on her way to Yosemite, but after needing to take a detour to a tire shop to replace the spare, she knew she wasn't going to make it there today. Plus, she wasn't on a real schedule, so she might as well take her time and enjoy all the other sights there were to see along the way.

Before taking off, Hailey looked through her camping apps to locate some dispersed camping sites in Sequoia National Forest. She was a little nervous to head into the woods on her own for the first time, but at least it wasn't going to be a complete shot in the dark to figure out where to camp. Before Hailey left on her trip, she had downloaded several camping apps onto her phone, as well as researched which websites provided the most information about places to camp. She had found one site that gave directions to several good dispersed camping sites in the forest, so it was time to test out how accurate the website actually was.

After hearing the latest information about Hannah on the news, Hailey was eager to get to her campsite and pull out her laptop to investigate the latest findings. Even though her body was just found, Hailey was hoping she would be able to dig up more information about the crime scene where Hannah's body was discovered. Hailey wasn't sure if her interest in the case was growing because her passion to become an investigative reporter was pushing her forward, or because she was close to Hannah's age and was also traveling along the same route she was when she had gone missing. Either way, Hailey knew she wasn't going to be able to let the incident go without finding out more.

The night washed over the sky before she pulled onto the forest road. It wasn't ideal to find a camping site at night, but after driving for five hours, Hailey was more than ready to get out, stretch her legs, and make something to eat.

Luckily, her maps from the free campsites website didn't steer her wrong, and she was able to find what appeared to be a fairly decent spot, as far as she could tell in the dark. Once she pulled into the spot, she switched off the headlights and the ignition. Her heart jumped at the sudden darkness as her eyes took a moment to adjust. Hailey remained in the front seat for a moment to take in her new dark surroundings. The moon was almost full, allowing her to see the silhouettes of the trees surrounding the site. Maneuvering herself between the front seats to get to the back of the van, she grabbed an apple and a box of crackers from the shelf. She plopped onto the bed and flipped open her laptop. During the entire drive to the campground from the gas station, Hailey's mind swirled with questions about Hannah's case. Turning on the hotspot on her phone, she connected her computer to the WIFI network, where she would be able to dive deep into the pool of information she could find about Hannah on the internet.

"Oh come on," she moaned as the icon in the bottom right corner of her computer continued to read *No Internet Access*. Aggravated, she toggled the hotspot connection off and on to see if restarting the hotspot would strengthen the connection but had no success.

Hailey's patience was wearing thin. She knew if she wasn't going to be able to research anything online, her mind would remain wide awake with questions all night. She decided to try a different approach; maybe the signal was being blocked by the van. Maybe if she went outside, on top of the van, she would receive a stronger signal.

A chill danced down her spine as she stepped out of the van onto the soft graveyard of brown pine needles. The night was still and peaceful. Unlike her stay in Joshua Tree, there were no other campers in sight. Clutching the flashlight, she swung her laptop case over her shoulder and began scanning her surroundings.

She yanked the door shut, sending a loud screech into the silent forest. She clenched the flashlight between her teeth as she grasped the metal frame and ascended the ladder.

"I sure hope higher ground leads to a stronger connection," she whispered optimistically. Once she made it to the top, she pulled out her laptop, closed her eyes and pleaded to the sky as she, once again, clicked on her hotspot. "Please work. Come on. Please connect."

Her plea must have worked. The service was stronger on top of the van, and she was able to connect to her hotspot, allowing her to open up the web browser.

Once the Google homepage loaded, she began typing in the search bar: *Hannah Chamber's body found near Cow Creek, California*. She hit *Enter* with more force than necessary and waited.

The screen blinked, loading dozens of articles from various news stations and reporters from across the state. Hailey clicked on the second article titled, "Authorities Confirmed Body Found in Cow Creek to be Missing Woman from Sacramento."

Her suspicions were settled. Being a journalist at heart, Hailey enjoyed reading news articles, but she knew they typically only provided the bare minimum when it came to high-profile cases, which is what Hannah's case had become. Her eyes searched the article for the highlights and more intimate details regarding how Hannah had died.

Stanislaus County Coroner's Office determined the cause of death to be blunt force trauma to the head. Deep ligature marks on each of Chamber's wrists lead investigators to believe there was foul play involved.

"I knew it," Hailey declared her certainty as she continued reading.

"This is not the outcome we were hoping for, but at least the family can now have closure," Lead Officer Heartman stated.

Hailey scoffed at the statement. *You can't have closure when foul play is involved and the suspect is still at large.*

Just as she began reading again, a loud snap reverberated through the trees behind her. Hailey gasped as a branch cracked somewhere in the darkness. She whipped her head around and clicked on the flashlight to peer into the wooded landscape. Nothing but still trees and branches filled her line of sight. Her heart was beating rapidly as her stomach stirred with panic.

Faint footsteps crossed the forest floor. The glow of the bright moon gave just enough light to the forest where her light couldn't reach, allowing her to see the silhouettes of the giant trees stretching towards the sky. When Hailey first pulled into the site, she liked the light of the moon, but now she realized it only made her surroundings appear more eerie and intimidating.

"Hello? Is someone there?" her voice quivered.

She sat still as she waited for a reply, one she wasn't entirely certain she wanted to hear. After a minute of silence and the rise of unease, Hailey decided it was time head back into the van. Leaving the webpage open, she slammed her laptop shut and shoved it back inside the case. Keeping the flashlight directed towards the unidentified sound, she descended the ladder as fast as she could. Just as her second foot touched the ground, the sound of rustling leaves came from the opposite side of the van. Something was out there. Hailey wasn't as secluded as she thought she was. Taking in a deep breath, she darted to the handle on the side door, yanked it open, and leapt inside.

As soon as she was fully in the van, she slammed the door shut, locking it tight behind her.

Chapter 9

"Can you believe it?" Hailey laughed at her own expense. "It was a deer."

"Well I am glad it was just a deer," Sarah said. "I don't want you to end up on my autopsy table."

"Nor do I!" Hailey agreed.

It felt good to catch up with her friend again. Ever since Hailey moved to San Diego and Sarah started her demanding job as a medical examiner, they didn't have as much time to catch up as they used to in college.

"So, I'm dying to hear about your journey so far! How's living in the van going? Have you met anyone on the road? Tell me everything."

"How about I start with one question at a time." Hailey laughed, although she did always enjoy Sarah's enthusiasm. "Living in the van has been better than I expected so far."

"Really? Well that's good!"

"Yeah, I mean it's sort of like living in a dorm room again. Remember how tiny ours was sophomore year?"

"How could I forget?" Sarah said with a giggle. "We were basically living inside of a closet."

"Well, imagine that, but with a tiny kitchenette added."

"I saw your post, your van remodel looks awesome. Way more glamorous than our dorm room, that's for sure!"

"Thank you! It certainly was a challenge to put together, but I think it turned out pretty good." Hailey looked around the van as she spoke, smiling at her work.

"So, the next question on my list is, have you met anyone yet?" Sarah asked.

"Not really," Hailey shrugged. "Except for a guy that helped me change my tire when it blew out on the highway."

"Oh yeah? Was he cute?" Sarah was excited to hear about a man other than Jeremy for once. She had never been keen on Jeremy ever since Hailey started dating him in the middle of their sophomore year, so it was safe to say she wasn't surprised or upset to hear they had broken up.

"On a side note, I'm fine, thanks for asking," Hailey teased. "But I guess you could say that I didn't mind him helping me out." She smirked as she recalled the moment.

"I'm glad to hear it. Well you know you can always call me if and when you need someone to talk to or don't feel safe and need to have someone on the phone with you. Well, when I'm not busy working that is," Sarah stated.

"Work keeping you busy?" Hailey asked.

"Very busy." Sarah paused then added, "Good for me, bad for those who end up on my autopsy table."

"Hey, speaking of autopsy and your work," Hailey began, "I'm assuming you know about the missing girl's body they found in Cow Creek the other day?" Hailey had no problem switching gears and prodding her medical friend for details.

"Oh yes. Especially since the girl was from here. Pretty terrifying isn't it? I'm worried about you traveling alone through those woods after learning about that incident."

"Yeah, I can't deny that last night I saw my life flash before my eyes when I heard those footsteps," Hailey commented.

"You know, the girl was traveling in a van just like you," Sarah said.

"Yeah, I know," Hailey glanced over at her open computer at the edge of the bed. "I...may have actually found her on Instagram and stalked her page."

"I would expect nothing less from you, or from a reporter I should say," Sarah teased.

Hailey never admitted it, but she loved that Sarah always referred to her as a reporter. Even though she may not have gotten the job she was aiming for out of college, Hailey still had her sights set on becoming an investigative reporter.

"And did you find anything interesting?"

"Well actually, when I was reading a news article about the crime scene and the details they have so far about it all, I noticed that the investigation was through Stanislaus county, isn't that the county you work for?" Hailey asked.

"No, I'm working in Sacramento County, but since the girl happens to be from Sacramento, we actually did receive her body to do the autopsy."

"For real? Why didn't you mention that to start!"

"You know I'm not supposed to share the inside details of cases with the public. Nor did I think you would be questioning me about it," Sarah stated.

"So I'm just part of the crowd?" Hailey asked.

"Oh come on, Hails, you know that's not true. I just really like this location and company, and I didn't want to risk saying anything that could get me in trouble. Not to mention I had absolutely no clue that you would be asking me about a murder victim."

"Alright, I suppose that's fair. But you know you can trust me. I mean, I don't even have a job," Hailey replied.

"I know, you're right. Honestly, I'd rather share these things with you than the media-hungry reporters out here anyway. They don't even care about the victims, just the story they can create out of them to make themselves look like they are the number one crime reporters." Hailey could picture Sarah rolling her eyes in disgust. She always hated the reporters who entered journalism just to be in the limelight.

"So when did you find out you would be examining Hannah?"

"Well I actually received the paperwork first from the forensics officers in Stanislaus County, since they were the ones at the crime scene, and honestly, it was hard to read."

"What do you mean? Was the scene gruesome?" Hailey questioned.

"It was bad, Hailey, what happened to that girl." Her voice was serious. "I see a lot of things, but this...this was done by someone with a lot of anger."

"How could you tell?" Hailey was all ears.

"Brace yourself because it's not pleasant." Sarah let out a sorrowful sigh as she relayed the details. "When the forensics arrived on the scene, they noted both of her shoulders had been dislocated. Each wrist was ingrained with purplish-red ligature marks, indicating that she was held in some sort of tight binding and was fighting to break free from it. Her feet were pretty beat up with scrapes and splinters. There were also cuts and bruises that covered the lower half of her legs, indicating that she was most likely running through the woods barefoot. She also showed signs of strangulation."

"That's awful. Definitely sounds like she was tortured."

"That's not even the worst of it. She had been stabbed seventy-three times between her chest and abdominal area."

"Seventy-three times?!" Hailey gasped. "I'm clearly not a professional examiner, but isn't that major overkill?"

"Complete overkill," Sarah confirmed.

She shook her head in disbelief. "How could someone stab another person that many times? Is that even possible?"

"It would certainly take a lot of persistence." Sarah paused. "And anger."

Hailey cringed. "That is bad. Do you think this was a wrong place, wrong time, scenario?"

"It's hard to say at this point, but the nature of the wounds make me think this was personal."

"You think she knew her killer?" Hailey stood up and put the kettle on the stove.

"From my experience, I think it's highly likely, but there just isn't enough evidence to support that theory right now." The line fell silent between them.

Hailey considered the information for a moment. "There must have been some sort of a trigger that really set this guy off then. Something had to be pushing that anger."

"I can't tell you what the motive was for this murder, or why he chose Hannah, but I will see what she can tell me from her wounds."

What she can tell me from her wounds, Hailey replayed Sarah's sentence in her head.

From the first day she met Sarah, in an ethics class freshman year of college, Hailey knew they would become great friends. With Hailey being interested in criminology and Sarah going into medical school to become a medical examiner, they both found a common interest in researching and solving crimes. Unfortunately, Hailey wasn't quite as lucky as Sarah was when it came to landing a promising job after completing their master's programs.

"There is one more thing that was found on Hannah at the scene that I think is definitely worth noting." Sarah commented, pulling Hailey out of her head. "There was a Polaroid picture that was taken of Hannah found with the body."

"A Polaroid?" Hailey was confused, yet intrigued.

"Strange, isn't it? I didn't even know people used those cameras anymore," Sarah stated.

"I think they are making a comeback through the younger generation in an ironic way, like old school is new school."

"Well, the picture was taken before he killed her, and it looks like it was taken in some sort of concrete room."

"A concrete room? Are you sure?" Hailey questioned.

"That's certainly what it looks like." Sarah confirmed. "Hannah is hanging by her wrists from what looks like a water pipe in a basement, maybe a warehouse of some sort."

"That could explain the dislocated shoulders," Hailey suggested.

"I sent the image over to the lab to see if we can get any fingerprints off of it."

"And where was the picture found?"

"I mean, it was tucked into the back pocket of her shorts. My guess is that he did that because it was just about the right size to fit into her pocket without falling out. He definitely wanted us to find it."

"How do you know?" Hailey asked.

"It was clearly placed into her pocket after he killed her. It wasn't crinkled or torn, and there is no way if she was still alive or awake when he put it in her pocket that she wouldn't be squirming uncontrollably. Or if he dragged her into the forest after he murdered her, and the picture was already in her pocket, then it would have gotten at least wrinkled or dirty."

"Yeah I suppose that makes sense," Hailey agreed.

"There's one more significant detail about the picture. It had a caption written on it in the thick, white border beneath the image."

"What did it say?"

"It said: *How picture perfect is your life now? #vanlife.*"

"Hmm, it sounds like he's up to date with social media if he added a hashtag at the end. And this guy is definitely trying to get some sort of point across if he went through the effort to take the photograph and dump the body where he knows it would be found."

Hailey took a minute to write down all of the details into her notebook. Even though she had originally planned to use the notebook as her travel journal, Hailey decided this information was more important to keep track of. It was a lot to take in, and she didn't want to forget any bit of it. Besides, she always had her photographs to look back at to remember the locations she had stayed at.

"Exactly what everyone is thinking here, too," Sarah replied. "I will forever wonder how you didn't get any of those reporter jobs you applied for."

"Thanks, Sarah." Hailey smiled. "Me too."

"It's not too late, you know. I just got lucky with my job since it's certainly not for everyone, but maybe after your journey you can get back out there and look for a reporting gig," Sarah suggested.

"Yeah. Maybe."

"You know, speaking of your journey," Sarah began switching gears, "I was thinking about you all alone out there, and I think you should get a dog." She paused, waiting for a response. When she didn't receive one, she continued, "I think it would be good for you to have a companion and maybe a little more protection, considering you wouldn't get a little ankle-biter."

Hailey considered it for a moment. "I was actually thinking the same thing last night."

"Could have saved you from those ferocious deer." They both giggled at the comment, lightening the mood.

"Did you know Hannah had a dog?" Hailey asked. "When I was looking through her Instagram, I noticed she had a dog in almost every picture."

"Really? Huh." Sarah searched her memory for any mention of a dog from the detectives on the scene but couldn't remember anyone saying anything.

"Yeah, I thought it was a little interesting that it wasn't mentioned in any of the news stories."

"I don't think it's been mentioned around here either, as far as I know."

"So I wonder where that dog is now."

"I'll be sure to keep an ear out."

The line fell silent again as they each retreated into their own thoughts. That was the best thing about good friends; there was nothing awkward about silence between one another, just mutual comfort.

"In all seriousness, aren't you lonely out there?" Sarah asked, pressing the matter.

Looking around at the empty, compact space, Hailey considered the question. "Sometimes. I certainly talk aloud to myself a lot more often than I used to."

"Then maybe it really would be a good idea for you to get a dog. I know several rescue shelters in town! If you came through here, I could go with you." Her enthusiasm radiated through the line.

"Let's not get ahead of ourselves here." Hailey learned her lesson after moving in with Jeremy that she shouldn't make rash decisions; they didn't seem to end up in her favor.

"At least consider it, Hailey. I'm even more convinced now that you need one after talking about this case."

"I will, I will." Hailey poured steaming water into a mug from the kettle and watched it cascade over the tea bag.

"Hey, um, the coroner's office is calling, I've got to go. Love you. Be safe. We'll talk soon to pick out your dog!" The line clicked as Sarah hung up.

Hailey rolled her eyes and laughed at Sarah's positive spirit. For being someone who worked with dead bodies day in and day out, she still managed to have one of the brightest personalities.

After finishing her tea, Hailey decided to slip on her hiking shoes and go for a walk. She had found a trail not too far from her camping spot that led to some decent-sized trees, at least according to the reviews.

As she wandered down the trail, she recounted the details Sarah had given her about Hannah's murder. Hailey was thankful she happened to have such a good friend on the inside of the justice system working with similar cases she someday hoped to be the lead investigative reporter on.

It wasn't long into the trail that Hailey found herself surrounded by enormous trees. She wasn't sure they were as big as the giant sequoias deep within the forest, but she had never seen anything like them. The immensity that each one had was breathtaking. Unlike in Joshua Tree, there was no problem finding protection from the sun beneath the towering trees. With nowhere to be, beautiful surroundings, and new information on the case filling her mind, Hailey kept a slow pace as she strolled down the trail. She walked slightly off the trail and up to one of the enormous trees. She ran her fingers across the bark, noticing the smooth, almost polished sheen it had from being touched by the hundreds of curious hands that had crossed it before.

As she stood at the base with her hand gently resting on a deep crevice that ran vertically up the tree, she couldn't help but wonder if Hannah's hands had met this same tree. And if they had, was the killer close behind? A shiver ran up her spine at the thought as she pulled her hand back.

Hailey glanced up and down the trail; no one in sight. Shaking the unsettling feeling from her mind, she continued back on the trail. It was still summer, but the elevation of the forest created much lower temperatures than the desert she had traveled from. Hailey removed one of the straps from her backpack off her arm, allowing her easier access to the pocket that held her sweatshirt. As she pulled out her jacket, her phone slipped out of the pocket and tumbled to the ground.

"Dammit." Swiftly picking it up from the forest floor, she blew the dust off it, then rubbed it against her shirt. She analyzed the screen to be sure it wasn't broken or cracked as she whipped off that excess dirt with the cuff of her sleeve. As she fumbled with the phone, the screen illuminated, showing a new text from Sarah. Surprised to see a message so soon after they had talked, Hailey furrowed her brown in confusion as she opened the text.

'Another body was just found.'

Chapter 10

A red exclamation point popped up next to her message after she hit send. *'Message Delivery Failed.'*

"Of course," she huffed as she rolled her eyes. "No service." Hailey pushed her phone towards the sky, as if the connection would be stronger two feet above her head. Wishful thinking.

Out of nowhere, a voice called out from behind her shoulder, "Are you lost?"

Startled, she pulled her arm to her chest, cradling her phone in her hand. Immediately realizing she needed a better defense stance, she straightened her back and brought her arms to her sides.

"No, I..." her voice trailed off as she turned to meet the inquisitor. "Luke?" A smile mixed with shock began to cross her face before she caught herself and bit her lip, trying not to show her excitement.

"I thought that might have been you," he said as he approached closer.

"Are you stalking me?" Hailey asked half playfully.

"Just making sure you didn't need my help again." He smirked as he pulled out his canteen and brought it to his lips. "Did you find a good place to get that tire replaced?"

"I wouldn't say it was the nicest place, but one hundred and fifty dollars and one new tire later, I am back in business." She felt her muscles relax as she spoke.

While sliding his canteen back into the side pocket of his backpack, he smiled lightly and looked up at the canopy of leaves high above them. "Pretty incredible place, isn't it?"

Her eyes followed the trunk of a tree up to the sky. "Yeah, these trees are pretty unbelievable."

"And these aren't even the giant sequoias that this place is known for," he stated. "So, are you staying around here?"

Unsure of how many details she wanted to give away, Hailey considered her answer before she replied. She was a little on edge, considering just minutes earlier she learned that another body had been found. She was absolutely convinced now that there was a serial killer currently on the loose in the forests, and for all she knew, it could be Luke. Pushing the negative thoughts out of her mind, she chimed back into the conversation before the silence grew awkward. "Yeah, I found a pretty nice boondocking site not too far from this trail."

"Nice. I'm boondocking not too far from here myself."

They continued walking down the trail together making chit chat, but in the back of her mind she was pondering if he wanted to murder her, he would have done so when she was stranded alone on the side of the road. Right? At least that's what Hailey was trying to convince herself for the time being. She didn't want to admit it to herself, but she was enjoying his company. It hadn't been long since she started her journey, but she was already starting to miss the daily human interactions that she had become so accustomed to.

"So, how long have you been on the road?" she asked.

"About nine months." He lifted his eyebrows as if he was shocked by his own response. "What about you?"

"I'm still in my first month." She felt a hint of embarrassment at her lack of experience.

"Well, you know, time flies by when you're living on the road. Seeing so many incredible places makes the days go by quick," he replied.

His response prompted Hailey to peer down at her watch. She was surprised to see an hour had already gone by since they started walking together. "I don't mean to cut our time short, but I need to get back to my van soon." She had been enjoying her walk with Luke so much that she had almost forgotten she was on a mission to find cell phone service.

"Maybe I could move my van closer to where you're parked?" Luke suggested, unsure if he was being too forward.

Hailey considered the proposal for a moment, reminding herself, *If he wanted to murder me, he would have done so when I was stranded alone on the side of the road in the desert.*

"You don't like the spot you found?" She couldn't simply agree to his proposition without questioning him first.

"It looked like I had some rowdy neighbors pulling in nearby this morning." He shrugged his shoulders as he looked up at her and continued, "It would be nice to have some familiar company."

"I suppose I could use some help starting my first fire," she replied, trying to act coy.

"I can certainly help you with that." The corners of his lips pulled into a smile.

"Great, I will see you at my site then." Hailey could feel the heat in her cheeks. Was she really that out of practice talking to men that this simple interaction was making her nervous? Hailey pivoted to walk away before he would notice the pink in her cheeks.

"Wait." Luke called out. "How will I know where you're parked?"

"Oh, right. Good question." Hailey laughed at herself and added, "Might be hard to find me if you have no idea where I am in this giant forest."

Hailey reached around to the small pocket in the front of her backpack and pulled out her map. Since she had planned to keep a journal of all the places she stayed at and visited along her journey, she had circled the coordinates of where her campsite was when she arrived the previous night. Lucky for the both of them.

"This is where I am," she said, pointing at the highlighter pink circle on the map.

Luke pulled out his phone and snapped a picture of her map. "Perfect," he said as his eyes met hers. "I will see you there then."

He turned and began walking back towards the direction he had originally come from.

Hailey felt slightly guilty that they had been walking towards her van all this time, and he would have a much longer trek back to his spot. But the feeling quickly faded as Hailey realized that would give her time to phone Sarah before he arrived at her site.

As she neared the site, she felt her phone buzz several times in a row, confirming she was back in range of service. "Yes!" she cheered, pulling her phone out from her pocket.

Hailey dialed Sarah, her apprehension growing stronger with each ring as her van came into view. Sarah's voicemail filled the line, and Hailey let out a disappointed sigh before leaving her message: "Hey, it's Hailey. I got your message, call me as soon as you can."

Hailey swung open the door to the van and went straight for her laptop. It appeared the service was somehow better than it was the night before and she was able to get a couple of bars of connectivity from inside of the van.

She decided to start with a broad search and typed in the search bar: *body recently found in California forest. The results were overwhelming.*

"Wow," Hailey exhaled. The amount of articles regarding bodies that had been found in the forests of California was astonishing, to say the least. She was going to need more details to narrow down her search. She picked up her phone and switched on the screen, hoping to see Sarah's name pop up. Nothing. Feeling defeated, she opened up Instagram and began scrolling through the feed. She found herself back on Hannah's page. She still couldn't shake her curiosity about Hannah's fate, and especially her growing interest in the internet troll that appeared on several of her posts.

Gravel crunched outside the van and Hailey knew that meant her research time was up. She slid her laptop back under her pillow and glanced out the window to see Luke's van pulling into the site. Hailey grabbed the sweater hanging by the bed and threw it over her shoulders. The sun was beginning to fade beyond the trees, bringing in the cool evening air. She peered at her phone screen one more time just to be sure she didn't miss anything before shoving it into her pocket and jumping out of her van to greet Luke.

"You found me," she said with a smile.

"Indeed I did!" He climbed out of the front seat and surveyed the surroundings. "You have a great spot here."

"Not a bad find for my first time boondocking," she said with a grin.

As the evening grew darker, Luke tucked in handfuls of dried pine needles and twigs from the ground under the larger pieces of firewood Hailey had bought from the gas station.

"That should do it." He lit a match and held it in the center of the stack, then gently blew on the tiny glowing flame.

Hailey sat in her camping chair, leaning forward to observe his work. "Well, that seems easy enough. I think I could do that on my own if I needed to."

"If you're planning to be on the road for a while, I'm sure you'll pick up all sorts of camping skills that you don't already have," he commented, keeping his eyes focused on the fire as he spoke.

Hailey leaned back into her chair as the flames took hold of the wood. His work was done. It felt good to have some company for a change, but her mind was still spiraling with questions about the new body that had been found and if it was related to Hannah's death.

"Have you ever felt unsafe during your time on the road?" She looked over at him as he appeared to be admiring his work of lighting a perfect fire. Hailey smirked at the sight.

Luke crossed his arms and took a moment to search his memory.

"Only a time or two," he answered, shrugging his shoulders. It was hard for Hailey to tell if he was just trying to come off as manly or if the moments he was thinking of truly weren't that frightening.

Hailey looked up at him with raised eyebrows. "Do I sense a story there?"

Luke smiled and walked over to his camping chair to sit down, tossing one last twig into the fire that he had left in his hand. "Well, I've never felt directly threatened by anyone, but you could say I've seen some interesting things since I've been on the road."

"What do you mean by interesting?"

"I don't want to spook you out, seeing that you're a newbie to this lifestyle."

"I think I can handle it," she replied smugly.

"Alright, well, the one that I still question was from the time I was camping in southern Colorado. It was a couple of months ago, when I came across a beautiful campground. It was right next to a still lake, surrounded by a deep forest of tall, healthy trees, and there appeared to be no one else in sight, so it was ideal for someone like me who was looking for some peace and quiet for a bit."

"Sounds like a great spot," Hailey agreed.

"And it really was. I discovered there was a trail that went around the lake, so naturally, I decided to go for a walk and check it out. It was so serene and peaceful, I was like, 'Sweet, I got this all to myself, jackpot.' "

Hailey could tell this is where his sweet campground was about to turn sour.

"Then as I came around the last bend in the trail, I spotted another campsite that *appeared* to be occupied."

"Appeared to be?" Her brows furrowed in confusion.

"It was the strangest thing." He ran his fingers through his dark hair as if he was still baffled by the scene. "There was a tent set up, a nice bike leaning up against the picnic table, and tons of food boxes and containers laying across the top of the table. It looked like whoever was staying there had been there for a long time and wasn't too concerned about picking up after themselves. But that wasn't the weirdest part." He shook his head and leaned forward in his chair, resting his elbows on his knees and clasping his hands together. "There was piano wire that was stretched and pulled tight between the trees around the site."

"To hang clothes on?" Hailey questioned.

"Initially, that's what I thought, too, but these wires were stretched around the complete perimeter of the site. As if he was booby-trapping the area or something."

"Okay, that does seem a little strange." Hailey was now leaning in, too.

"I thought that maybe it could have been to keep animals away from the site, but the position of the wire on the tree was just..." he paused searching his mind for the right word, "odd."

"So there wasn't a person there when you walked by?"

"That's the part that put me on edge," he continued as Hailey leaned in, completely captivated. "I didn't see anyone come or go from that site the entire four days that I stayed there."

Her eyes widened with surprise. "No one at all?"

"Not a single sound or movement. No sign of life."

She leaned back into the chair and took a deep breath, going over all the details of his story. Her arms prickled with goosebumps. "That would certainly creep me out," she said as her eyes focused on the flames.

Luke let out a chuckle. "Isn't it funny how the lack of someone's presence can be so creepy?"

"I mean, especially when there are clear signs that someone was there at some point," she added.

"Exactly. Like where were they? Did they abandon it? Or was it a hiker gone missing type of scenario? Did an animal get them, or even another person? I have no idea, but they clearly had some fear about who or what was in the area, hence the wired fencing they put up. It had me on edge the entire time I was there."

Hailey's thoughts drifted off to Hannah and the new mystery body that had appeared. It was true, she wasn't afraid to hear about murders or frightening events. The fear was created by the mystery of it all. If people knew who the murderer was or why these individuals were being targeted, it wouldn't be *as* scary. The lack of leads or motives leaves people at the mercy of their own imagination. And nothing is scarier than one's own imagination.

"So what? You just left the last day and that was that?" she asked.

"Actually, the day before I left I called the forest service to let them know what I observed. I waited around the next day to see if anyone would show up, either the mystery camper or a forest ranger, but no one did."

"That's really weird. I think I would be freaked out for sure, especially if I was camping alone."

They both shook their heads in unison, as if to shake the chilling thoughts from their minds.

As the hours passed and they became more acquainted. Hailey was surprised at how easy Luke was to talk to and how much they had in common considering they had just run into each other in the woods. Or on the side of the highway, to be more precise.

During their time sitting by the fire, Hailey learned that Luke had gone to business school to study finance. But after three years of working as a financial advisor, he decided that traveling was his real passion. He made the decision to begin saving up money at the start of his third year with the company, and by the end of it, he had saved enough to buy a Sprinter van and support his travels for at least six months. When he hit the road, he began teaching himself how to code and create websites. Eventually, he got proficient enough to market his skills to others, providing him with a sufficient income to continue traveling past his original six month mark.

"It was hard at first. I would stay up all night watching YouTube videos and doing research online about how to create different web designs. Finally, I got to a point where I was able to create them on my own and began to market my skills through several freelancing websites."

Hailey felt a tiny tinge of contempt flicker inside as he spoke. She was unsure whether it was because she was subconsciously upset with him for choosing to leave a well-paying job to live a life on the road, or envious of him for following his passion and making a career for himself while traveling. Or maybe she was still holding a grudge because she didn't have a choice to leave her job in the city.

"What about you?" he asked, returning the question. "What led you to the vanlife?"

Pulling a beer to her lips, she took a generous sip as she stared into the flames. If she told him the truth, would he think she was just running away from the real world? That she was just a coward, running away from her problems? Then again, maybe if those were his judgments, they would be accurate. Maybe she was running away. Hailey began to question herself in the wake of his inquiry.

"Oh you know," she began, "just your basic heartbreak story." She decided to go with the truth but play it off casually, hoping he wouldn't ask too many follow up questions.

"Is that so?"

"Yeah. I decided to take the leap and move in with my boyfriend, but he didn't turn out to be the Prince Charming I thought he was," she replied, taking another drink.

Luke tilted his head up from the fire. An orange glow flickered across his face as he pulled his lips into a half smile. "Sounds to me like you had the perfect reason to start a new adventure."

Hailey felt her body relax and, for the first time since leaving Jeremy, she felt a glimmer of pride. "I thought so, too."

Smoldering red and orange coals glimmered beneath the pile of charred logs as Hailey and Luke mutually decided it was time to call it a night. As Luke shoveled mounds of dirt over the hot embers and stirred in some water, Hailey gathered up their empty beer cans, tossing them into a trash bag. She was only planning on having one drink when he offered her a beer, but good conversation and four hours later, one had turned into four. It had been awhile since she'd had more than one drink, and she could feel the warm buzz of alcohol coursing through her veins.

"Alright, I think that's everything." Hailey tossed the trash bag onto the floor of her passenger's seat and slammed the door shut.

"Thanks for tossing those out," Luke said, as he stood next to the now dark campfire ring, holding a shovel in one hand and pulling the headlamp off his head with the other.

"Thank you for the drinks," she replied, making her way back over to where he stood.

They stood face to face with nothing but the silvery glow of the moonlight reflecting off their skin. Hailey felt her body waver as she stopped just a few feet away from Luke, unsure whether it was the beer or the uneven wooded ground that set her equilibrium askew. She felt a glint of nerves rustle in her gut as she searched for the right words to say to her new acquaintance.

"I guess I'll be seeing you for breakfast then?" Hailey asked, instantly regretting her choice.

"Yes, I would guess so." Luke chuckled. "And I look forward to it. Goodnight, Hailey."

"Goodnight, Luke," she replied with a moonlit smile and retreated to her van.

Chapter 11

Hailey was jolted awake by rhythmic vibrations humming across the counter of her kitchenette. Beneath the dense canopy of trees that soared over the campsite, the inside of the van was still dark, making it hard to tell how long the sun had been up. Groggy from sleep, Hailey stretched out her arm trying to reach her phone without having to leave the comfort of her bed. She wrapped her fingers around the thin edges and held it just above her as she laid her head back into her pillow. Squinting her eyes at the bright screen, Sarah's name came into focus and Hailey suddenly felt wide awake.

"Sarah! Hey, I've been waiting to hear from you after getting your last message. What's going on?"

"Sorry, it's been a little hectic here with another homicide victim showing up only a couple days after Hannah."

"Yeah, no kidding, I was shocked to see your message, to say the least. I tried to message you back, but I didn't have service at the time."

"Well, in a nutshell, the department is ninety-five percent sure that it's the same guy," Sarah declared.

"How do they know?"

"They found another Polaroid on the victim."

"Then it's got to be him! Where was it found?"

"It was tucked into the back pocket of her jeans," Sarah stated.

"Similar placement to the one you found in Hannah's shorts."

"Exactly. And it was the same type of picture. Her hands were tied behind her back and her feet were also bound together at her ankles. She wasn't wearing any shoes, and you could see scrapes across her arms, legs, and face, which I would assume would be from running through branches and bushes in the woods."

"Hearing all that just makes my stomach churn."

"I know, and here's the kicker. Beneath the square photograph, there was a hand written caption that read: *'How perfect and beautiful does my life look now? #VANLIFE'.*"

"Okay, that has got to mean that it's the same person who killed Hannah." Hailey sat up in her bed.

"We don't have any DNA evidence yet, but with another Polaroid picture being found tucked in the victim's pocket, I think it's safe to say there is more going on here than a coincidence."

"Do you think you will get any fingerprints from the photographs?"

"I was really hoping we would be able to, but unfortunately when we ran the tests, nothing showed up."

"Damn, he must have been wearing gloves," Hailey inferred.

"That's my guess too."

"So I'm thinking maybe this guy has something against the lifestyle," Hailey commented.

"It's possible," Sarah continued in a dry tone as she read more details from the report: "*The girl was only twenty-three years old. Her acrylic nails were chipped and broken, indicating she at least put up a fight.*"

"Acrylic nails? That seems odd to have those if you're living on the road getting your hands dirty all the time."

"Yeah, my thoughts exactly. But definitely could play into the 'vanity victims' theory. We are waiting for the DNA results to come back from the lab from the swabs taken beneath each nail. Acrylics are good for picking up skin cells, so they may have been a good choice after all. Her left ankle was broken, and her legs were blotched with fresh scrapes and bruises, confirming my thoughts that she was running through the woods. Although, unlike all of the scrapes on Hannah's body, some of the lacerations on her legs ran vertically instead of horizontally. That typically indicates to me they were created from a dragging motion. Meaning the attacker must have had a hold on her upper body as he pulled her through the jagged terrain. She does seem to weigh a bit more than our first victim, so maybe he wasn't strong enough to pick up her whole body. But the rage was still apparent, making it similar to the other case. She was stabbed forty-six times, but the stab wounds aren't what killed this victim."

Hailey was listening intently, jotting down details in her notebook as Sarah spoke. There was silence on the line before Sarah flipped through some pages and continued, "She died from a deep laceration across her neck."

"Can you tell what type of weapon was used?"

"My guess would be something he found laying around, maybe a large piece of glass or a sharp rock? The wound wasn't clean; it was jagged and sloppy."

"Hmm, that's interesting." Hailey put a star next to the detail as she added it to the page.

"Something else came up in her results, too, that I didn't find in Hannah's. Flunitrazepam was in her system, or Rohypnol, as you might know it."

"Roofies?" Hailey was surprised. "So she was drugged." She stood up and peered out the window to see if there was any motion from Luke's van. No movement yet.

"That's correct."

Hailey began to think out loud. "If she was drugged, then that means she must have run into him under circumstances where she felt comfortable. Somewhere he could have slipped her the drugs without her being suspicious of him." She began thinking of the beers she shared with Luke the previous night. Some of the saddest cases are those where the victim trusted their assailant.

Sarah continued, "And the results that came back from Hannah's case showed that there were no toxins in her system. So he could have used them on our second victim because she was larger, maybe stronger, and he needed more to knock her out compared to our first victim. Also, neither one of the girls showed any signs of sexual assault."

"Well, that's at least good news."

"But we did find fibers on Hannah's shirt that weren't from any of her own clothing."

"That's got to give you something, right?"

"Too soon to tell. We will have to wait for lab tests to come back from the most recent victim and see if there are any of the same fibers on her clothing."

Hailey flipped to a new page in her notebook. "Okay, so let's go back to our latest victim for a minute."

"Alright. What do you want to know? Remember, I'm not a detective, so I don't exactly have all the details of what happened. Nor should I even be sharing any information about the cases really."

"I know, but you certainly get a lot more information about the case than the public does, considering you're working on the bodies. And you know you can trust me, I wouldn't say anything to jeopardize your job."

"That's true, and I know you wouldn't, " Sarah acknowledged.

"Okay, so let's start with where her body was found." Hailey put Sarah on speakerphone as she pulled up the map on her laptop.

"Um, let's see." The sound of rustling papers shot through the speaker as Sarah flipped through the report again. "Looks like she was found by a camper who was hiking near Lake Spaulding in Tahoe National Forest."

Searching Google Maps, Hailey located the lake. "That's not that far from where Hannah's body was found."

"Not far at all," Sarah confirmed.

Hailey heard a door slam and pulled back her curtain to see Luke walking towards her van.

"Dang it, I gotta go. Luke is coming," she blurted out, her voice rushed. "Thanks for all the info, Sarah, we'll have to continue this conversation later, but keep me posted on anything you hear, okay?"

"Wait, did you just say Luke?" Sarah could always switch gears in a heartbeat if there was a boy involved. "Is that the same guy that helped you with your flat tire?"

"Yeah...We sort of ran into each other in the woods yesterday afternoon and decided to camp in the same spot last night." The words collided together as she tried to rush them out as Luke was inching closer.

"Sounds like fate to me."

Hailey rolled her eyes. "It was just a coincidence."

"Uh huh, I'm sure it was," Sarah taunted.

"I'm hanging up now, I'll talk to you soon, okay?" Hailey knew she had to end the conversation before Sarah began asking more questions.

"Okay, okay. I'll talk to you soon. Be safe, Hails."

Hailey ended the call just before Luke approached the side of the vehicle. Before he could knock, she swung open the side door. "Good morning." She greeted him with a disheveled smile as she tried to mentally collect herself. It didn't take long for her welcoming look to fade once she realized she had yet to look at herself in the mirror.

"Morning." His smile was just as charming in the daylight as it was beside the flames. "Catching up with someone?" he questioned with a raise of his brow.

"Oh, yeah." Hailey looked to the ground caught off guard by his question. "Just making the daily call to my mom." She figured he must have heard her talking to someone but was really hoping he didn't hear more than muffled words.

As the words left her lips, she realized she really did need to call her mom before she began to worry about her again, which she would now have to do when Luke wasn't present being that she just lied to him about the whole interaction. Hailey wasn't very good at lying, but she didn't want Luke to know she was snooping around murder investigations involving women she had no tie to other than the fact that they were other solo van travelers.

"I try to make a call to my old man every day, too." Luke swatted a fly off his arm as he spoke. He turned around and began walking back towards his van as he called back over his shoulder, "I hope you like pancakes."

Hailey quickly changed into her day clothes, pulled her hair up into a ponytail, and brushed on some mascara. A flicker of adrenaline ignited in her chest as Luke came around his van holding two plates full of pancakes. She couldn't tell if it was the hunger she was feeling or the faint attraction for someone new kindling inside her stomach.

They each devoured their plate of pancakes in a matter of minutes, and with each bite Hailey couldn't keep her mind from mulling over all the information she had just received from Sarah. The second victim was drugged by ingesting a date-rape drug—that was certainly something she hadn't thought about before. She took a bite of her pancakes, hoping Luke didn't slip any unusual ingredients into her breakfast.

"So I was thinking about something this morning," Luke started.

"And what's that?"

"I know we barely know each other, but I enjoyed spending time with you last night and I feel like we get along well, at least judging from our conversations." He tilted his head towards her, searching her face for signs of affirmation. Hailey nodded in agreement with his statement, so he continued. "I remember you mentioning that you were heading towards Yosemite next, and, if you're interested, since I am traveling towards Yosemite too, maybe we could continue traveling together?" He jabbed two pieces of pancake together onto his fork and shoved them into his mouth as he waited for her reaction.

Hailey picked up a blueberry from her plate and popped it into her mouth. Her mind had gone back to her conversation with Sarah, blurring Luke's words. He waited for a response, but when one didn't come, he was beginning to regret his suggestion.

"Hailey?" he asked hesitantly.

She blinked rapidly, as the sound of her name brought her back to the conversation.

"What?" She looked at the ground, embarrassed that he caught her lost in her thoughts.

"What do you think? About us continuing our travels together?" He was trying to keep his cool, afraid he was going to be rejected.

"Oh, I..." her eyebrows lifted with surprise as she fumbled to find the right words. "I like that idea," she replied with a smile.

Luke visibly relaxed and grabbed her empty plate from her lap. As he walked away to toss out the plates, Hailey thought about their new plan to travel together. It wasn't a bad idea, right? After all, she was enjoying his company, and it didn't hurt that he was easy on the eyes.

"There is one thing I would like to do along the way," she called out to him from across the site.

"Yeah? Well, alright, I've never been one to say no to a little detour."

They exchanged a smile before Hailey pulled out her phone and opened up the web browser to start a new search. She began typing into the search bar: *Animal Shelters in Fresno, California.*

Chapter 12

Hailey kept glancing into her side mirror, making sure Luke's van was still in tow behind her. She was happy they had made plans to head to Yosemite National Park together, but Hailey was even more excited about the detour she had decided to make through Fresno along the way.

Hailey barely knew Luke, and she had yet to reveal anything to him about her interest in the murder cases, since she wasn't even sure at this point what her own plans were regarding the information she was gathering. It had only been a couple of days since she had been in contact with Sarah about the cases, but she had a feeling she wouldn't be able to keep her newfound obsession a secret for much longer if she and Luke continued to travel together.

Between the hours she spent with Luke and researching the murder cases the past couple of days, Hailey had been searching Craigslist and animal shelters in the cities near Yosemite for a dog. Even though she felt less lonely and safer traveling with a guy, she knew there was no promise they were going to continue traveling together long term. There was no promise, either, that he would even stick around after their next destination.

"Are you ready to do this?" Luke jumped out of his van with overwhelming excitement.

"You know I'm the one getting the dog and not you, right?" Hailey snickered.

"But since I'm traveling with you, I get to play with the dog, too," he replied lightheartedly.

"If you're lucky." She batted her eyelashes at him and walked towards the entrance. She almost forgot how fun it was to be playful with someone.

As they stepped through the two glass doors, an aroma of kibble, wet dog, and cleaning supplies hit them like a wall. As Hailey approached the desk, an older woman with strawberry blonde hair and deep red lipstick greeted her, "Good morning, are we looking for a new companion today?"

"Yes, I believe I am." Hailey matched the woman's bubbly tone. "I am hoping to find a medium-sized dog that is already potty trained, but that's not a complete deal breaker." She felt her nerves rise as the words left her lips. It was as if saying the sentence aloud to someone working at the shelter made the situation seem more real.

"Wonderful. I think I may have some great pups for you to see today." The woman cracked a small smile, nodded her head, and waved Hailey towards a hallway behind the desk.

As they walked down the hall, Hailey glanced into the rooms through the large viewing windows placed in each of the doors. As she passed by, one of the rooms was closed. Curiosity pushed her to peek through the window, knowing it meant there was a first time meeting happening between an animal and their potential new family. As she peered through the window, she saw a mother and her son, about six years old, sitting on the floor of the room. He was holding a kitten in his arms as he giggled and rubbed his face against its fur. The sweet sight of a family happily bonding with their new pet was just the warm fuzzy feeling she needed to confirm she was making the right decision.

Luke placed a hand on her shoulder and looked through the window, curious to see what she was involuntarily smiling at. "Soon that will be you." His warm breath against her neck sent goosebumps down her back.

"Miss," the woman said, standing at the end of the hallway, motioning to one of the open rooms. Hailey glanced back at Luke and flashed him an anxious smile. She walked to the end of the hall and stepped inside the bare room. Hailey sat in the nimble blue chair placed in the corner as Luke stood near the door.

"You two wait here. I will go retrieve our furry friend from the back." The woman's jovial tone was encouraging. They patiently waited as the woman left them alone in the room.

"Are you nervous?" Luke asked as he stood with both hands in his pockets and his sunglasses hanging from the collar of his shirt just below his neckline.

"More than I thought I would be," she answered, nodding her head as she tapped her foot on the linoleum flooring.

"Come on, honey." The woman returned sooner than expected, tugging on a leash behind her.

A medium-sized black, white, and brown dog with shaggy hair trotted through the door. "This here is Sadie. She's about three years old and completely potty trained."

Hailey held out her hand with her palm to the floor, allowing Sadie to sniff her fingers before reaching out to pet her head. Sadie hesitantly sniffed her hand before pushing her head into Hailey's arms, wiggling her body with excitement. Hailey laughed as pure joy rushed through her body, the dog continuing to rub against her legs.

"Looks like we may have a good match here." Luke bent down and Sadie trotted over to meet his welcoming stance. Sadie closed her eyes and leaned into his hands and he scratched behind her ears. The scene would make any woman's heart ache.

After several minutes alone with the dog, the woman reappeared in the doorway. "How are we doing in here?"

"She's such a sweet dog," Hailey responded with a grin.

"So do we think Miss Sadie found her forever home today?" The woman pulled her lips into a tight smile and winked.

Hailey held Sadie's head in her hands and looked into her eyes, one bright blue, the other golden brown. "I believe she did."

The women walked back from the file cabinet as Luke and Hailey stood at the front desk with Sadie by their side.

"Here is a folder with all her medical records, starting from the day she came into our rescue about a year ago." The woman placed a folder on the counter. "Let me print a receipt for you and then you guys will be all set to take home your new family member."

Hailey blushed at the woman's assumption that she and Luke were involved, although neither of them bothered to correct her. As Hailey gathered all the paperwork, Luke took hold of Sadie's leash and headed out the doors. She liked how easy things seemed to come with Luke, as if they had already known each other for a long time.

After a quick stop at the local pet store to pick up supplies for her new dog, Hailey and Luke each hopped into their vans and left Fresno to head towards Yosemite National Park.

"So do we have a last name for this Luke fellow?" His voice was teasing, but Hailey knew her father was serious.

"I'm not telling you because I know you're just going to go into *FBI Agent Mode* and do a complete background check on him," Hailey said, making a note to herself to figure out Luke's last name for her own sake.

"You know we just want to be sure you're safe, dear," her mother chimed in, clearly supporting the idea of a background check.

"Well, I at least have Sadie now." Hailey looked over at her new companion sitting in the passenger seat as she looked out the window. It was as if she knew it was where she was meant to be all along.

"Oh yes, you must send us pictures!" Her mother was elated.

"I think it was a great idea for you to get a dog, but remember, you still have to stay alert and make smart decisions out there." Despite her efforts, the FBI agent in him was still present.

"I know Dad. I'll be sure to pin my location and send it to you guys when I get to my camping spot."

"And please remember to send that tonight this time. You had your mother worried half to death last time you forgot."

"I know, I know, I'm sorry, it was just a busy day." The last thing she wanted to do was tell her parents that on top of traveling alone, she was also tracking murder cases of other young, female vanlifers.

"We know, we just worry." She could picture her mother standing in the front of their bay window staring out at the street, just the way she always did when Hailey and Daniel would walk home from school, waiting and worrying until they walked through the front door.

"You still remember all those martial arts skills I taught you, right?" her father inquired.

"Never missed a day of practice, Dad."

Hailey's father had seen all kinds of horrible things in his line of work. Kidnappings, homicides, gangs—name the crime, he'd investigated it. As early as she could remember, her father began teaching her and her brother martial arts; good skills for anyone to have throughout their life.

"That's my girl," he said, his tone soft and proud.

"Oh, Hailey, I almost forgot to tell you how beautiful your pictures are!"

"Thanks, Mom. I've been really enjoying capturing all these amazing places I have visited so far."

"Next to your writing, you've always been such a great photographer," her mother gushed. "You must get that skill from me."

"Oh, yes, from the woman who has yet to figure out how to take a selfie." She always teased her mom about her lack of knowledge about technology. "I'm getting off the freeway and need my directions, so I gotta go, guys."

"Okay, we love you. And remember to send us your location," her mother reiterated. "Bye, honey."

"I will, I will. Talk to you guys soon. Love you, too. Bye."

Hailey ended the call and patted Sadie on the head. Some days were harder than others when it came to missing her parents, but at least she now had Sadie to help fill the hole. It had only been a couple of hours since Hailey had picked up Sadie, but her heart was already filled with love for her new travel partner.

Luke had taken it upon himself to look for a pet-friendly campground in Yosemite when Hailey was checking out at the shelter, so he was driving in the lead this time. Hailey was thankful for him taking initiative, but she still had her map pulled out to follow along with the route. Better to be safe than end up lost and without service if she lost him on the road.

When they pulled into the campground, several spots had already been taken. As they continued down the gravel road, they were able to find a spot large enough to fit both of their vans. After they pulled into the site and parked, Hailey put on Sadie's leash so they could go on a walk to check out their new surroundings. They had only taken a couple steps down the road when Hailey's phone rang. As she pulled it out of her pocket to check who it was, Luke glanced down at the screen, too.

It was Sarah.

Chapter 13

"Do you need to get that?" Luke asked.

"Uh, no," she responded, shaking her head. Hailey tried to act casual, but with a clenched jaw and pursed lips, she was doing a poor job.

The deeper she would get involved in the cases, the harder it was going to be to hide them from Luke. Between Sarah taking breaks and Hailey having good enough service, it was challenging enough to get Sarah on the phone to talk about the details. Hailey also knew Sarah was risking a lot even sharing any bit of the details with her.

"Was that your mom again?" Luke questioned her, even though he already knew the answer.

"It was just a friend from college. I'll shoot her a text." She tugged on Sadie's leash and began walking down the road while texting Sarah.

Hey, I can't talk now. Chat later?

Hailey sent the message then slid the phone into her pocket, but that didn't stop her mind from composing a list of questions. She wanted to talk to Sarah, but she knew with Luke standing close by and walking through a busy campground, it wasn't a good time to take a call regarding details of a murder.

Luke didn't want to be pressing, but he could tell Hailey's mind was focused on something other than their stroll.

"So have you joined any Vanlife meetup groups?" he asked in an effort to recapture her attention.

"I actually did join a couple of groups before I hit the road." She paused to allow Sadie to sniff a tree. "But I haven't really checked any of them out yet."

"I've attended a couple of events by different groups," he stated.

"Are they any good?"

"Surprisingly, yes. I've met some pretty cool people." Seeing that he had regained her attention, he continued. "I saw there is an event coming up next weekend. That's actually why I was headed this direction. Maybe we could check it out together?"

Hailey debated the idea for a moment. Meeting strangers and participating in small talk had never been one of her strengths. She was a good reporter, which meant she was good at prodding people for information, but when it came to casual conversations with people she didn't know, she found herself fumbling to keep the conversation going. Maybe attending the event with Luke would help relieve some of her social anxiety, and it wouldn't be a bad idea to meet some other travelers. Hailey turned her head to face Luke, who cracked a side smile as their eyes met.

"Where is the event?" she asked.

"Sacramento."

Hailey thought about it for a moment before responding. "Alright, you can count me in." She felt a flutter in her chest at the thought of her confirmed attendance.

Just as she opened her mouth to ask him more details about the meetup, a vibration went off in her pocket. Hailey didn't have to take it out this time to know that it was Sarah again. Calling twice in the span of thirty minutes wasn't something she normally did. Something pretty important must have come up for her to reach out so urgently.

Hailey pulled out the phone and gave Luke an apologetic look. Reading her mind, he held out his hand to take the leash from her. She mouthed the words *'thank you'* as she answered the call. "Hey, Sarah." She placed the leash in his hands and patted Sadie on the head before she turned her back and walked away from the other campsites and from

Luke, far enough that he wouldn't be able to decipher her conversation.

"What have you got?" There was no time for pleasant exchanges.

"You're never going to guess what turned up today," Sarah began. "Remember that dog you said you saw in Hannah's Instagram pictures?"

"Yes, of course." Hailey could feel her pulse accelerate.

"They found it," she said, then stopped to let suspense linger. "Alive."

"For real? When? Where?"

"Our department got a call from the Calaveras Humane Society in Angels Camp earlier this morning. They said a couple who was driving down the highway saw a dog covered in blood walking along the side of the road. They assumed the dog had been hurt and was bleeding, so they picked him up and took him to the vet. After the vet took a look at him, she discovered he only had a sprained leg, but there were no open wounds."

"So the blood was from someone else," Hailey cut in, her voice almost a whisper.

"Exactly."

Sarah mirrored Hailey's quiet tone as she continued. "Luckily for us, the vet knew something wasn't right when she saw a lot of blood, but no open wounds, and called the M.E.'s office in Stockton. They went straight down to her office and took swabs of the blood from the dogs hair as well as swabs from under the dog's nails."

"And?" Hailey asked with anticipation.

"The blood that was on the dog's hair was a DNA match to Hannah," Sarah stated.

"I knew it. I knew that dog had to be somewhere out there! So that means the dog was there when Hannah was attacked," Hailey spoke aloud as she pieced together the information.

"That's right. But that's not even the surprising part," Sarah began as Hailey turned her head to peer around the tree to check on Luke and Sadie. "The lab tests that came back from the swabs taken from under the dog's nails weren't a match to Hannah's DNA."

"Really? Does that mean you have the killer's DNA then?"

"It can't be confirmed. There is no telling what the dog may have gotten into while wandering around in the woods and along the road. And they don't even have a main person of interest yet to compare the DNA to. Nothing showed up in the system."

"Damn. Well I guess that makes sense." Hailey pushed the dirt around with her foot as she considered the details.

"But I am also waiting for the results to come back from our other victim who was found by the lake. If we get skin cells from under the acrylics she was wearing, and compare the results from the dog's nails and get a match, then the forensic evidence will prove that we officially have a serial killer on our hands," Sarah stated.

"Especially considering the Polaroids you found tucked into each of the victims clothing," Hailey added.

"Exactly. Too many similarities to be two different murderers at this point."

"I'm going to see what I can find online. There has to be more details we're missing." With the new information Sarah had just revealed, Hailey knew these cases were related but, just like the detectives on the case, she didn't have enough hard proof to back up her suspicions yet.

"I have to get back to the lab. The latest victim's parents are coming in to identify the body. We have a hunch of who it is, but we need the next of kin to confirm."

"That has got to be awful to see."

"It's definitely one of the worst parts about my job," Sarah confirmed.

"Keep me updated on what you find."

"I will. Talk soon." The phone clicked as Sarah ended the call.

Hailey took a deep breath as she processed the new information. As she thought about the parents coming in to identify the body, it reminded her of the day her family had received the news about her brother. It had been just a normal Friday evening. She'd had a friend over to spend the night and they were playing up in her room when her father knocked on the door with a solemn face and tears welling in his eyes. Hailey had never seen her father cry before and knew something was terribly wrong.

After they laid Daniel to rest, her mother continued to cry everyday for months. For a while, Hailey thought they were never going to be able to heal from their loss. That one phone call had changed their lives forever. Hailey could feel a lump beginning to rise in her throat as the pain from the memory began to resurface.

Before she walked back over to Luke and Sadie, she took a moment to take in the scene. She couldn't help but wonder if these girls were traveling with a man they knew, or thought they knew? It made her question how much should she trust this guy she had only known for a short amount of time. Given the timeline of the murders so far, she didn't suspect Luke was dangerous, but it wasn't unreasonable to assume that the killer wasn't too far away if he was hunting in the California forests for his next victim.

As thoughts of paranoia began to creep into her mind, Hailey decided it would be a good time to check in with her parents. Not in the mood for a lengthy conversation over the phone, that would no doubt result in them bombarding her with questions about her travels, Hailey opted for a simple text instead. She wrote a brief message updating them from the last time they had spoken and reassured them that she was in a safe location and would call them soon. Pinning her location on the map, she hit send and slid her phone back into her pocket.

Hailey made her way back to Luke. He was kneeling down on one knee, smiling as he rubbed Sadie's neck. He looked up as he called out to her, "Is everything alright?"

"Oh yeah, we just haven't caught up in awhile." She was hoping he wouldn't catch her fib.

Hailey checked her watch then looked up at the sky. "Do you mind if we head back to the campsite? I'd love to get a picture of Sadie in the van before it gets too dark."

"Sure, no problem." Luke handed Sadie's leash back over to Hailey, and they began walking back.

Hailey sat down in her camping chair, handing Luke a plate of chicken, risotto, and cooked vegetables as he brushed his hands off after tossing one last log onto the fire.

"Wow, do you always cook like this?" He examined the plate, impressed with the spread.

"Actually, this is the most complicated meal I have made since being on the road."

"Then I feel honored." He forked a piece of chicken into his mouth, holding a closed mouth smirk as he chewed.

Hailey couldn't remember the last time she felt appreciated for cooking a meal; it was a good feeling for a change.

When she was almost done eating, she kept aside one last piece of chicken for Sadie, who was lying peacefully on a rug beside her chair. She got up to retrieve her camera.

"Did you get some good pictures of Sadie today?" Luke asked as he tossed his empty paper plate into the fire.

"I think so," Hailey turned on the camera and began scrolling through the photos.

"What do you think about this one?" She passed the camera over to Luke.

"Wow, that's really good," he said, almost sounding shocked. "You take really good pictures. I'm impressed." He continued scrolling through the photographs when an image of Hailey popped up on the screen.

"Uh, I was just testing the different filters," she blurted out, thankful the sun was down far enough that he couldn't see her blushing.

"Looks like they turned out pretty good," he said with a grin.

Hailey felt a shy smile across her face as he passed the camera back and her fingers brushed up against his hand. A rush of adrenaline flooded into her chest as she pulled the camera into her lap.

"Thank you," she responded as she turned off the screen.

"I think I'm going to turn in, I'm pretty tired from all our adventures today." She glanced down at Sadie who had her eyes closed as she rested her head on her paws.

"It looks like someone else is exhausted from the day, too."

They put out the fire, said goodnight, and retired to their vans.

Hailey washed her face, brushed her teeth, and placed a bowl of fresh water on the floor for Sadie. It wasn't a lie when she'd said she was tired from the day, but Hailey needed to come up with something to say to hide the fact that she really wanted to get back to her van to do some research on her laptop after gaining new information from Sarah.

The browser opened up to the Google homepage, and she began typing in the search bar: *girl's body found near Lake Spaulding CA*. As the page loaded, she pulled out her notebook and turned to a new page. The Google search returned with dozens of results. To her surprise, the first article on the list read "Polaroid Killer Strikes Again"

"Great." Hailey let out a sigh. "Looks like the media has officially gotten a hold of the cases."

As she scanned through the article, she began to wonder if the detectives on the case were upset that the media had labeled him with a name. If her hunch was right and he was targeting influential young women from social media because he felt the attention was being taken away from him, then the media was giving him just what he wanted—putting him in the spotlight.

Hailey knew she wouldn't be able to search Instagram for the girl's account yet without a name, considering the parents had only made it to the coroner's office that afternoon. After jumping through several articles, she decided they weren't providing her with any more information that she didn't already have from Sarah. Hailey decided she would text Sarah and ask if the family had confirmed or denied the identity yet. When a reply never came, Hailey accepted the fact that she was just going to have to patiently wait to hear from Sarah when she was in a position to share the information with her. Then maybe she would be able to see if there was any connection between the two victims on social media.

Sadie sat up on the rug and looked at Hailey with big eyes, hinting she wanted to come up onto the bed. Hailey thought about it for a minute, debating if she wanted to allow the dog onto her bed and what kind of precedent that would be creating, but she folded easily. After all, living out of a van didn't provide a lot of indoor space to begin with, and there were sure to be plenty of cold nights ahead when a warm body would be welcome to both.

"Come on." Hailey patted the side bench that was closer to the ground encouraging Sadie to jump up, knowing she wouldn't be able to make the direct jump from the floor to the bed. With a little wiggle and dip to wind up, Sadie leaped onto the side bench, then up onto the bed and licked Hailey's face. After Sadie got settled in the corner at the bottom of the bed, Hailey slipped her legs under the covers and rolled back onto her pillows.

It was only her first day with Sadie, but between her cellphone and camera, she already had dozens of photos to go through to decide which one she wanted to post to Instagram. After an hour and a half went by, she finally picked out her three favorite images and edited each one to have the same filter. Hailey had learned that many users on Instagram were beginning to use themes on their images to make them look uniform. So naturally, Hailey decided she would give it a shot. She plugged her phone into the power cord beside her bed and pondered a clever caption to introduce her new dog to the world. After typing and deleting several caption ideas, she finally created one that she was satisfied with.

Meet the newest adventurer to life on the road—Sadie! #dogswhotravel #vanlife.

Hailey read the caption one last time, hit post, and closed her screen as she placed it in the basket. Laying her head back onto her pillow, she already felt anxiety beginning to rise, anticipating how many people would like her post by morning. She stared up at the ceiling, thinking about the millions of people who were on Instagram. *So strange how social media has created a way to connect with strangers from all over the world,* she thought to herself. Pulling the blanket up to her chin, she snuggled into her pillow, being careful not to kick Sadie with her feet.

As she closed her eyes and turned away from her phone that was already illuminating with notifications, she wondered, *Does Luke have an Instagram?* She began brainstorming and formulating different possibilities in her mind of what screen name he would have. Would it be humorous, the type of screen name that's a play on words? Or maybe it would be related to his newfound life on the road. Or maybe it was as simple as making it his name, which reminded her, she needed to find out his last name. Not for her father, but for her own notes. Succumbing to her exhaustion, Hailey drifted off to sleep.

Chapter 14

"Mancini," Luke stated as he took a sip from his coffee mug.

"Ah, so you're Italian?" The dark hair and tan skin now made perfect sense.

"One hundred percent! I still have some family over in Italy that I used to go stay with during the summers growing up."

"But not anymore?" Hailey asked.

"Well, I went off to college and started working during the summers. Then after graduating, I got a 'real world' job, so I didn't really have the opportunity to go as often as I used to." He paused and looked towards the ground as he continued. "And after my father got sick, I couldn't bear to leave my mother home alone to take care of him on her own."

Hailey could sense the pain in his voice as he spoke. It was comforting to know he was close with his family, as if it were a trait that made him less threatening as a stranger and more relatable.

"Oh, I'm so sorry to hear that." Hailey held her coffee mug between both her hands as she looked at him with apologetic eyes.

He looked up at her as he leaned back in his chair and ran his fingers through his hair.

"Yeah, it was a tough couple of years. But thankfully he got better, and I felt like my family was in a place where I could travel and not have to worry as much about them constantly. Even though my dad wasn't exactly thrilled that I wanted to leave my finance job." He looked down at his feet then back up at her. "What does your family think about you hitting the road full-time to travel?"

"It took some convincing, but I think they support me. Well, at least I know my dad does. My mom is a bit of a helicopter parent."

"Ah, the overbearing type?" he asked

"Sort of, but I can't blame her." Hailey looked down into her mug at the light brown liquid, counting the swirls of vanilla creamer that glided across the surface. "We lost my brother when I was younger. My mom was always protective of us, but after losing Daniel, she went into extremely protective mom mode over me."

"I'm sorry, Hailey." Luke laid a hand on her knee. "I can't blame her for wanting to make sure you're safe then."

Luke removed his hand as he leaned back into his chair. Hailey followed suit, leaning back in silence. Several minutes passed as they sat gazing up through the branches at the wisps of clouds that drifted across the sky. Hailey was surprised at herself for sharing such an intimate detail about her life with Luke. It was something she didn't share with many people, especially with someone she had only known for less than a month.

"Speaking of losing loved ones..." He hesitated, creating suspense before he continued. "Have you heard about those girls that were murdered out here, near Yosemite?"

Hailey gradually sat up, wondering if this was her opportunity to come clean about the research and investigating she had been doing on the victims of the murders, or if she should just act casual. She decided to go with the latter.

"Oh yeah. I saw the news articles pop up in my news app. Sounds pretty scary." She was hoping he didn't see through her fib.

He shrugged his shoulders. "I wasn't sure if I should mention it or not, in case you hadn't heard about it. I didn't want to freak you out since you're a young girl who is technically traveling alone too."

"Yeah, I mean, it's definitely a little unsettling." She patted Sadie on the head, who was nestled between their chairs. "I think it's safe to say I feel safer having a dog with me now, so I'm not completely alone in the van."

"Not to mention your new human travel partner, too," he said with a cheeky grin.

"Oh well, of course," she added, smirking.

"You know, I was thinking, since we have been traveling together for a little bit now, maybe it would be a good idea to exchange numbers," Luke suggested as he retrieved his phone from his pocket.

"I suppose that's not a bad idea, just in case I need your muscles again in time of need." She smiled, slightly embarrassed at her attempt at flirting.

Luke opened up the number pad and handed his phone over to Hailey to enter in her contact information. As she passed back his phone, she searched her pockets for her own phone until she realized she had left it inside her van.

"I must have left mine in the van. I'll be right back."

Hailey stepped into her van and grabbed her phone out of the basket beside her bed. It was unlike her not to check it first thing when she woke up in the morning, especially after posting to Instagram the night before, but waking up to take the dog out had become her priority that morning, and Luke was already awake with coffee waiting.

Rushed and focused on pulling her phone off the plug, she didn't realize that her journal had been sitting on top of the cord. As she yanked the cord, it unraveled beneath the journal, flinging it onto the floor and landing in an open position. Being in such a rush, Hailey didn't even realize what had happened.

As she walked back over to where Luke was sitting, she saw 233 notifications from Instagram, one missed call from '*Home*', and a text from an unknown number, which she assumed was Luke.

"I'm guessing this 303 number is you?" she questioned, already knowing the answer.

"Yep, that's me."

"303?" She looked up at him quizzically, "Is that a Utah area code?"

"Colorado, actually. That's where I'm from."

"Oh nice, that is definitely a place on my list to check out!"

"It's pretty great, but unless you ski or like the snow, you should probably only go there during the summer," he suggested.

"I'm from Chicago, so I definitely know what it's like to be in cold weather, but that's also the reason I wanted to move out to Southern California. I prefer warmer weather and a more consistent climate."

"Yeah, it's hard to beat this place," he agreed. "So the next logical question in this day and age would be: Do you have an Instagram?"

"Ha, yeah, it almost seems like people these days exchange account information and screen names more than phone numbers, doesn't it? I have one, but I'm still working on getting it up to date," she replied. "I'm guessing you have one too?"

"I do now. I didn't used to, until I started traveling and became more involved with social media," he responded.

"I got one in college," she said, placing her phone into the empty cup holder in the arm of her chair, "but I was never that active on it either until I started this trip."

"So what's your screen name?"

"Hailey roaming, but all one word. " She leaned in close enough to see his screen to confirm he had the right account before clicking the 'Follow' button.

He clicked it and looked up with a teasing grin. "I hope I am interesting enough to get a follow back."

"I guess you will just have to see," she replied with a flirtatious smile.

Hailey opened her Instagram to follow him back and was pleasantly greeted with 64 more likes, eight comments, and nine new followers. It looked like her most recent post of her new dog in the van attracted even more attention than her first vanlife post. While Hailey was admiring all the attention her post had received, Luke was also scrolling through her

Instagram page.

"Wow, did you remodel your van?" He had clicked on one of the first images Hailey had posted when she had started her renovation.

"Yes, I did!"

"That's awesome. I've been seeing how a lot of new vanlifers are remodeling their RVs and vans. Yours looks really great in these pictures," he said, clearly impressed.

"You know, if you want, you could see it in person." Hailey gestured towards her van.

"Yeah, definitely. I'd love to!"

They stood up and walked over to her van. Hailey was hoping she didn't leave any bras or underwear laying out since he promptly took her up on the offer. As she swung open the door, she scanned the room to make sure it was presentable. Although, even if it wasn't, she wouldn't have had time to relocate anything before he saw it considering how close he was standing beside her. She instantly noticed her journal on the floor, scooped it up, and tossed it over to the bed.

"This is awesome!" Luke stepped into the van without hesitation. "I mean truly, you did a great job in here."

Hailey was a little surprised at his forwardness to just walk into her van, yet they did just share intimate details about their lives with one another, so she supposed he wasn't exactly classified as a stranger anymore. Still, her van wasn't just her mode of transportation, kitchen, or living room; it was also her bedroom, and this was the first other human to enter her personal space.

She stepped into the van after him as they began to discuss the details of her renovation.

"I can take your mug and rinse it out if you want." She held out her hand to take his mug as she continued relaying the details of how she got the van and where she had found all of the ideas for the interior layout. As she spoke, she rinsed off the mugs in her sink, allowing Luke's eyes to wander around the space, taking in all the personalized details and the

DIY decor she had crafted. He took a step over Sadie, who had decided to lay right beneath his feet, to take a look at the pictures she had hanging above the foot of her bed. As he browsed the photographs and noted the well-done shelving she had mounted, his eyes crossed over to the journal.

When Hailey had hastily tossed it onto the bed, she hadn't noticed the notebook had flipped open as it hit the comforter. Out of curiosity, he skimmed the words on the page. It didn't take him long to realize she had been lying when she said she had only seen the news articles about the murders. These notes had a lot more details than any news article would provide.

"Yeah, it was a lot of hard work, but it was definitely worth it to make this tiny space feel more like home." Completely unaware of Luke's wandering eyes, Hailey was still carrying on about the renovation process.

As she turned around to grab a towel to dry the mugs, she caught his gaze directed towards her open notebook.

"Did you open my notebook?" Simultaneously, she placed the damp mug and towel onto the counter as she lunged past Luke to grab it.

"What? No way, it was just open on your bed. I swear." Luke held up both his hands in surrender.

"But you were reading it." Hailey could feel the blood begin to rise in her cheeks.

"It was open and I just glanced at it. I didn't touch any of the pages or anything." Luke tried to take a step back but realized he had no room to do so in the tight space.

Hailey's heartbeat began to quicken as she tried to piece together her words. Was this her opportunity to come clean to Luke about all the research and investigating she had been doing? Or should she try to concoct another tale? She decided to go with the truth this time, at least most of the truth, that is.

"I'm a reporter," she declared, loosening her grasp on the notebook and looking down at the cover as she continued, "At least I was working towards becoming one."

"What do you mean?" Luke's arms fell back down to his sides.

"The reason I wanted to go on this journey isn't just because I had a bad break up." She paused and took a calming breath. "Another reason is because I lost my job."

Luke took a step towards her and laid a hand on her shoulder, his voice almost a whisper. "Hey, I'm not going to judge you. This is a part of what this vanlife is all about. Figuring out who you are and being able to work towards your passion without someone else stomping on it with their opinions."

Hailey began to feel guilty for not being up front with him when she had the chance the first time. But to be fair, she didn't know him that well yet and wasn't sure what his reaction would be.

Luke leaned back against her bed, sitting on the edge with his feet still touching the floor. "Remember how I told you I design and create websites for people?"

Hailey nodded her head.

"Well, one of the sites I made was for the first girl that went missing, Hannah."

"Wait, what?" Hailey was dismayed.

Luke exhaled. "Hannah's parents found me online, and they liked my work. They reached out and gave me a brief synopsis about how their daughter had gone missing while traveling and asked if I would create a website for them about her. You know, describing who she was, where she was last seen, and setting up a GoFundMe link for people to donate and contribute to the search."

"Wow, I just..." Hailey shook her head and looked down at her notebook. "I just wasn't expecting that."

"Yeah, it's not exactly a good discussion topic. Naturally, I built a bit of a relationship with the family when I was working with them, and it was pretty heartbreaking when they contacted me to notify me they wanted to change the description on the donation page from contributing to the search to her funeral service instead."

"I can imagine that would be pretty tough on everyone, no doubt."

"So, you're working to be some kind of crime reporter?" He paused as she nodded to confirm. "And you're reporting on the girls that have gone missing in the forests and parks these last couple of months?"

Luke looked at her with a furrowed brow. Hailey leaned against the bed beside him. "It all started when I happened to see the missing poster for Hannah in the visitor's center in Joshua Tree. It really captured my attention and curiosity, causing the reporter in me to just take over and go into investigation mode."

"But how did you end up with such in-depth information about the cases?"

"I happen to have a good friend who works as a medical examiner in Sacramento and due to the location of where the bodies were found, she has been working with the lead examiner on the cases."

"I suppose if you're going to report on the cases, it's good to have an inside connection," he stated. "Seems like the media is really running amok after that second girl was found."

"Yeah, no kidding. I hate those kinds of reporters," Hailey stated.

"So since you aren't working for anyone directly, you just take notes for yourself?"

"I guess that's one way to look at it. I've been using this journal to keep track of all the details I have received from Sarah and the other information I have gathered from doing research online about each of the victims."

"Makes sense. So then, what do you plan on doing with all the information you're gathering?"

"I'm not completely sure yet. Maybe write up my own article about everything? But of course I have to be careful about what I write or release to the public since I am not technically an accredited reporter right now."

"You know," Luke began as he folded one arm across his chest, resting his elbow on it as his hand rubbed against the scruff of his beard.

"I could create a website for you. You could think of it as your own news reporting site."

Hailey pondered the offer for a moment. She liked the idea of taking all the information she had gathered so far and piecing it together on an organized website, but that would also be risky. Most of the information she had gathered was done in questionable legal circumstances. If she started writing about everything she had gathered about the cases online now, she could get both her and Sarah into some major trouble, and that was the last thing she wanted to happen. Getting Sarah fired and losing any potential she may have of getting into the reporting world was the last thing she wanted to do.

"I wouldn't even charge you for it," he said with a side smile.

Sadie stretched out her legs and stood up to drink some water, then hopped out of the van onto the dirt. Hailey watched her as she trotted over to the rug between the camping chairs and laid down.

"I just might have to take you up on that offer." She didn't have the heart or the patience to explain to him why she couldn't have a website that revolved around the current information she had on the cases. "Are you hungry?" she asked changing the subject.

"Starving," he said as he placed his hand over his stomach.

After fixing up some sandwiches, Hailey and Luke retreated to their vans to change into their hiking attire. As Hailey slipped into her leggings and a workout shirt, she decided to check in with her parents. She wasn't sure how long they would be out on their hike and figured it would be better to call home sooner rather than later, especially after missing their call earlier that morning.

Before stepping out of her van to meet Luke, she opened up Instagram one last time to check the notifications on her post. As she scrolled through the notifications, there was a name and a comment that made her do a double take. *@camping_merkins57* had commented: *oh great another f'n vanlifer.*

Chapter 15

Hailey's stomach dropped as she read the comment. Did she just get a target drawn on her back? She clicked the username, just in case it wasn't him. When the profile marked "private" filled the screen, she knew it was the same internet troll that had commented on Hannah's posts.

"Are you ready?" Luke jogged over to her van as he called out.

"Um, yeah, let me just grab Sadie's travel water bowl," she responded as she fumbled to grab the bowl off the shelf.

"Are you okay? You look like you've seen a ghost or something."

"I'm fine." She paused as she shoved the bowl into her backpack. "I just think I'm totally overthinking a comment someone made on my post."

"What was the comment?" He looked at her with one eyebrow arched.

"I'll tell you in the car," she replied.

Hailey hooked Sadie's collar to the leash and hopped out of the van, making sure the doors were locked behind her since they were going to drive Luke's van over to the trailhead, leaving hers behind.

Once they got settled in the car, she explained what had caused her sudden feeling of unease. It took the whole car ride to the trailhead for Hailey to explain to Luke how she had found Hannah's Instagram and lost herself down the rabbit hole of stalking her page, all the way down to the details of how she had discovered the internet troll who had been commenting and harassing Hannah on more than one occasion.

"So you think this guy is targeting you now?" Luke asked.

"I don't know. Maybe. Maybe I'm just being dramatic, but it does make you wonder, doesn't it?"

"Have you found any comments he has made on the other victim's Instagram?"

"No, but I still don't know what the other victim's name is." As she said it, she remembered that she had yet to hear anything from Sarah about whether the parents had confirmed the identity of the girl.

"I'm surprised the media hasn't released any information," he commented as they all jumped out of the van and began walking towards the trail.

"I think they have to wait for the family to confirm the identity before releasing any names to the media, since she didn't have any ID on her."

"I guess that makes sense."

"Not that it stopped the media from swarming the case the minute it leaked that another Polaroid was found on the victim." Hailey replied, rolling her eyes.

It took about two hours for them to walk up and down the trail, making several stops along the way to enjoy the scenery, take pictures, and let Sadie drink some water. Hailey was enjoying their hike, not only for the beautiful views, but she found she did her best thinking when she was walking outside in a space that had little distractions.

Just as they were descending the last portion of the hike into the dirt parking lot, Hailey's phone buzzed. It was a message from Sarah.

I've got a break for about 10 minutes, are you in a position where you can talk?

Without hesitation Hailey responded: *Yes!*

The second after she hit send, her phone began to ring. She looked over at Luke. "Do you mind if I take this? It's my friend who's the medical examiner."

"No problem at all, I'll take Sadie." Luke grabbed the leash from Hailey and walked over to a rock near the trailhead that was large enough for him to sit on, while Hailey walked towards the other side of the parking lot where she could get some privacy from the other hikers.

"I was beginning to think you forgot about me," Hailey said as she answered the call.

"Sorry, it has been even more hectic around here." The stress in Sarah's voice was evident.

"What's been going on? Did the parents identify the girl? Was it their daughter?" Hailey had been thinking about the case ever since she admitted her involvement to Luke just a few hours earlier.

"Yes." Sarah's voice was solemn as she continued, "It was their daughter, Allison. They reported her missing after she didn't call or respond to any of their messages for two days."

"I can't imagine what they must be going through," Hailey said, shaking her head.

"No parent should ever have to see their child like that. Pale, cold, and naked on a metal autopsy table. I don't think I will ever be able to emotionally detach myself from this part of the job."

"I don't blame you. Parents aren't supposed to outlive their children." Hailey thought back to the pain her own parents had to endure when they had to identify Daniel's body after the accident.

There was a moment of silence before Hailey began unraveling her spool of questions, "Do you think you can give me the last name? I want to see if I can find her social media accounts. I really feel like we might be able to learn a lot from their online habits, maybe determine if I can find any similarities between Allison and Hannah."

"Let me take a look." Hailey could hear Sarah opening up a file drawer. "Danwick. Allison Danwick."

Without her notebook in hand, Hailey repeated the name several times over in her head making a mental note so she would remember it and add it to her journal when she got back to her van.

"Are there any more leads?" Hailey asked.

"Remember those blue fibers I found on Hannah's clothing? Well, I found matching fibers on Allison's clothes. My guess is that they each contracted the fibers from either the secondary location he held them at and took the picture, from something in the vehicle he used to transport them, or possibly from an item of clothing that the perp wore during both of the abductions."

"Makes sense," Hailey agreed. "So it looks like you have to wait for them to find this guy before you can find the source of that blue fiber."

"Unfortunately, yes."

"Oh! Since I know you don't have a lot of time, I have to at least tell you who liked my latest post on Instagram today."

"Who?"

"The guy that I found trolling Hannah on her page."

"Oh my God. Are you serious?"

"Yes! I am one hundred percent sure that it is the same guy. Especially because he made an unnecessarily rude comment on my post."

"He did? I have to see this. Is it still there or did you delete it?"

"It's still there. I didn't want to delete it in case this guy really is behind these murders and I need evidence of his surly comments on social media," Hailey stated.

"Good idea. Wait, if he commented on your post and he is the assailant, are you afraid you're on his radar?" Sarah said aloud the thoughts Hailey was afraid to. "I mean, I'm honestly worried about you myself."

"That certainly crossed my mind. I have to say having a dog and Luke nearby has helped subside my fear a bit."

"Ah so you're still traveling with this Luke fellow?" Sarah mused.

"Well you certainly go from concerned to nosy, real fast," Hailey teased.

"We don't have time to talk about it now, but you know I want all the dirty details about your new travel partner."

"And I want more details about these cases," Hailey countered.

"Don't worry, I'm on it. Trust me, myself, along with all the detectives on these cases, want to get this guy before another life is taken by his hands."

Hailey could hear a door opening in the background on Sarah's end of the line and knew that meant their time was up.

"We'll touch base again soon," Hailey said.

"Sounds good, stay safe."

"I will."

Hailey ended the call and looked around the area, not realizing how far she wandered until she spotted Luke and Sadie sharing a granola bar by the trailhead across the lot. She wished she had more time to talk with Sarah, but at least now she had the name of the most recent victim and was eager to get back to the campsite where she could do some digging on her.

Before walking over, Hailey pulled up her Instagram page on her phone and selected her most recent post. She scrolled through the comments until the username *@camping_merkins57* came into view. Part of her hoped it was gone; a hope that maybe he changed his mind and deleted the comment. Or better yet, she just imagined the whole thing and it was never there to begin with. But there it was: *"oh great another f'n vanlifer,"* typed in the same font as all the other comments—the same fonts that displayed compliments, friendly questions about her adventures, and wishes of "safe travels." A knot began to form in her chest and her pulse quickened each time she re-read the words.

A car alarm startled Hailey out of her growing anxiety, causing her to drop her phone onto the gravel.

"Shit." Without hesitation, Hailey swiped up her phone from the ground and brushed off the remnants of dust from the screen.

The high-pitched, rhythmic sound rang in her ears as she grasped her fingers tightly around her phone and began walking back towards Sadie and Luke. She looked up to see a car not too far away with flashing orange lights dancing along with the pattern of the alarm.

As Hailey approached, Sadie jumped up, putting her paws on Hailey's forearms to greet her after their short separation. A man appeared from the restrooms holding his hand high above his head while clicking a key fob until the beeping stopped.

"Ready to head back?" Luke asked while looking at the man.

"Yeah, I have some things I'd like to look up," Hailey responded while running her fingers through Sadie's fur.

"Maybe I can help you out." Luke looked at her sideways as they walked towards the van. "Since I'm practically part of the investigation now."

Hailey smiled as she opened the passenger door allowing Sadie to jump in before her.

"Oh, you're part of the investigation now, are you?"

"Well, I am pretty good at researching on the computer and learning new things," he boasted.

Hailey smiled and leaned her head back against the head rest as they drove back to the campsite. The ride was mostly silent on the way back, but it didn't feel awkward; the silence felt natural between them. Maybe it was due to all the questions and concerns filling her mind, or maybe they were over the jitters and nerves of their new friendship, or new attraction—she still wasn't sure which side of the line her feelings stood on regarding Luke.

As soon as they returned to their campsite, Hailey went straight for her laptop and began researching Allison Danwick. Now that the identity had been confirmed, the media swarmed in on the investigation like bees to honey. There were several articles that popped up with the same sorority photograph of Allison that was used as the featured image. Hailey enlarged the image and couldn't help but feel a pang of sadness for the young, attractive girl. Her hair framed her face in curls that flowed beside her cheeks and landed just above her black, off-the-shoulder shirt that encompassed her upper body. Big pearls in each ear matched the necklace hanging around her neck. She appeared sexy, yet classy. As the evening drew near, Hailey was getting frustrated at the fact that she still wasn't able to find Allison on Instagram. A Google search of her name only brought back news reports.

Luke had tossed some chicken with vegetables wrapped in tin foil onto the grill for dinner and cracked open a beer. Hailey closed her laptop and grabbed her phone to join him and Sadie, who had been enjoying a rawhide bone on her blanket in her favorite place between their camping chairs.

"Maybe she doesn't have an account?" Luke suggested as he flipped a piece of chicken that laid across the chard grate.

"I just find it hard to believe that this girl wouldn't have one. I mean, her photograph was clearly a sorority picture from college, so I can't imagine a sorority girl not having any social media accounts," Hailey replied as she scrolled through all the 'Allisons' on Instagram.

Luke sat back in his chair and pulled out his phone while placing his beer into the cup holder. "That's true, how are they supposed to get all the attention they crave without Instagram?"

Hailey shot him a look, although he wasn't wrong.

"Maybe there is a different way you can search for her." Luke picked up his phone and opened Instagram.

"What do you mean?"

"Have you just been looking through accounts? Or have you searched through the tags, too?" he asked.

"Just the accounts."

Hailey could hear the clicks of his keyboard as he began typing on his screen. Disappointed in herself for not thinking of that first, she began attempting the same search. They each scrolled through the tags, searching for any resemblance of Allison in the posts.

"Jeez, who knew there would be so many posts under these tags that are completely unrelated to the word." Luke shook his head as he spoke and continued scrolling.

"I know, shows you how many people are out there trying to build their following any way they can."

Several minutes passed as they each scrolled through the feed to the sound of fire crackling and sizzling vegetables. Just as Hailey was about to give up, Luke reeled her back.

"Take a look at this." Luke held his phone out for Hailey to see his screen.

"No way. That's her! You found her!" she confirmed.

Without hesitation, she grabbed Luke's phone from his hands to take a closer look. "And it looks like you found her under the hashtag 'vanlifegirls,' " Hailey lifted her eyebrows at Luke.

"What?" He smirked. "I've been in this vanlife on Instagram for a little while now. I've seen all the different tags people like to use."

"Uh huh," Hailey replied, directing her eyes back to the screen. "Well it definitely fits the type of victims we think this guy is targeting, so I guess I'll let this one slide."

Luke stood up to check the meat, unphased by her swiping his phone from his hands. "Sorry, I totally just snatched this from you." Embarrassed by her lack of consideration, she handed his phone back over to him.

"Don't worry about it. I get how passion can control our actions sometimes and I can see how invested you are in this case," he said nonchalantly as he flipped the chicken. He sat back down, taking the phone from Hailey with the phone still opened to the photograph of Allison.

"Kind of crazy, isn't it? Looking at her picture like this, knowing what happened to her." He shook his head in disbelief.

"Social media is sort of weird how it seems to almost freeze people in time. Seeing an image like that of her almost makes it seem like she's still happily smiling out there somewhere," Hailey replied.

Relieved and slightly surprised by his casual response for grabbing his phone, she regained focus. "What's her account name?" Her fingers hovered over her keyboard in anticipation.

"Um, let's see." Luke brought the phone closer to read the small print of the username at the top of the image: *"@danwicksdestinations"*

Hailey typed the username into the search bar and, sure enough, there she was at the top of the list. Hailey tapped the circle with Allison's cropped photograph and was redirected to her Instagram page.

"Public profile—just what I was hoping for," Hailey commented as she began analyzing the page.

Judging by the sixty-three thousand followers, six hundred posts, and one hell of a conceded Instagram feed, she looked like the perfect victim for someone who hates vanity. Allison was young, beautiful, and athletic. By the amount of lululemon workout outfits she wore, and the brand new Mercedes van she had, money didn't appear to be a problem, either. By the look of her feed, it would appear she had everything she needed—and wanted—to be an Instagram influencer.

Similar to the photographs on Hannah's page, each image seemed to be staged and taken at the perfect angle, with just the right lighting, every time. Allison appeared to have more photographs of her out hiking and exploring the places she visited compared to Hannah, who only had images of her around or in her van. Hailey also noticed that Allison appeared to be traveling completely alone. No pets and no other people in any of her images. That definitely made her an easier target. Not only did traveling alone make her the perfect victim, but she seemed to post a lot more often. And based on her captions, it seemed she would post her current location while she was still staying there. Not exactly a wise move when you were a young girl traveling alone.

"See any similarities?" Luke questioned as he began using his knife and fork to unwrap the hot foil to check on the broccoli and zucchini.

"Other than the fact that she is another young, attractive girl traveling alone? No, nothing is really sticking out to me," Hailey responded without her eyes leaving the screen.

"Are there any comments from that troll guy?" he asked.

"I haven't really been looking through the comments yet. Maybe after dinner." She looked up to see Luke plating the vegetables and chicken.

"Would you like another glass of wine?" he asked.

"Sure, since this one is my favorite." Hailey tilted her head back, allowing the last of her drink to stream down her throat from the plastic wine glass.

Luke smiled as he began refilling her cup, then looked at the bottle to read the label. "Let's see what we have here. A Kim Crawford Sauvignon Blanc. I can't say I've ever had it. Although it does sound very sophisticated."

"My mom always drank it, so I suppose I got hooked on it, too." Hailey shrugged one shoulder as she took a sip from her freshly poured glass. "Thank you for cooking. It's been nice to have someone to have dinner with."

Luke plopped down into his chair and began cutting into his chicken. "No problem," he said as he popped a piece into his mouth. "I must admit, I have met several people on the road so far, and I have enjoyed your company the most."

Hailey smiled as she pushed some vegetables onto her fork. "I never expected to meet someone this early on in my trip, but with everything that has been going on in these forests, it's been nice having someone close by. I never imagined that when I began this trip I would be jumping into an investigation revolving around a potential serial killer."

Luke nodded his head. "Yeah, I'll bet. I mean, I never imagined I'd be creating a webpage for a girl who went missing and was murdered in the same woods I would be traveling through."

They each cut into their chicken and took a bite as pensive silence lingered between them, until Luke switched gears.

"So, tell me—What is one of your favorite places you have traveled?"

Hailey was caught off guard by his question but liked his attempt at lightening the dinner mood.

Before she knew it, the bottle of wine sat empty beside several crushed beer cans on the table Luke had improvised out of an upright tree stump placed between them. When he began making dinner, she figured it would be a quick meal. Eat, have a glass of wine or two, feed Sadie, and then head in for the night to do some more research on Allison. Somehow the casual, quick dinner turned into fireside drinks and an exchange of adventure stories. She was starting to see a trend.

Hailey didn't normally drink that much, but she was enjoying the warm feeling of the alcohol coursing through her veins and how her confidence rose with each sip she took. And conversations with Luke came easy. It felt good to drink with someone and know it wasn't going to turn into a pissing match of who did more chores that week, or who messed up or said the wrong thing. No malice, no regret, just contentment with each other's presence.

As the night grew later and the wine settled in her system, Hailey could feel her eyelids growing heavy. She looked down to see Sadie had already surrendered to the night and had fallen asleep on the blanket between them.

"I don't know about you, but I am worn out," Hailey announced as she stared into the fire.

"I am too. Maybe we should pack things up for the night?" Luke suggested.

"That sounds good to me, since we want to head towards Sacramento for the Vanlife meetup event tomorrow."

Hailey gently woke up Sadie and collected her blanket and water bowl in her hands. With her hands full, she attempted to pick up Sadie's food bowl too, but Luke cut in to lend a hand.

"Don't worry, I got it," he insisted, scooping up the bowl without waiting for a response and following her towards her van.

Hailey placed the blanket on the floor beside the bed. Sadie, who was still groggy, curled up onto the makeshift bed without hesitation and fell back into her slumber. Luke placed the bowl on the floor of the van beside the water bowl as Hailey placed her empty wine bottle and plastic cup inside the sink, deciding she would deal with it in the morning.

As she turned around, she found herself standing face to chest with Luke. As he exhaled, Hailey could feel the warmth of his breath against her forehead. She had never stood close enough to him to realize how much taller he was than her. Six one, maybe two? His fingertips were cool against her skin as he hooked his index and middle finger into the front lip of her jeans and pulled her hips into his. Without resistance, she tilted her head back as he pressed his lips against hers. The hairs stood up on the nape of her neck as a surge of adrenaline raced through her chest. The slight taste of beer lingered on her tongue as he pulled his lips away and brought his hand to her cheek. His thumb was rough against her smooth skin as he glided it down from her cheek bone to her chin, while pulling his mouth into a seductive smile. "Good night," he whispered as he dropped his hand back to his side and his fingers fell from the waistband of her jeans.

He turned on his heel and began walking back towards his van with a presumptuous stride. It wasn't until he was several feet away that she caught her breath and settled her swirling emotions enough to compose a response, "Good night, Luke."

Chapter 16

A cold, moist nose nudged against Hailey's hand, pulling her out of a deep sleep. She rolled over and managed to open one eye to see Sadie sitting beside the bed, patiently waiting to start the day. Her head was swirling. Whether it was from the wine or the kiss with Luke, she couldn't be sure. The one thing she was sure of was that she needed water.

The inside of her cheeks were sticky with thick saliva as her tongue clung to the roof of her mouth, waiting to be rehydrated. She knew that her last glass of wine was one too many. Even though she may have been regretting finishing off that bottle, she wasn't regretting the late night moment she had with Luke. Just the thought alone awakened the butterflies in her stomach.

After she gave Sadie her breakfast and chugged three quarters of a bottle of luke-warm water, she fell back onto her bed and stared up at the ceiling as the water sloshed into place.

Allison's face flashed across her mind, and her eyes widened at the thought. The night had slipped away from her and she had almost completely forgotten about the mission to search Allison's Instagram account for any suspicious activity. She looked over at Sadie as she pulled her phone out of the basket, taking note that she had about ten minutes before she would need to let her outside.

She had Allison's account information now and it still sat at the top of her most recent searches. She clicked on her page and waited for the images of the beautiful brunette to fill her screen. Hailey began scrolling through the images one by one and opening the comments. With over 200 comments on each photograph, this search would take more time than she was expecting. For all she knew, there may not even be anything to raise an eyebrow at, just repeated compliments and emojis expressing their praise or envy. But she knew that was one of the challenges of research and reporting—frequently, you came up dry and empty handed.

Sadie began whining at the door. It was time to put the search on hold, throw on a bra and sweatshirt, and head outside. Before the door was even open all the way, Sadie wiggled through the gap and shimmied out onto the moist dirt. Just as Hailey stepped out into the morning air, she heard the rolling of a sliding door. Luke was up, too. She suddenly felt self-conscious about her morning hair and her poor choice of a sports bra she had decided to put on.

"Good morning," Luke mused as he walked over to hand her a cup of coffee. "I wasn't sure how long you had been up, but I figured an extra cup of coffee never hurt."

"This is just what I needed, thank you." Hailey accepted the warm plastic mug from his hand and took a generous sip.

"How ya feelin'?" Luke asked in a tone indicating he already knew the answer.

"I've certainly felt better." She took another sip. "But I've definitely felt worse."

A flashback from the night in college when she had stayed out too late and drank too much before her mid-term psych exam popped into her mind. She had never felt so miserable trying to label all the parts of the brain while fighting the rising nausea in her throat. At least in this moment, she felt better than that.

Luke chuckled at the thought of his own memories of an overindulged evening or two. "I know what you mean."

The sound of birds chirping and a car driving down the dirt road not too far away filled the space between them as they stood sipping coffee.

They stood comfortably watching Sadie trot around the campground, sniffing every rock and bush to see if any visitors had meandered through their site overnight. Hailey debated if she should bring up their encounter from the night before. Did he even remember it? He had to, considering he was only drinking Bud Light and weighed at least twice as much as she did, and she managed to remember every little detail.

"Did you find what you were looking for on that girl's account?" he chimed in, shaking Hailey out of her thoughts.

"I didn't really have time to look through her account last night." She shook her head as a smile tugged at the corners of her mouth. Could she really be that out of practice that a simple drunken kiss had her mind this distracted? No. She was not about to let a school girl crush distract her from these cases.

"Maybe you can help me look through her page." She walked over to her van and sat on the edge of the doorway.

Without any questions, Luke pulled out his phone and sat beside her. "Sure. I can do that. What are we looking for?"

"Go to Allison's account." Hailey paused as Luke typed in the name and waited for the page to load. "Okay, so we are going to scroll through all of the comments on her posts."

"All of them?" Luke raised his eyebrows.

"All of them," she confirmed. "I will start from the first image she posted when she appeared to have started her vanlife and work towards the top. You start at the most recent post and work backwards."

"Okay. What image should be our middle point?"

"Let's go with this one." Hailey clicked on an image of Allison standing in the middle of her van, facing her newly refinished kitchenette and pouring herself a glass of red wine, laughing and looking away from the camera. Hailey wondered how many takes it took for her to capture that "candid" moment.

"And what exactly am I looking for again?"

"We're looking for any comments from the username *@camping_* *merkins57.* But maybe take note of any other comments that look out of place or demeaning." Hailey was now officially in business mode.

Heads down, thumbs scrolling, and eyes fervently searching through the comments, they were on a mission. It wasn't exactly the type of research she had ever imagined she would be doing, let alone with the help from a financial advisor gone nomadic web designer, but she knew she had to work with the resources she had. For a moment, she wondered what leads the detectives had on the case. Were they searching Instagram, too? Did they see the same connection between the victims that she had? Had they discovered the similarities in their social media accounts? Or maybe they were following a completely different lead, with details Hailey knew nothing about.

That was one of the challenges of being a reporter, especially a reporter who wasn't technically employed with an official agency. You had to find loopholes, be pushy, and maybe cross the line a little bit to get the dirty details. She was lucky she had Sarah on the inside, but there would be a time when she was going to need to figure out how to get in contact with the detectives who were working the case; get the real inside details on the investigation.

"Hey," Luke said abruptly, "I think I've got something here."

"Let me see." Hailey filled the small gap between them and leaned in to see Luke's screen.

Naturally, she read the comment first:

sure, vanlife looks easy when you have daddys money to support your expensive, prissy taste

Then her eyes jumped back to the username, and sure enough, there it was: *@camping_merkins57.*

"That's it! That's him," she said with certainty. "This guy clearly has something against young women joining the vanlife scene. And he's not afraid to show it."

"I bet he's some low-lifer who just lives in his mother's basement and has nothing better to do."

"I've got to get a hold of Sarah and tell her what we've found. Maybe she has more information too and we can compare notes. Maybe fill in some gaps and answer some questions."

"That's a good idea. So, what time do you think you will be ready to hit the road?" Luke asked as he rose from his sitting position and began walking towards his van. "Assuming that you still wanted to head to the meetup event today?"

"Oh, yeah, I almost completely forgot that was today." Hailey stood and looked at herself in the mirror. "I was hoping I could get a shower in before we go, but I forgot to fill up my water bag before we left our last spot."

"You know, I take most of my showers at the gym. I have a guest pass if you want to look one up on the way and stop there?" Luke offered.

Hailey raised her eyebrow. "I didn't think about that. What a good idea."

"I actually got the idea from someone I met at the first Vanlife meet-up I went to in Arizona. It's worked out pretty well for me so far."

Her eyes trailed down to his defined biceps. The mystery of his toned arms and fit physique may have been solved. "I can call Sarah from the road if you want to get a start on our day."

"Okay, yeah, that sounds good to me."

After making sure their vans were 'mobile ready,' their engines roared to life. Hailey was feeling anxious, yet excited, to attend a Vanlife meetup event. She was also feeling thankful she had Luke with her to help ease her nerves at her first event.

Once they hit the main road, Hailey dialed Sarah, hoping she would catch her at a good time to talk so they could catch up on each of their latest findings.

The line rang and rang until finally her voicemail came through the speaker. It wasn't what Hailey was hoping for, but since it was out of her control, she left a brief message. "I found something on Instagram. Call me as soon as you get this. I'm on the move again, but should remain in cell phone range." She knew she shouldn't leave too many details in her voicemail because if something were to happen to her and her messages were searched, she didn't want it revealed that Sarah had been sharing confidential information with her. After she ended the call, Hailey propped her phone up in her cup holder as she eagerly waited for a call back, continuing to follow Luke to the gym. But a call never came.

"So, how was it?" Luke's hair was still wet from his shower and she could smell the sweet, musky pine scent of his shampoo as she approached him in the lobby.

"It feels so good to be clean and to be able to just enjoy standing in the warm water. It's amazing how re-energizing a good shower can be." Her cheeks were still flushed from the heat of the shower.

"Definitely one of my favorites stops while traveling on the road," he agreed as they began walking through the exit.

Before they hopped back into their vans, Hailey let Sadie out to stretch her legs while Luke plugged in the address to the meet up.

"So, are you going to meet up with your friend in Sacramento since we will be in the area?"

Holy shit. How could Hailey have completely forgotten this whole time that the meetup was in Sacramento? Not only where Sarah worked, but where the first victim was from? Embarrassed by her lack of awareness, she tried to hide her shock and responded coolly, "Definitely. As long as Sarah is able to step away from her work for a bit."

"I mean, she has to go home at some point, doesn't she?" he asked.

"Of course, but you know what I mean." She fluttered her hand at him as if to dismiss the conversation.

"I think I'm actually going to hook up with a friend from Santa Rosa later tonight," he added.

"Oh." Hailey was surprised by the pang of jealousy she felt in her gut. "That sounds nice."

"Yeah, he grew up on the same street as me when we were kids, and somehow we have managed to stay connected all these years."

Hailey felt the jealousy subside as Luke confirmed he was meeting with a male friend. "It's great to have friends like that," she replied as they approached their vans.

With Luke leading the way, they hopped back into their vans and headed towards Sacramento. As soon as Hailey was settled into her seat, she picked up her phone and dialed Sarah again.

Chapter 17

"I am so happy you decided to get a dog. Is she an Australian Shepard?" Sarah asked as she knelt down to give Sadie a rub on the neck.

"They think she's a mix between an Aussie and a lab." Hailey smiled down at Sadie as she wiggled from side to side with excitement. "I think they call it an Aussiedor."

"Well I love her!"

Sarah held the door open with her arm, allowing Hailey and Sadie to walk into the entryway from the garage. Before she closed the door behind them, she hit the lock button on her car, and the horn rang in their ears as it echoed against the concrete walls.

"You can never be sure," she said with a shrug of her shoulders.

Hailey nodded in agreement. Just because your car was in a garage didn't mean it was safe. As they stood in the entry, her eyes trailed up the long flight of dark grey carpeted stairs that stretched before them. "That's quite the entry," she stated.

"Keeps me in shape," Sarah replied, ascending the steps.

Sadie weaved between their legs and beat each of them to the top. She stood looking down at them, wagging her tail vigorously as if she was telling them she had won the race. It was a lot easier with four legs and the energy of a 45-minute nap in the car ride over.

"How have I never seen your place?" Hailey gushed as she ran her fingers across the black quartz counter top. "I love it!"

The bright white kitchen cabinets reflected the light streaming in from the long windows that took the place of a wall in the living room, allowing for light to pour into the room despite the overcast day. The open layout created the illusion that the condo was bigger than just the thousand square foot space that it was.

"Is that a deck?" Hailey asked aghast as she peered up at yet another staircase.

"Yes! That's my patio. We could have a glass of wine and sit out there while we catch up if you want?" Sarah suggested as she began pulling down two wine glasses.

"That sounds great, but preferably red if you have it. I sort of drank too much white last night."

"Sounds like we have more than just murder cases to discuss." Sarah smirked.

Hailey kicked herself for slipping and revealing too much. She hadn't even processed her own emotions about Luke yet and certainly wasn't ready to get someone else's opinions on the matter.

Sadie sat as close as she could to the edge of the patio with ears perked as she watched the hustle and bustle of the street below. Meanwhile, Hailey and Sarah settled into the brown wicker chairs, each taking a sip of their wine. For just a moment, they enjoyed the peace of the day before jumping into the unpleasant details of the murder cases.

"So, let's start with Instagram," Sarah started as she placed her glass on the table between them, initiating the business portion of their meeting. "Tell me about everything you found on there."

"Well, did you get a chance to look at my post and see the comment that guy made?" Hailey asked.

"I did. It was totally uncalled for, for sure. Especially considering that he's a complete stranger. But his profile is private, so I didn't really get a good look at the guy. And the name just says *S. Merkins*. Not a whole lot to work with."

"Not to mention his profile picture is blurry and he's wearing sunglasses," Hailey added.

"Which says to me that he is maybe older? Not exactly an expert at social media?"

"Or that he wanted his identity to be hard to decipher," Hailey said with a raise of her brow. "Make his features unrecognizable or unidentifiable."

"That's possible too. And you have seen this same guy make snarky comments on each of the victims' posts as well?"

"Yes." Hailey almost dropped her phone onto the ground with the amount of urgency she used to pull it out of her pocket. "I took screenshots just in case he removed his posts, but you can see them for yourself on each of their pages."

She opened up Instagram and pulled up each of the girls accounts, showing Sarah the comments *@camping_merkins57* had made on their posts. Sarah held Hailey's phone in her hand reading each comment twice to be sure she read them correctly. After she finished reading the comments, she scrolled through each of the victim's accounts, shaking her head with a look of sorrow.

"What is it?" Hailey asked.

"These girls," Sarah's voice was quiet, "I never really get to see the victims like this."

"What do you mean?"

"I don't get to see them before...before they were victims. I never see the life they led. Whether they were popular, or the star athlete at their school, or whether they were bubbly and kind, like all their friends and family say they were. When they show up in my lab, when they are lying on my table, I just see the devastation, the aftermath. The only time I even come in contact with the families is when they come to identify the body. I don't have conversations with them, I don't get to know them, I only decipher how the victim died. How they ended up on my cold, metal table." Sarah shook her head in dismay.

"This line of work isn't easy," Hailey continued, laying a hand on

Sarah's knee. "It can be grotesque and mournful, but it can also be rewarding. You play a huge role in putting these low-life criminals away."

Sarah handed the phone back to Hailey. "We better get this guy."

"Do the detectives on the case have any leads? Any suspects?"

"At this point in time, it seems that any individual these girls came in contact with while traveling are suspects."

"That certainly narrows it down," Hailey replied sarcastically. "There could be tons of people these girls met while traveling across the states."

"Yeah, no kidding. And the media isn't helping the situation. The department tried to keep the first case under wraps for as long as they could, but once word gets out that yet another affluent, young, beautiful girl goes missing in the woods and winds up dead—"

"The media swarms in packs," Hailey interjected. "Not to mention these girls were media influencers. They were already in the spotlight."

"But I know the detectives on the case are doing everything in their power to not let the media get a hold of those Polaroids. Someone leaked information that Polaroids had been found on the bodies, but luckily the actual images and quotes written on them haven't been exposed," Sarah stated.

"Do they have the same suspicion that this guy is targeting these women because he has something against their livelihood, prosperity, or even their vanity? Or maybe he feels this is a game to redirect the attention onto him?"

"They definitely think it has something to do with his own motivation wanting to be in the spotlight. Why else would a criminal leave behind a clue in the form of a message?"

"Yeah, very interesting..." Hailey leaned back and took a sip of her wine while formulating her next question. "You mentioned before on the phone that these Polaroids appear to be taken in the same place?"

"That's certainly what it looks like. The concrete walls and dirt floor look the same. There was also what I would assume to be a water pipe that was only visible in one of the images. The lack of lighting in each picture also leads me to believe there aren't any windows at the location."

"Maybe a basement or warehouse?" Hailey suggested.

"Seems like those are the most plausible places to me."

"So he kidnaps the girls, then takes them to a secondary location where he tortures them and takes their photograph. Then he dumps their body somewhere he knows they will be found?"

"That's right. We're dealing with a seriously messed up and evil person here."

Hailey nodded as they each took a sip from their glass and gazed out into the overcast sky. It had been over a year since they had spent time together face to face even though they lived in the same state and this wasn't exactly the situation or circumstance Hailey had in mind when they would be back together again. Although Sacramento and San Diego did seem worlds apart, between the L.A. traffic and the working hours each of them had to put in to prove their place at their "big girl jobs" after college. Unfortunately, even working overtime and weekends didn't allow for Hailey to hold her spot as a Public Relations Specialist. Whether it was a blessing or a curse, she still couldn't be sure.

"It's interesting that he doesn't hold them for ransom," Sarah said. "But, then again, I guess that would support the theory that he doesn't care about the money. He cares about the vanity. He hates their vanity and feels that they are taking away all the attention from him. Because he wants to be an influencer?" Sarah questioned, as she tried to piece together the information they had gathered thus far.

"Or maybe he doesn't want to be an influencer necessarily, but he does feel that they are intruding on his domain. That he should be the one people look to for camping advice. I mean, his account name is 'Camping Merkins,' " Hailey proposed.

"Assuming this guy really is *our* guy."

"True," Hailey agreed before asking her next question. "You also found matching fibers on the girls' clothing, right?"

"Yes. Each of the victim's clothing had traces of a blue fiber that came from the same source."

"Okay, so he was either wearing the same shirt, or pants, or gloves when he kidnapped them. Or it could be from the vehicle he used to transport each of the girls to and from the basement or warehouse or whatever this secondary location is."

"I think it might be important to note that there were no signs of sexual assault either. Which, from my professional experience, it's extremely rare for a young woman to get kidnapped and held captive and not get sexually assaulted," Sarah stated.

"Rare, but at least a small silver lining if there is one at all," Hailey replied. "But anger was definitely involved by the amount of stab wounds each victim had, right?"

"Definitely. Forty-six stab wounds isn't just an act of murder, but an act of extreme animosity."

"Isn't there a chance of the perpetrator cutting themselves during stabbing incidents?" Hailey asked, cocking her head to one side.

"Yes, it can happen, but there was no blood other than the victims' found at the scene or on their clothing." Sarah sat back in her chair with her arms and legs crossed, pondering her own question. "How old do you think this guy is?"

"Judging by the age of the women, their presence and involvement on social media, and his apparent disdain for their vanity, it leads me to believe he is in his twenties. Potentially early thirties," Hailey answered.

Sarah nodded her head in agreement. "That sounds on par with what the detectives think, too. Something about the rage in these cases also shows immaturity and disorganization."

"Now we just have to figure out how to get in contact with this guy. Or at least figure out how to see his profile to get a real name, so we can look into his background."

"I would say I could talk to the detectives on the case, but they would find it odd that I was digging into the case, seeing that it's not exactly my specialty to be the one questioning people. Forensics, yes. Investigating, no," Sarah stated.

Hailey contemplated the predicament for a moment. "Maybe Luke has some ideas of how to look him up better or find him somewhere else online. I mean, he does create websites and uses coding, so maybe he knows some inside research skills."

"Ah, so the infamous Luke is a web designer?" Sarah curved her lips into a half-smile.

There was no getting around this one. Hailey debated her response as she took a generous gulp from her glass. "Yes. Well at least now he is. He used to be a financial advisor before he started his vanlife adventure."

"An entrepreneur. Even better."

"As I was saying," Hailey pressed as she attempted to redirect the conversation back to the real matter at hand. "I think maybe he would be able to get more information on this Merkins guy."

"It's at least worth a shot, right?" Sarah asked.

Hailey nodded. At this point, anything was worth a shot.

"So let's go back to this new travel buddy," Sarah began. Hailey knew Sarah wasn't going to allow her to just glaze over the new intriguing traveling partner she had managed to partner up with. "Tell me about this entrepreneur, Luke. And why are you in Sacramento? Weren't you going to Yosemite after Sequoia?"

Hailey decided to answer the question she knew how to best answer to first. "Yosemite is definitely still next up on the destination list, but there is a Vanlife meetup here in Sacramento this weekend that I thought would be fun to check out." Not to mention it was all Luke's idea.

"What is a Vanlife meetup?"

"It's an event that brings together a bunch of people who are traveling in vans across the country. It creates a place where you can network or meet like-minded people. Sort of a way to give people a sense of community even though they are on the move all the time and traveling alone."

"That actually sounds pretty awesome."

"Yeah, I thought it might be a good way to connect with other women travelers. Maybe even get some ideas of topics to write about on my website."

"Oh, you have a website, do you?" Sarah asked, surprised.

"Well, not yet. Luke offered to make one for me and I thought maybe I would take him up on it. Start a blog or something like that to write about my travels. I don't know. Just a thought." Hailey felt embarrassed at her lack of employment ever since she lost her job and wasn't sure what Sarah would think about her plan to try her hand at becoming a digital nomad.

"I think that's a great idea, Hailey!" Hailey let out a sigh of relief as Sarah continued. "You're a reporter; it's in your blood to write stories, and you are so good at it. You should definitely take advantage of having someone with website-building skills at your fingertips and start creating."

Hailey knew there was a reason Sarah had remained such a good friend after all this time and separation. Even throughout college, Sarah was always encouraging Hailey to chase her passion for writing; she always pushed her to follow cases that she worked on during her internship right to the end, even if they didn't seem to lead anywhere. Maybe if she was lucky, Sarah could be her ticket to getting to the bottom of these murder cases too.

The evening began to grow cool as the sun set into the ocean, painting the clouds with hues of orange and pink. Sarah closed and locked the door behind them as they descended the stairs back into the living room.

"I don't really have much to offer for dinner, but I'm sure I can scrounge something up if you want to stay," Sarah offered as she placed the empty glasses into the sink.

Hailey looked down at her phone to check the time and saw a message from Luke on her screen. He had sent a message supplying her with the location he had found at the meetup for them to park their vans beside one another.

"Thanks for the offer, but I should probably get back to the van to feed Sadie."

"Of course, you have a child to take care of now," Sarah teased.

They both laughed and began walking down the steps back towards the doorway.

"I'm glad we were able to do this. I think this really helped line up some of the details to see what we have and what parts are still missing." Hailey placed her hand on the doorknob. "It's been really good seeing you and catching up," she added with a heartfelt smile.

"I'm glad you're doing this, Hailey. And I'm happy we could make this work. Let me know if you'll be in town for a while and maybe we can get together again. Whether it's to discuss the case or not."

"Absolutely. I will keep you updated on this whole meetup thing."

They embraced each other in a hug and Hailey could feel tears beginning to prick in the corner of her eyes. Between the breakup with Jeremy, moving out of their house, packing up her life to hit the road, meeting Luke, and jumping into murder investigations, there had been a lot of emotions Hailey hadn't had time to process. She had always been good at pushing her emotions under the rug, but in this moment, being held in Sarah's embrace, all her emotions rushed to the surface and a single tear slid down her cheek.

A vibration hummed between them, pulling them out of the moment. Hailey brushed the tear from her cheek before Sarah could see as she pulled her phone from the pocket of her jacket.

"Sorry," Sarah said as she clicked on the screen to view the message. "This job is sort of an around the clock gig."

"I get it," Hailey replied.

"Oh my God." The words left Sarah's mouth before she even had time to think about it. Her eyes darted up to meet Hailey's.

"Another body was just found."

"Are you serious?" Hailey asked with wide eyes.

"Looks like I'll be heading out with you." Sarah pulled on her jacket and swiped her badge and car keys off the hook from the wall. "At least it was nice to get out of the office for a bit."

Before Sarah hopped into her car, they pulled each other into one more hug. This time it was an embrace of security, a way they were able to feel that the other was safe.

As Hailey walked to her car, she waved goodbye to Sarah as she drove past her down the road. Once her tail lights faded into the distance, Hailey suddenly felt more alone and began to quicken her steps towards her van. Once inside, Hailey clicked the locks before Sadie had even made it over to the passenger seat. Even though she knew there was almost no chance that the killer was walking down the very street she was on, Hailey couldn't stop the anxiety from rising in her chest. She needed to get her mind off the victim, so Hailey decided to check in with her parents as she drove back to the meetup event.

"So explain this meetup thing to me," her mother requested. "What exactly is it?"

"A place where people like me who are also traveling alone can meet other travelers who are doing the same thing. It's basically an event created for all the other vanlife travelers out there to get together in one place and network with one another."

"Sounds like it could be a good opportunity to get some tips on where to stay and what places to avoid," her father commented.

"Exactly. And maybe I will meet some other solo women travelers too that are going the same direction I am that I could meet up with along the way."

"Oh that would be wonderful!" her mother cheered. "It would be great for you to find some other girls to travel with so you aren't alone out there."

"I mean, at least have Luke with me for now."

"But he's just a boy that you barely know," her father added.

"Yes," Hailey replied, rolling her eyes. "I suppose it would be nice to have other women to travel with on the road as well."

"You know we just worry about you being so far away from home and going out on this adventure all by yourself."

"I know, Mom, but don't worry, I am being cautious." Hailey felt the guilt get heavier with every word. She could only imagine the state of concern her parents would be in if they knew she was inserting herself into the investigation of two vanlife women who had been murdered in the areas that she was planning on traveling through.

"Just be sure to send us the location again once you get there. I liked that I had a map to look at the last time you messaged us where you were," her dad commented.

"I will be sure to do it as soon as I park in my spot," Hailey assured.

"So I am assuming we won't be hearing from you much this weekend?" her mother asked.

"Probably not, but I will be sure to check in next week."

"I'm happy to hear you were able to see Sarah while you are there too."

"Me too," Hailey agreed.

"Gives your mother comfort knowing you're near someone we actually know," her father added.

Hailey bit her tongue as guilt washed over her. She couldn't imagine how her parents would react if she told them one of the reasons why she had been over to see Sarah. Staying silent about the murders when talking to them was only going to get harder the more she dug into the cases, but she knew that if she wanted to continue her investigation, then she didn't have a choice.

"I'm pulling into the lot now, I'll be sure to pin my location once we hang up."

"We will keep an eye out for it. Have a fun weekend at your event. We love you," her father replied.

"Love you guys too."

"Stay safe," her mother added.

"I will."

Hailey ended the call and promptly pinned her location, sending it to her parents. She placed her phone into the cup holder and looked over to see the space beside her van was still empty. Assuming Luke must still be out with his friend and not sure when he would be back, Hailey decided to turn in for the night. She changed into her pajamas and snuggled into the sheets, with Sadie following closely behind as she nested at the bottom of Hailey's feet.

Hailey tossed and turned as thoughts of the new victim swirled through her mind. Finally, she settled into a position on her back and stared up at the ceiling. Exhaustion began to win the battle as Hailey closed her eyes to welcome it. Just as she began to slip into unconsciousness, a burst of light flashed across the windshield. Hailey opened her eyes with alert speed just in time to see a faint yellow glow casting through her side windows before they turned back to black as the lights switched off. By the sound of crunching rocks beneath tires, Hailey knew that it was Luke pulling in beside her. She glanced down and tapped her phone to check the time. Three a.m.

Chapter 18

Luke's mouth was stretched agape with a long yawn as Hailey eagerly jumped out of her van ready to experience her first Vanlife meet up.

"Late night?" she asked, already well aware that he hadn't returned back to their site until three a.m.

"Much later than I was planning," he said with a groggy tone.

"What time did you even get back?"

"Oh man, I don't even know. Maybe two-ish?"

"Must have been enjoying your time catching up with your buddy."

"Yeah, Nick was always the partier out of my friends, and it's safe to say nothing has changed there."

"So are you going to survive today?" she teased.

"I think I will make it," he responded with a half-smile as they began their walk.

The sun was warm against her skin as they strolled along the asphalt that was lined with vans and other travelers from all over the country. Sadie was overwhelmed with excitement of all the people and other dogs walking about, causing her to pull ever so slightly as if to tell Hailey to pick up the pace. Hailey was relieved Sadie was responding so well to all the commotion of unfamiliar people and animals. Being in a shelter can change a dog for the worse, but Hailey was happy to see that it looked like Sadie had beat the odds.

"This is incredible." Hailey was stunned at how many people had come out to the event. She had a hunch that vanlife was becoming more popular, but she wasn't expecting such a huge turnout.

"See, I told you it would be fun," Luke said with a playful grin. "Traveling alone in the vanlife doesn't actually mean you're alone. There is a whole community out here."

A *whole community of potential victims*, Hailey thought as they walked by a girl, no more than twenty-three, who was checking her reflection in the sliding door window of her van.

"Hey there!" Hailey and Luke came to a halt as a young man jumped in front of them with a giant smile painted across his face. "Name's Mika." He thrust his hand towards Luke, while simultaneously brushing a curly, blonde lock of hair away from his eyes. "I'm having a bonfire tonight and would love it if you guys could make it! I'll be playing some live music with my buddy, Alex." He gestured to another young vagabond with shaggy brown hair chatting up someone else across the street.

Luke shook his hand, responding with just enough enthusiasm to make the kid's day. "I'm Luke, and this is Hailey. That sounds like an awesome way to spend the evening. We will be sure to stop by."

"Great! See you guys later!" Without missing a beat, Mika jumped off with the same childlike grin to greet another group of people who were walking by.

"People aren't shy at these things, are they?" Hailey asked, clearly already knowing the answer.

"I wouldn't say they are all quite as energetic as Tom Petty over there, but I'd say most of the people you meet here are genuinely friendly individuals. Or else they probably wouldn't be here."

"I guess I wasn't sure what to expect from this event, but I think this is going to make a great topic to write about on *my* website." Hailey smirked as she waited for Luke to catch her subtle hint for him to create a website for her.

"Are you officially taking me up on my offer?" Luke turned to her with a surprised look stretched across his face.

"Well, I thought about it, and I love to write, so having a website where I can blog about all my adventures sounds like the perfect thing for me to do on the road." Hailey was hoping he wouldn't bring up the investigations, since she didn't want to have to explain to him why she couldn't publicly share any of the details she had obtained regarding the cases.

"Maybe after we stop by our new friend's bonfire tonight, we can sit down together and you can tell me what style and designs you like," Luke suggested.

"That sounds perfect. I definitely don't want to miss Alex and Mika's jam session." She flashed Luke a playful smile and continued down the road.

After spending a couple of hours checking out all of the different food trucks and entertainment that would be available at the event for the weekend, they decided it was time to head back to their vans to get ready for the evening. Even though the day was warm, the evenings were chilly once the sun went down.

Hailey slipped into fitted jeans, a white t-shirt, and a dark red leather jacket. With one more look in the mirror and a swipe of lip gloss, she was feeling confident and ready to mingle. As she jumped out of her van with Sadie, she looked up to see Luke leaning coolly against the hood of his van. As she walked over to greet him, she wondered if she had ever seen another man make jeans and a grey fitted t-shirt look so good.

"All set?" He pushed his foot against the bumper and stood with his hands in his pockets.

"All set. We're ready to check out the nightlife." Hailey was surprised by her own enthusiasm as they set back out into the crowd of vanlifers.

The air was filled with the smell of campfires and the hum of chatter as new friendships were being formed. They each volunteered waves and smiles to each group they passed as they sauntered down the road. It was a strange yet comforting feeling to be surrounded by complete strangers and not feeling out of place. She finally felt okay—hell, she felt thankful with where she was in her life. Thankful she was given this opportunity to travel and find this community of digital nomads, a bunch of individuals who were just trying to find their way through life by way of adventure and unconventional means.

The turquoise van with yellow painted writing came into view just as the sound of the song "Sitting, Waiting, Wishing" by Jack Johnson being played by a guitar and bongos filled their ears. The jam session had begun and Hailey loved the warm, welcoming energy that radiated from the group surrounding Mika and Alex as they played.

Before they knew it, Hailey and Luke were mixed among the group enjoying drinks, hot dogs, and stories with the other travelers while sitting fireside. As the night grew later, the crowd slowly dwindled as people receded back to their vans. Soon, there were only seven that remained around the fire: Luke, Hailey, Alex, Mika, and three others who had been enjoying their company.

Luke spent most of his time talking with Alex, Mika, and the other guy, Steven, who spent his days creating survivalist videos and posts on social media. Hailey didn't mind that the group had been divided between the sexes. She enjoyed learning about how Julie was a life coach and helped clients all over the country, and how Rachel spent her time making jewelry from her van and selling it on Etsy to support her traveling lifestyle.

"Wow, so you guys met on her first day on the road?" Mika asked with wide eyes.

Luke looked over at Hailey with guilt in his eyes. Clearly their conversation had shifted and they were no longer discussing how they make a living on the road. Hailey didn't break eye contact with Mika as she responded, rejoining the group conversation. "Well, technically...yes, but we didn't start traveling together that day. We continued on our separate ways and then ran into each other again in Sequoia."

"Then it was fate for sure, man," Alex chimed in with a goofy grin on his face as he slapped Luke on the arm with the back of his hand.

Hailey could feel the temperature rise in her cheeks and was thankful that it was dark enough that no one would notice. She wondered if Luke felt the same way as she discreetly glanced in his direction just enough to see a smile touch his lips.

"Hey, I was just happy to have one new follower on social media," Luke teased, clearing the awkwardness.

Everyone chuckled at his comment, including Hailey, who began to question if she believed in fate. Or if it really was just a lucky coincidence that they ran into each other soon after her flat tire incident.

"Aye, speaking of social media, you guys should all subscribe to me on YouTube," Mika said with a beaming grin.

"You mean to *us,*" Alex slapped his hand against Mika's shoulder. It was clear who ran the show in the band.

"Same thing," Mika chuckled as he proceeded to explain to everyone why they should follow their channel. "We mainly do covers of other songs, but sometimes we write our own and play them in the places we travel to." He was like a kid with a new toy, describing it to his preschool class, overjoyed and more excited about it than anyone else. "We have over five thousand subscribers and get over ten thousand views on our videos."

"It's pretty rad," Alex piped up again, nodding his head in agreement.

"Maybe we can do a social media support swap," Julie suggested.

Hailey wished she would have taken Luke up on his offer sooner to create a website. All she had to show for herself at this point were a couple posts on Instagram from her short travels so far. But at least she would have five new followers whom she had actually met in person that she could promote her website to when the time came.

"I'll go first!" No one argued with Mika as he perched himself at the edge of his chair and waited for everyone to pull out their phones.

"To find *us* on YouTube," he turned to give Alex a look as he emphasized the word before he continued, "search Mika and Alex's Musical Quest."

He waited until everyone had successfully found their pages on You-

Tube, Facebook, Instagram, and Twitter. They certainly wanted to make sure they reached their audience from every platform possible, and clearly it was working with the amount of followers they had. Alex informed everyone that they shared their music Instagram account, but also each had their own accounts they would like to connect through, as well. They made sure to emphasize that they were very selective with who they followed, so everyone should consider themselves lucky. Hailey couldn't tell if they were joking or not, but what did she care? At least she would have three more accounts to add to her own following.

Julie and Rachel were next, each sharing their Facebook, website, and Instagrams, both personal and business accounts, with the group. Hailey soon realized that if she was going to be serious about her website, she may need to consider making a Facebook page and a whole new Instagram account for it. She cringed at the thought of managing so many social media accounts. She had only just begun to manage and get the hang of her personal Instagram account.

Next up was Luke. "Alright," he said, leaning forward and placing his elbows on his knees, "I don't have a Facebook page for my business, or a special Instagram account, but I do have a website and a personal Instagram account that you can all follow."

A simple man on the surface. Not overly involved in social media outwardly, Hailey knew there was a reason she liked this guy. Everyone stared at him blankly, awaiting his account name.

"*take-a-luke-skies*. All one word," he said with a smirk.

Hailey laughed out loud when she first saw his screen name follow come through during the night of their campfire. Hearing him say it again still made a small smile inch across her face.

Julie asked, "Really, that's your real screen name?"

"Yep, why not?" he shrugged while letting out a huge grin. "It's a clever way of telling people that my business is getting them looks online."

It was now Hailey's turn and she was feeling less embarrassed now that Luke went before her and confessed that he only had one social media account.

"My Instagram account name is *haileyroaming*." She watched as everyone typed it in their phones and felt compelled to add, "and I have a website coming soon, so I will be sure to send that to you all through Instagram when it's live." Luke turned his head and smiled at her as the flames painted his face in deep orange. Hailey bit her bottom lip and curled her toes, trying to control the fire that had just ignited in her core.

Last, but not least, it was Steven's turn to wrap up the circle of social media support—or whatever Julie had said they were doing.

"Similar to Luke, I only have YouTube and Instagram. No website or Facebook." Everyone nodded, waiting for him to proceed.

"You can find me on YouTube by searching Steven's Survival Guide." He paused as everyone's heads were down, fingers tapping their screens. He waited until everyone's eyes were focused back on him until he proceeded onto the next account. "Alright, and my Instagram account is *at camping underscore merkins*, spelled m-e-r-k-i-n-s, then the number *fifty-seven*."

Hailey felt the blood drain from her face. Did he just say what she thought he did? Had her prime suspect really been sitting across from her all night? Sitting with the group, joking, laughing, sharing stories, playing the part of your basic happy vanlifer? Hailey was sick to her stomach. She couldn't decipher whether she was more angry, scared, or happy that the identity of the internet troll she had been trying to hunt down had just been revealed, and right in front of her nonetheless. She thought of the victimized girls in the Polaroids and anger took over and her blood began to boil. Without looking up, she discreetly moved her foot next to Luke's and nudged him with enough force for him to recognize that something was wrong.

He received Hailey's signal, loud and clear. Luke did the honors of pretending he didn't hear him correctly to confirm he was the callous internet troll that Hailey suspected he was. "Wait, I'm not sure I typed it right," he lied as he held up the phone in Steven's direction.

Steven leaned in and squinted his eyes to see the small print. "Yep. S. Merkins. That's me," he said, as if he wasn't some demeaning psychopath.

It didn't take long for the anger to turn into fury. Her skin was boiling and she was about to blow her top. This was her guy—this could be the killer.

Luke looked over and could see the vengeance in Hailey's eyes as she crossed her legs and began to twitch her foot hastily from side to side. She wanted to berate him for being so smug and demand where he was on the nights the girls went missing. But she couldn't. She knew a good reporter didn't just start sputtering out questions, no matter how badly she wanted to. A good reporter meticulously chose her words to formulate inquisitive questions. Questions that would catch the suspect off guard and allow him to spill details. Questions that would uncover the truth.

Hailey tried to act casual as everyone stood up and began to say their goodbyes. At least as casual as one can be in the midst of a potential serial killer. She watched Luke stiffly shake Steven's hand while wearing an awkward smile across his face; he was doing just as good of a job as she was at playing it cool.

After saying her final goodbye to Mika and Alex and thanking them for such a wonderful evening, aside from inviting a murderer to the shindig, Hailey turned on her heel and headed back towards the van. Luke followed in her wake as she darted down the road, weaving in and out of others who were still roaming the street. Her hand began to cramp before she noticed how tight she had been holding onto Sadie's leash. As she switched the handle to her other hand, a red indentation of the rope was left behind, imprinted on her palm.

"Hailey! Wait up!" she heard Luke call from behind her but didn't bother to slow her pace. She didn't have time to waste; she had a name and was ready to pull an all nighter digging up all the dirty details she could on Steven Merkins.

Chapter 19

A mere six years old and stuck at home for five days with strep throat; most people would feel miserable, but she was more than happy to enjoy her endless meals of mint chocolate chip ice cream and cherry Jello-O as she laid curled up beneath her pink-flowered comforter. Her mother sat beside her on the edge of the bed and placed a cool, wet cloth across her forehead to suppress the fever before opening the pages to Hailey's favorite book. She pulled the soft pink flowers up to her chin as the ice cream glided down her throat while she listened to the hum of her mother's voice. After the last soothing bite, Hailey rolled over to her side as her mother gave her a kiss on the forehead and left the room. She caught a glimpse of herself in the closet door mirror and could see a stream of pastel green dripping down her chin. Just as she lifted her hand to wipe away the creamy liquid, loud pounding reverberated agaist the bedroom door.

Hailey was jolted awake as she realized the pounding wasn't in her dream, but was coming from the side door of her van. A blue hue filled the van as the first light of the morning cracked the horizon. Sadie began to bark and Hailey leapt out of bed, with her heart racing and eyes wide. She was in such a deep sleep that for a moment, she was confused where she was, and it took her a minute to remember she was in her van and not her childhood room. Throwing on her robe, Hailey pulled back the curtain to peer out the window. It was Luke. What in God's name was he doing awake at this hour? Better question, what was he doing pounding on her door so aggressively at this hour?

"What are you doing?" Her voice was hoarse as she slid open the door just enough to poke her head out.

"Steven!" he said with urgency.

Hailey looked at him confused, still mentally half asleep.

Luke continued. "I couldn't sleep and have been up since five, so I decided to make myself some coffee around six. Then I realized I was out of coffee and—"

"Is there a point to this coffee story?" Hailey was in no mood to hear an aimless novel at six-thirty a.m.

"I saw Steven get out of his van, then look around as if to make sure there was no one else up or watching him. Then he hauled a giant blue blanket out of his van and threw it away in the dumpster at the end of the road."

Now that was the kind of information she would be willing to wake up for, despite getting a mere three hours of sleep after spending most of the night digging up all she could on Mr. Steven J. Merkins.

"Hold on." Hailey closed her door, leaving Luke to be the one confused this time. In less than two minutes, she managed to toss on the same pair of jeans she'd worn the night before, along with a sweatshirt and tennis shoes, before leaping out the door, with Sadie following closely at her heels.

"Where are we going?" Luke asked with a surprised look on his face as he followed her determined stride.

"To the dumpster of course. We have to get that blanket." Hailey didn't even bother to look back as she spoke. She knew that the sun was rising fast, meaning soon the other campers would be up too and she wouldn't be able to go dumpster diving without raising a lot of eyebrows and concern.

Luke didn't ask any more questions. He grabbed a trash bag from his van and followed Hailey to the dumpsters.

"Can you give me a boost?" she asked.

"How about I do the honors?" They each stood staring at the dumpster covered in streams of crusted juice and mystery food elements that had tried to escape their fate.

"Be my guest." Hailey gestured towards the bin with a wave of her hand.

Luke shook his head and took a deep breath to prepare himself for something he never imagined he would be doing in his life, let alone before seven in the morning where he was surrounded by vans full of people, people who could wake up and witness what he was doing at any minute. As they each took a hold of the enormous lid and lifted it open, a sour smell assaulted their nostrils, causing them both to wince.

"You owe me breakfast for this." Luke placed both hands on the edge of the bin and hoisted himself up onto the ledge. "At least when I get my appetite back." He sat on the ledge, peering into the bin and evaluating the contents. "Here it is." He hopped inside, crunching old potato chip bags and soda cans as he landed.

"Try not to touch it as much as you can," Hailey pressed as she stood on her toes looking into the bin.

"Don't worry, I'll bag it up."

"Good idea." Hailey swiveled her head to search the area around them to be sure the coast was still clear. The giant black plastic bag came soaring out of the bin, causing Sadie to jump out of the way of its path before it landed on the asphalt.

"Yikes, that was close," Hailey said with a slight scowl.

"Sorry, that was the most efficient way I could think of." Luke jumped back out over the ledge and tried to close the lid as gently as he could.

"Alright, now let's get out of here," Hailey said, tossing the bag over her shoulder.

"I definitely need to go wash my hands," Luke added, cringing as he looked down at his hands.

Sadie trotted ahead, leading the way as Hailey and Luke swiftly followed behind, trying to get back to their vans before they were spotted taking a strange morning walk with a giant bag of trash. When their vans came into view, Hailey felt a tinge of relief—the home stretch.

Out of nowhere, a figure jumped out before them.

"Shit." Hailey jumped and was certain her heart stopped for a moment. "Alex, you scared the crap out of me," she exhaled.

He pulled his lips into a sheepish smile. "Sorry, Hailey. I saw Sadie scamper by and figured you must be close behind, so I thought I would say good morning."

She could feel her heartbeat begin to slow as she no longer realized she was in danger.

"Mornin' Alex," Luke said, now standing at her side. "You're up early."

"Yeah, I'm always the first one up and thought I would grab a cup of coffee down at the Java Stop van that's parked at the end near the other food trucks. You guys want to join?"

Hailey and Luke exchanged a look, completely caught off guard, before Hailey quickly worked up a response. "I actually need to give Sadie breakfast, but maybe Luke could go with you? I'm dying for a good cup of coffee." Luke caught the plan of distraction and agreed to walk with Alex over to the Java Stop.

"Great!" Alex lit up like a kid on Christmas morning as Luke gave Hailey a *'you really owe me now'* look before turning to Alex and asking if he could wash his hands first. He didn't want to get his dumpster hands all over his fresh cup of coffee.

Hailey grinned before regaining her focus as to why the aversion had to be made to begin with. It wasn't everyday she found herself walking around with a giant black bag she had pulled from a dumpster. Not to mention the contents could potentially be evidence in a murder case. She had about thirteen more vans to walk by before she would make it back to where she was parked, and she didn't want to waste any more time standing around.

Sadie had already made it to the van and was waiting outside the door as Hailey approached. "Good girl, let's get this inside, shall we?" Hailey hooked her hand in the lock and began to slide open her door when a voice growled behind her.

"Saving that trash for later?"

Hailey felt her stomach drop as she turned around to see Steven standing behind her as an ominous smile creeped across his mouth. Hailey opened her mouth to respond, but no words came out.

"I didn't think you'd be up this early," he began, his eyes dark and steady as he spoke, "seeing that I saw light coming from your van at two this morning."

"What were you doing watching my van at two in the morning?" she asked with narrowed eyes.

"Couldn't sleep," he stated. "Curiosity encouraged me to look out the window, see if there was anyone else up, and I saw the glow of a light on coming from your windows."

"Guess I couldn't sleep either," she replied with a tight grimace.

He eyed the trash bag as she tried to push it behind her legs, as if her legs were remotely wide enough to hide the mass. "One person's trash is another man's treasure?"

"What makes you think I took this from the trash?"

"Because you were walking away from the dumpster and that doesn't look like old ramen wrappers and plastic utensils stuffed in that bag to me." He crossed his arms across his chest and widened his stance, rocking from one foot to the other.

Hailey was not about to let him intimidate her. What was he going to do? Kidnap her, steal the bag, or better yet, stab her in the middle of hundreds of vans that people were slowly waking up and walking out of? No. She had the upper hand here and she wasn't going to let him win.

"Why do you even care? Did you throw something in that dumpster you don't want to be found?" Her eyes locked on his, holding his dark gaze. Silence idled between them. Hailey felt the unease settle in her stomach as she squared her shoulders.

"What would it matter to you if I did or not?" His tone ticked up a notch.

"You're hiding something, Steven, and I'm going to figure out what it is." Hailey was losing her patience.

Steven stared at her, speechless. She had his attention now.

"Well aren't we a little hasty in the morning?" he mocked.

"Or maybe I'm just hasty when I'm being lied to," she retorted.

"Lied to? When have I lied to you?"

"Oh please." She rolled her eyes. "You act like you're some innocent vanlifer making survivalist YouTube videos, but I know what you've done. I know what darkness you're hiding."

Hailey searched his face for any indication that she hit a nerve, but his expression remained stone cold.

"I'm not hiding anything."

"Then why are you here, standing at my van, questioning me about what I was doing this morning when it's absolutely none of your business?"

In one swift motion, Steven thrusted his hand towards Hailey, grabbing her wrist in a firm grasp. Her confidence melted into panic as his grip grew tighter and he leaned his face close to hers.

"Give me the goddamn bag," he hissed.

Chapter 20

Luke came jogging over holding a coffee in each hand, one of which had spilled over and was dripping between his fingers. "Steven," Luke said with shock in his eyes.

Steven immediately dropped his grip on Hailey's wrist at the sound of Luke's voice, but a red imprint of his hand remained on her skin.

Hailey and Steven didn't break eye contact as Luke made his way to Hailey's side. With the blanket in her possession, there was no chance in hell she was going to let him intimidate her into giving it back. Especially now that she had Luke on her side and had regained her footing.

"I'm telling you, I have nothing to hide."

"Somehow I don't believe that, *@camping_merkins57*," she retorted.

"What does my Instagram screen name have to do with what I threw away in the dumpster? Or with anything else, for that matter?"

"Don't play dumb. I have the evidence. I have the proof that you have been using your Instagram to target and harass young girls living the vanlife." Hailey looked around, realizing she was beginning to raise her voice.

"I...I didn't do anything wrong." Steven stammered as he shifted his weight from one foot to the other and crossed his arms nervously. She knew she was striking a nerve now. He ran his fingers through his greasy black hair before he began defending his actions. "Okay, sure, maybe I lost my temper a little bit and made some comments I shouldn't have online, but it's not like I'm the only person who has done that. There are plenty of people who get worked up on social media."

He wasn't wrong, but Hailey also wasn't convinced that harassing vanlifers online was the only thing he was guilty of. "Tell me," she started, narrowing her eyes, "did you know who I was when we showed up to the campfire last night? Did you recognize me from social media?"

Sadie barked, drawing everyone's attention to the fact that she had been chewing on the plastic bag.

"I think your dog is hungry," Steven hedged.

"Don't change the subject," Hailey hissed.

Luke nudged his way behind Hailey, grabbed the bag, opened her door, and tossed it into the van. He then proceeded to give Sadie a heaping bowl of kibbles as the stand off continued.

"Look, I didn't know it was you, okay? It didn't even cross my mind until we all started exchanging social media accounts and you said your account name." He paused, waiting for her to respond. When she didn't, he continued. "Even then, after we all went our separate ways for the evening, I went and looked you up and realized I had commented on one of your posts."

"Why? Why do you do it? Is that your platform for finding your next victim? Am I on your list now?"

"Whoa, what? Next victim?" He scrunched his face in confusion. "And a list? What list are you talking about?"

Hailey squinted at his face and assessed his confusion for a moment. Did he really have no idea what she was talking about, or was he just a good liar?

"You see, I think that you find these young girls traveling alone on social media, stalk them, and berate them for joining the vanlife. It must really get under your skin that these girls get thousands of followers, whereas your page only gets a few hundred."

She could see his face beginning to change color with anger. Her interrogation was working.

"I'm sure you just can't wait for events like this where you can meet these girls in person and lure them into your grasp. Make them think you're some kind vagabond like them, get them to trust you, make them believe you're a nice guy." His hands began to turn into tight fists against his sides.

Hailey held her ground. She could feel Luke at her side and knew if it came down to it, Steven wouldn't stand a chance against him in a fight.

"Okay, look. I'll admit it," he stuttered, becoming frantic. "I hate these girls, and some guys too, who buy a van, remodel it, and just use it as their prop for photos on social media. They aren't real campers, they don't know anything about camping, and they ruin it for people like me who are out here doing it for the right reasons."

"And what are the right reasons?"

"To purely enjoy nature!" He was beginning to draw attention from people passing by. "I am a survivalist. I am out here to enjoy nature for what it is and teach people about the real side of camping. Not how to hang twinkle lights or how to match your bedspread to the damn rug. I hate these prissy little rich girls that come from their high-class lifestyle and steal my followers and get all the credit for living out of their van when they don't even know anything about camping."

"Hate them enough to want them dead?" Luke cut in and Hailey flashed him a glare. This was her battle.

"What? No! I'm not some murderer." Steven threw his hands up in surrender.

"Then why are you so concerned about what I took out of the trash?"

"I was painting last night," he said as he let out a defeated sigh.

"Painting?"

"Yes, I like to paint. Is that a crime?"

Hailey shook her head and waved her hand, motioning for him to proceed.

"I made a stencil to create signs to hang around the event. But I wanted to hang them in the middle of the night when no one else was up."

"Which is why you were really awake at two a.m."

"Yes."

"What did these signs say?" Luke chimed in, ignoring the scowl Hailey shot in his direction.

Steven took another deep breath in and looked over his shoulder to be sure no one else was listening in on their conversation. Then, in a low voice, he relayed his message: "Those who flaunt their lifestyle, ultimately lose their lifestyle."

"Sounds like a threat to me," Hailey snapped her head at him with a stern look. If Luke chimed in one more time, he was going to get the next berating.

"I just wanted to give the influencers a little fright. You know, maybe make them not want to be part of this life. I had no intention of physically hurting anyone."

"Then why did you throw away a giant blue blanket?" Hailey challenged.

"After I was finished with my signs and they were dry, that's when I looked out the window to see if anyone was out or still awake. That's when I saw your light on. I knew I couldn't go yet and turned around, knocking the dirty paint water all over the floor onto the blue blanket and all over my newly painted signs, completely ruining them." The frustration in his voice seemed sincere.

"So you're telling me that the trash can is filled with your ruined painted signs? And you're afraid that I found them and was going to expose you to everyone?" Hailey wasn't totally convinced.

Steven looked at Luke, back to Hailey, then to the ground before answering. "Yes. Especially if you made the connection that I was the one who made the mean comments on your Instagram post."

"Oh, I connected you to more than just mean comments on Instagram."

Steven had a nervous, yet confused look on his face.

"I knew you were hiding more than just making menacing comments on Instagram. I did my own research on you, Steven Merkins, and you know what I found?" This time she raised both her eyebrows, pausing for dramatic effect, knowing he wasn't going to have an answer. "You have two restraining orders against you for harassment, and I bet that you don't want to risk being sued or having the cops come after you again since your name is already red flagged in their system."

"Those were just complete misunderstandings," Steven tried.

Hailey rolled her eyes. "Ah, the motto of every guilty party in a harassment case."

Steven straightened his shoulders and puffed out his chest out. That last comment definitely hit a sore spot. "Look, there are some things I've done in the past that I can't erase, and, yeah, sure, I get a little short tempered and angry sometimes, but I am not a physically violent person. I would never lay a hand on someone."

Hailey considered the information for a minute. Steven didn't appear to be the athletic type and didn't look like he had lifted any sort of weight in quite some time. Moving a woman who weighed one hundred and fifteen pounds wouldn't be a walk in the park, especially for a man of his stature. If Steven wasn't capable of physical violence, then he wasn't her guy, and she would be back to square one. But Steven wasn't going to be let off the hook that easily. Whether he was being honest or not, she couldn't entirely tell. Either way, she decided she would still hold onto the blue quilt and get it to Sarah as soon as possible to take samples and compare the blue fibers to those found on each of the victim's clothing.

The three of them stood staring at one another, unsure whose move it was. Finally, Luke broke the awkward silence, "Okay, so it sounds like to me we have several misunderstandings going on here."

Both Hailey and Steven turned their attention to Luke.

"I think if anything, I am the victim here," Steven said in a brash tone.

"Oh, give me a break, you were up making hate signs," Hailey scoffed.

"Alright, you two," Luke placed himself in the middle. "I think that it's fair to say both sides have done wrong and we should all just call a truce."

"Whose side are you on?" Hailey hissed at Luke.

"I'm not going anywhere," Steven offered. "If I truly have done something wrong, don't you think I would want to get out of here as soon as possible? I have no plans to leave until the event is over tomorrow."

Luke turned to Hailey. "Don't you need to go see your friend in town anyway?"

Hailey stared at him with a puzzled look. That was a weird question to ask in this moment. He knew she had already gone to see Sarah, the same night he went to meet his friend.

He continued, "Remember, you were going to stop by your friend's place for lunch today?"

The light bulb switched on. "Oh yes, I almost completely forgot about that."

She didn't like how he cut in during her interrogation with Steven, but she did admire his quick thinking. Hailey could drop off the blanket to Sarah that afternoon, maybe during her lunch break if she could make it in time.

"What do you say, Steven? Can we call this a truce?" Luke held out his hand.

Steven squared his eyes with Hailey. "Only if she throws the bag back into the bin and doesn't report me for harassment."

Hailey opened her mouth, but before she could object, Luke jumped in. "Deal. Here is the bag, you can toss it away yourself so you know it really happened." Luke pulled out a black trash bag from Hailey's van and handed it over to Steven.

Steven grabbed the bag from Luke and nodded his head. "Deal."

Hailey stood staring at Luke, really hoping he had a good plan since he'd just handed back the only bag of evidence she had from this guy that she was going to drive over to Sarah at their impromptu lunch.

"And I'll delete the comment I made on your account. You're clearly more than just a bimbo wannabe influencer," Steven said smugly as he pivoted away and began walking towards the dumpster.

The second Steven was out of ear shot, Hailey turned to Luke and slapped him on the arm. "What the hell? Why did you give him the bag back?"

"I didn't," he said with a grin.

"What? I literally just watched you hand it to him."

Without saying a word, Luke slid open her van door wide enough for her to see the black trash bag with the blanket inside still sitting on the floor.

"Wait, then what did you give him?" she asked with a baffled look.

"Your trash." He pulled his lips into a crooked smile.

Oh, how she wanted to kiss that crooked smile.

Chapter 21

"The results came back from the blanket." There was silence on the line as Hailey waited with anticipation while Sarah pulled up the lab results. "The fibers weren't a match and the stain on the blanket was, in fact, spilled oil-based paint."

"Dammit," Hailey huffed. "I really thought I had something big here."

"I know it isn't the news you were hoping for, but I do have some other information that you may be interested in," Sarah offered.

"I'm all ears."

"Remember when you were here and I received that message about another body being found?"

"Of course. Where was it found? Near the same place as the last victim? And did you find out if you were going to be working on the case?" Hailey asked.

"Whoa there, Diane Sawyer. Give me a chance to answer at least one of the questions," Sarah teased.

"Sorry, you know how anxious I get."

"So the body wasn't found near the same dump sites as the other bodies. It was much further away this time. All the way near Crater Lake, as a matter of fact."

"Crater Lake? That's all the way in Oregon."

"Strange right?" Sarah asked. "As for examining the case, my answer is yes. My boss said that he needs to stay here in town since he is the lead examiner at our office, so he is sending me to Oregon to meet with the lead examiner there that will be receiving the body. They want me to get started ASAP. They called when I was on my way into the office and said the M.E. found a Polaroid rolled up in the victim's mouth during the autopsy, so I'll be heading up to their office in Douglas County, Oregon."

"It's got to be the same guy. That's his signature."

"That's what everyone is thinking, but it is strange that he would cross state lines."

"What was the picture of? Did it appear to be in the same location as the others? If he crossed state lines, I can't imagine he used the same hideout." Hailey couldn't hold back all the questions filling her mind.

"Let me pull it up again. They sent it to our unit to verify it was similar to the other pictures we found on the two previous victims." Hailey could hear Sarah typing into her keyboard as she pulled up the image. "Here we go. Yep, looks like the same place the other photographs were taken. Dimly lit space, concrete block walls, and unmaintained dirt floor."

"Hands and ankles bound?"

"That's correct. But this time her mouth was gagged too. Which would make sense if he was holding her in a moving vehicle," Sarah stated.

"True. He wouldn't want her to be able to call for help if they stopped anywhere along the way."

"But sadly, it sounds like it was the same result in the end. Victim was stabbed repeatedly. Although from the report, it looks like there were only about ten stab wounds this time."

"I can't imagine this guy suddenly figured out how to manage his rage," Hailey said sarcastically.

"Definitely not. The cause of death was asphyxiation. It appeared that he stabbed her premortem, so maybe she knocked the knife out of his hands and he had to resort to strangling her."

Hailey cringed at the thought. *What if he liked watching her gasp for air? Squeezing so tight until she stopped moving, until she took her last breath.* Not only was a serial killer on the loose targeting young women traveling alone, but he was figuring out different ways to take out his rage on each of the victims. This guy needed to be caught, and soon.

"At the rate he's going, if he doesn't already have another victim in his grasp, he's definitely identified and out on the hunt for one," Hailey said.

"That's everyone's fear here, too. You know, I think it might be a good idea for you to maybe warn women travelers at the event you're at," Sarah suggested.

"That might not be a bad idea. Today is the last day of the event, meaning most people will be hitting the road again tomorrow, potentially driving right into his playing field."

"Exactly, and I know that most of the vanlifers don't have TV and probably aren't seeing the broadcasts and warnings from the media about all this. Look, I wish I could talk more, but I better get going. I need to pack since I'm scheduled to leave in a couple of hours, and who knows how long I will be up there."

"Wait, one more thing. I'm assuming since you haven't referred to her by name that they haven't confirmed her identity yet?" Hailey asked.

"They are testing her fingerprints, but I haven't heard back from them since this morning. I'm sure by the time I get there they will have results," Sarah responded.

"Alright, well let me know when you get there and keep me updated," Hailey said.

"I will. As always, be safe, Hailey."

"I will, you too, Sarah."

The call ended and Hailey sat on her bed running over the fragmented details she just received about the new victim. Reaching across her bed, she retrieved her laptop out from under her pillow to pull up Google Maps. She typed in Cow Creek, CA as the starting point and Crater Lake as the destination.

"Whoa, four hundred and sixty-two miles," Hailey said in shock, as she looked at the screen. That was a large distance to travel from his other dump site. Hailey wondered what would cause him to travel such a great distance to commit his next crime when the first two were both committed in national parks and forests in California. Maybe he was afraid to get caught in California after committing two crimes which both made state news. Or maybe his next victim had already been chosen and was en route to Crater Lake and he followed her there. Whatever his motive was, Hailey was on a mission to find the answers.

Hailey opened up her notebook and looked at the pages scribbled with her notes, it was beginning to look messy and the last thing she wanted to do was mix up the information. It was time to create a link map. She pulled the California and Oregon maps from her bag and brought them to the bed. She looked around the small space, wondering where on earth she had enough room to piece together two whole maps onto the wall. Just as she thought she was going to have to use the back of the door, she realized that she surprisingly hadn't placed anything on the wall above her bed. Hailey held up the California map in her hands, imagining it against the wall. "It's perfect," she said as she retrieved the tape from the tool basket. After taping the maps together on the wall, she began to write down all the pertinent information she had so far onto sticky notes, placing them in their rightful positions on the map.

Not completely convinced that Steven could be fully ruled out yet, she wrote on a sticky note *Person of Interest A: Steven Merkins*, then stuck it in the top right corner of the map. Next, she wrote *Person of Interest B:* on another new note, leaving it blank before placing it beneath the other one on the map. Hailey then marked on the map where each victim was found and where they were last seen. There was still a lot of information she needed, but at least she felt like she had a better visual hold on her details of the cases now, especially since it was looking like there may be more murders to come.

It was almost eleven a.m., and Hailey decided that she had marked all the details on the map that she had at this point and that it was time to face her next challenge—figuring out how to warn other women at the event about the murders that had been taking place without creating panic or looking like she was crazy. She looked in the mirror and decided to pull her unwashed hair back into a tight pony tail and swipe on some mascara and blush. Maybe the more put together she looked, the more seriously people would take her.

With Sadie by her side, she hopped out of the van, gazing up and down the road as other vanlifers crowded the street. Luke had gone off to join a group of guys he had met the day before to enjoy the nice weather and play some football, leaving Hailey to take on the quest on her own. Hailey was unsure of how she was going to reach so many people in a casual and spread out setting.

A waft of seasoned ground beef and warm, homemade tortillas began to fill the air, and Hailey made the decision she would come up with her plan while consuming tacos from the food truck at the end of the road.

"Hailey?" a voice called from behind as she moved to the side to wait for her order to be called.

"Hey, Rachel," Hailey greeted her with a smile. "Are you waiting too?"

"Yes, I am! This truck has the best vegan tacos," she said with a grin. "Want to grab a seat together?"

"Sure, that sounds great." Hailey wondered if she was going to get an earful when their orders were ready and her plate consisted of nothing but meat tacos.

"I'm sad it's the last day of this event. I love coming to these and meeting so many other travelers," Rachel said as she took a heaping bite of her fried avocado taco.

Hailey nodded. "It has been great to see what a community there is among vanlifers and that I'm not the only girl traveling alone in my van."

"Not at all! There are tons of women doing the same thing." Just the segue Hailey needed.

"Do you ever get scared traveling alone?" she asked in a casual tone.

Rachel thought about it for a moment. "Sometimes." She picked up her lemonade and took a swig. "But I suppose that's because doing anything alone as a woman can be scary."

"Yeah, that's the truth, huh?" Hailey couldn't argue with that.

"I definitely think I take more consideration into where I am camping for the night and I never post where I am staying at the time I am staying there. I always post about a spot after I have moved locations."

"That's smart." Hailey was pleased she had managed to befriend someone who at least had some common sense when it came to safety. "Have you heard about the women who were found murdered in the national forests out here in the past couple of weeks?" Hailey asked bluntly.

Hailey barely finished the question before Rachel's eyes widened and she jumped in with her response. "Yes! I was in such shock when I first heard about the girl, Hannah, who went missing. I knew it wasn't a good sign that no one had heard from her, but I really was hoping she just took a wrong turn or was out boondocking somewhere without service and forgot to call home." Her eyes fell to the table. "I met her at a meetup."

"Really?" Hailey was stunned.

"Yeah, she was so bubbly and sweet. I was sad to see the news about her death."

"I've heard that there was another murder," Hailey said quietly, "and it was another single girl traveling in her van."

"For real?" Rachel put down her taco and was leaning in, matching Hailey's tone.

"Yeah, I don't know about you, but three murders that were all young girls traveling in their vans doesn't sound like coincidence to me."

Rachel shook her head. "Definitely not a coincidence."

"I wish there was a way to reach all the other women traveling alone. Just so they are aware of what's going on and to maybe be a little extra cautious while traveling."

"You know, there is a girl I met this morning while waiting in line for coffee who I happened to already follow on Instagram and YouTube because she is totally a vanlife celebrity. Maybe if we can get her to post something, she could reach a lot of vanlife women," Rachel suggested.

"Really?"

Rachel nodded.

"That's a great idea." Hailey's face lit up as she pushed the last bite of her taco into her mouth. "Any idea of how we find this celebrity before she leaves this event?"

"You're just in luck because she happened to give me a personal tour of her van after we got our coffee this morning," Rachel replied, grinning like a schoolgirl who just became best friends with the popular girl.

"Well, I hope she's home because we're heading over." Hailey smiled as she scooped up both of their empty white and red checkered trays and stood up from the table.

As they walked through the crowd, passing individuals and groups congregated around vans, Hailey wondered what secrets unfolded behind their steel doors. She had already caught one internet troll and wondered how many other villains may be camouflaged among them.

"Hey ladies," a familiar voice called out in front of them. "I thought I saw you two turn down this way." A bright grin crossed Luke's face as he stood shirtless before them.

"Take-A-Look-skies" Rachel whispered to herself, as her eyes trailed up and down his strong, tan torso. "Hey, Luke, how's it hanging?"

Hailey rolled her eyes. "Working on your tan?"

"Might as well with a beautiful day like this," he said, still sporting his cheeky smile. "Where are you two headed off to?"

"I'm taking Hailey to meet my friend Brianna Moore," Rachel said with a wide grin.

"No way. You're friends with Brianna Moore?" A broad-shouldered, red-headed guy stepped beside Luke with a surprised look on his face.

"Hailey, Rachel, meet Will, Peter, and Jordan." Luke gestured towards the red-headed body-builder and a tall, athletic man with dirty blonde hair that appeared by his side. Will and Jordan were like a walking billboard for how to stay fit while traveling full-time, while Peter was tall and gangly and evidently wasn't on their same workout regiment.

"Am I supposed to know who this Brianna Moore person is?" Luke asked, darting his gaze from Will to Rachel.

"She's, like, the self-proclaimed 'Queen of Vanlife,' " Peter said while rolling his eyes.

"I guess I better pay more attention on Instagram," Luke replied in a sarcastic tone. "Well, we're heading to get some lunch. Maybe we can catch up with you ladies afterwards?" he asked, flashing a half smile at Hailey.

"Absolutely," Rachel replied eagerly.

They continued on their separate ways and Hailey was happy to be back on task. She wasn't exactly looking to spend her day fraternizing with the cast of The O.C., but if she at least got the word out to other female travelers about the serial killer, then she would feel somewhat productive.

After walking for a while and listening to Rachel go on and on about the latest trend in her jewelry making, they approached a pink van with yellow cursive writing across the side that read, *"Not All Who Wander Are Lost."*

"How original," Hailey muttered under her breath, luckily quiet enough that Rachel didn't hear.

"This is it!" Rachel said with excitement as they approached the van.

"She certainly isn't hard to find in this van, now is she?" Hailey commented.

"Isn't it beautiful?" Rachel said, ignoring Hailey's remark. "She even got a decal made of her social media sites to put on the back of her van, so people can easily find and follow her pages."

Hailey couldn't help but wonder how a serial killer was running loose targeting young female vanlife influencers and this girl hadn't managed to be at the top of his list. As they reached the back of the van, a group of about ten people were crowded around the opened back doors, listening intently to a beautiful blonde sitting on the back bumper. Rachel walked ahead, confidently adding herself into the group as Hailey trailed behind.

"Hey Rachel!" Brianna stood up, greeting Rachel with a hug and bright white smile.

As they pulled out of their embrace, Rachel turned her shoulder and waved Hailey over to the middle of the group. "I wanted you to meet my friend, Hailey."

Hailey awkwardly made her way through the barrier of followers to meet the acclaimed influencer.

"Hi, Hailey, I'm Brianna. It's nice to meet you." She was just as bubbly as Hailey had expected. "Are you a solo woman traveler, as well?"

"Yes, I am." Hailey hesitated as she looked around the circle. "That's actually why I wanted to meet you. I've heard so many wonderful things about you and your life living on the road alone," Hailey said with a genuine smile, trying to establish a positive relationship before asking for any favors. It was one of the first techniques she learned in her journalism course; if you build rapport, you are more likely to get more of what you need from people.

"I love meeting other solo travelers. You should join my Facebook group for solo woman travelers. I have built a great community of women on there, where they all share their tips and travel advice with one another," she stated with enthusiasm.

Hailey couldn't deny that she was impressed with Brianna's stamina and self-marketing acumen. Rachel was right when she said she knew the perfect candidate to reach a large audience of vanlife women travelers.

"That's awesome, I will definitely check it out." Hailey's smile faded as she contemplated the best way to piece together her next sentence.

"We were actually hoping to get your help with something," Rachel said, beating Hailey to it.

"Absolutely, what is it?" Brianna looked at Rachel, who directed the response to Hailey.

"This may sound a little morbid, but I'm not sure if you're aware of the murders that have taken place recently here in California involving young women in the vanlife community." Hailey paused searching Brianna's face for a reaction.

She immediately cupped her hand around her mouth and furrowed her brow in shock and sadness. "There has been more than one?" she asked as her hand fell from her mouth to her chest.

"Yes, and the killer is still out there," Hailey added. "Rachel mentioned to me that you have a large following and I thought maybe you could create a post to warn your followers and other solo travelers about what's going on. You know, remind them to be extra cautious and always aware of their surroundings."

"Yes, absolutely, I would love to help get the word out. That's terrifying. I will put a post together on all my social platforms and post it tomorrow morning so it reaches the majority of my followers."

"Thank you so much, Brianna. I knew you would be the perfect person to come to," Rachel said, clearly trying to prod her way into Brianna's inner circle.

After an exchange of social media links and thanking Brianna for her help, Hailey and Rachel made their way back to meet back up with the guys.

As much as Hailey wanted to sit in her van and see if there was any new information leaked about the most recent murder near Crater Lake, she knew there wouldn't be any detailed reports yet, especially considering her most accurate information would come from Sarah and she hadn't heard from her since their phone call earlier that day. Despite her mind being occupied, she decided to try her best to enjoy her last evening at the meetup with her group of new friends before they all left to go their separate ways in the morning.

It wasn't long after Hailey and Rachel joined Luke, Will, Peter, and

Jordan that she had learned all about how Will utilized YouTube and Instagram to promote his workout brand that he had created for remote workers and travelers who did not always have access to a gym, which certainly explained the broad shoulders and muscular build he managed to maintain after being on the road for over two years. Peter joked that he just joined the group to meet girls, but he had a full-time job in Oregon and could only travel when he could get away from work. Meanwhile, Jordan worked as a part-time as a forestry technician building trails and fighting fires in the Sierra National Forest then spending the other half of his time traveling around the country in his van taking pictures of scenery and wildlife and selling them online for some extra cash.

The diversity amongst the group made Hailey feel even more inspired to create her website so she too could have something to brag about to fellow travelers. She was also beginning to realize that these events were just as much networking events as they were a way to make new friends. She took a mental note to find more of these events as she traveled up the west coast.

"So where is everyone off to next?" Luke asked as he grabbed another beer and sat down.

"I'm heading south towards Las Vegas to see some friends down there for a couple of days," Will said with a grin that said he was going to be doing more than just seeing friends while he was in Vegas.

"I have to get back to work in Oregon, but my next weekend getaway will probably be up to Mount Rainier," Peter said, then looked over to Rachel.

"I'm heading towards Huntington Beach. Definitely need to work on my tan," Rachel said with a giggle as she rotated her pale forearm for everyone to see.

"I honestly haven't decided yet. I have to be back at work in two weeks, so I might just go to Tahoe or somewhere close by," Jordan commented as he took a sip of his beer. "And then I'll be back to fighting fires. Hopefully not too many this season though. What about you, Luke?"

Luke glanced over at Hailey. "I think I'm just going to keep heading north." He shrugged his shoulders. "Maybe up to Oregon next."

"That's what I was thinking, too," Hailey added. "I have heard amazing things about Crater Lake and I want to keep heading north through Seattle and probably up to British Columbia."

"O.M.G. Yes." Rachel just about spit out her wine at the mention. "Crater Lake is one of the most amazing places I have been along my journey. So beautiful."

"There's nothing like it," Peter agreed.

"I think it's overrated, but definitely worth a visit," Jordan added.

Navy blue coated the sky as the sun fell into the ocean once again. The hours passed easily as they exchanged tales of their lives before travel and the confused judgments from their family and friends as they left their old lives behind. They had only known each other for less than twenty four hours, but to any outsider it would appear their friendship had been established for years.

Hailey looked around the circle at her new friends and wondered if they joined the vanlife because they wanted to explore, or if like her, they were running away from a former life they wanted to escape.

"Whoa, time sure goes fast when you're having fun," Rachel said looking down at her illuminated Fitbit.

"What time is it?" Hailey asked

"A quarter past one."

"I thought it was only like eleven p.m.!" Will commented with wide eyes.

"Well, I think it's safe to say we had some successful networking and some good friendships were made at this event," Luke said, flashing a smile.

They each stood up and said their goodbyes before collecting their chairs and heading back to their vans.

"It was so great meeting you, Jordan," Hailey said as he pulled her into an embrace.

Jordan held her tight and whispered into her ear, "Be careful about the company you keep."

Hailey pulled away and furrowed her brow in confusion. He darted his eyes towards Luke and Hailey followed his gaze, observing Luke as he said his goodbyes to Rachel and Will, displaying his ever-so-charming smile across his face. She looked back at Jordan as his dark eyes remained fixated on hers. She parted her lips to question his comment, but before the words could leave her mouth, Luke was at her side.

"It was great hangin' with you man," Luke said, holding his hand out to Jordan.

Jordan returned the gesture and shook Luke's hand firmly. Hailey's eyes remained focused on Jordan as she contemplated his statement.

She felt a gentle hand on her back as Rachel pulled her out of her trance to say goodbye.

"Promise me you'll keep in touch," she said with a genuine smile.

"Absolutely," Hailey responded, even though her mind was elsewhere.

Luke and Hailey stood side by side as they watched their friends meander out of sight and back to their vans. As his hand brushed against hers, a wave of unease washed over her. Maybe Jordan was just getting in her head. Or maybe Luke wasn't just the charming guy she thought he was. Maybe there was a darker side to his story that he had yet to tell.

Chapter 22

Sarah pulled into the parking lot of the Douglas County Medical Examination office, collected her files from the passenger seat, and headed into the tan block building.

A woman with a warm smile greeted her at the front desk. "Hi, there. Do you have an appointment with someone today?"

"Hi, I'm Sarah Archer," she said, retrieving her badge from her purse and showing it to the woman. "I'm from the Sacramento County Medical Examiner's office."

"Oh yes, we have been expecting you. Just head down the hallway. Your team is set up in the last room on the right. I'll let Brian know you're here so he can direct you to the autopsy room."

The woman pressed a button on her outdated beige landline to notify Brian of Sarah's arrival. Sarah thanked the woman and began walking down the plain hallway with empty walls until she made it to the last room on the right. The room was empty, but she could see the board had already been set up by her team with the gruesome images and details from the cases they had gathered thus far. Since no one was in sight, Sarah assumed they were already out at the crime scene, gathering more information from the Oregon police department and the couple who had found the body on their hike.

"You must be Sarah," a soft tone rang from behind her. "I'm Brian, head examiner here." A man with dark brown hair and a salt and pepper beard stood in the doorway with a gentle smile.

Sarah crossed the room to meet him. "Yes, it's so nice to meet you."

"Wish it was under different circumstances." He nodded as he shook her hand. "If you're ready, I can take you to the lab so we can get started."

"I'm as ready as I'll ever be," she said, still clutching her files in her arms.

Sarah followed Brian up the hall to the elevator that carried them down to the bottom floor. They exited into another hallway lined with giant blue metal doors and loud, buzzing fluorescent lighting, a sure sign they had successfully made it to the autopsy floor. They passed two offices and an observation window before entering the frigid autopsy room. As soon as she stepped into the brightly lit space, the heavy, vile odor of death molested her nostrils. No matter how many times she had walked into an autopsy room, it still took her several minutes to adjust to the moist stench of decay that was emitted into the air from a dead body. Luckily, she had already put on her lab coat in hopes of keeping as much of the smell as possible from settling into her clothes.

"It is my understanding that there is no need to recap on the situation since your team has been called up due to the possibility that this case is related to two others you have open at this time," Brian stated while handing Sarah a medical mask and gloves.

"Correct. I am hoping this victim will be able to tell us more about the person we are looking for and help us bring him down before another young woman ends up on our tables."

Brian nodded in agreement before he began. "I received the results from the fibers you sent over from the other victims' clothing and compared it to the fibers that we found under this victim's nails." There was a slight pause, causing unease to rise in Sarah's gut. "They were a match."

"Well, that's definitive proof to tie these cases together and that there's not a copycat killer out there too," she said, letting out a sigh of relief. "Do you mind if we take a look at the wounds on the body?"

"The original examination done at the scene of the crime documented there were ten stab wounds. I found twelve, but ten of those twelve were directed towards her lungs and heart," he stated.

"This person was aiming to kill," Sarah said.

"It would appear so, but not with the weapon he used to create these wounds. It was too short to puncture deep enough through her skin to cause any damage to her vital organs."

"And what about the two other wounds you found?"

"One was staggered across the victim's forearm, deep enough to cut her extensor digitorum muscle."

"Indicating she must have been holding her arms up in front of her head. A self-defense wound," Sarah determined.

"Exactly. But the other was a bit more curious." He placed his hand on the victim's cold, pale shoulder and rolled it towards them, revealing another wound across the top of her shoulder blade. "It's odd that all other wounds were on the front of her body, but this one is also more staggered, similar to the lesion on her forearm."

They both examined the wound for a moment as Sarah took note of the details. "What type of weapon do you think we're looking at?"

"Judging by the diameter and length of the wounds, I would say we're looking at maybe a small pocket knife. Or something similar to that size. Could also be a type of box cutter knife, maybe."

"That could make sense if this person is traveling through or living in the woods," Sarah agreed. "The report said she died of asphyxiation?"

"That's correct," he replied, as he began to point at the victim's neck. "Judging by these marks around her neck, it looks like he strangled her with his hands."

Sarah shook her head in grief as her eyes trailed from the bruised marks around her neck to the purple ligature marks that circled around her wrists.

"These marks appear to be fairly wide in diameter as well, and after looking at the Polaroid, my guess would be that he used a type of rope to restrain her," Brian stated.

"It was also said in the report that the Polaroid was found in her mouth?" Sarah asked.

"Yep, I have it right over here. The examiners at the crime scene didn't even see it. No one had thought to look in her mouth until she was brought here. Of course, after I discovered it, I notified the detectives and that's when they called your team."

"So I'm assuming you ran it through DNA analysis," Sarah stated.

"Yes and unfortunately the only DNA on the photograph was the victim's."

"What about the toxicity reports? Anything turn up there?"

"There was some alcohol in her system, but other than that, nothing out of the ordinary."

Sarah considered the information. If there was alcohol in the victim's system, was she drinking alone? Or did she enjoy what she thought were innocent drinks with her killer before he struck?

"She appears to be slightly smaller than the previous victims. Wouldn't be too challenging for a decently athletic individual to restrain her, or carry her body somewhere," Sarah said, thinking aloud. "Especially if she had some drinks in her, maybe causing her to be less stable and alert."

Brian nodded his head in agreement as he stepped over to the table that displayed all the bags of evidence that were taken and neatly labeled with the time and date they were removed from the victim. Sarah accompanied him to take a look at all of the clothing and accessories that lay across the cold metal slab.

"What's this?" Sarah held up a bag with a small rectangular paper inside.

"It's a business card."

"May I?" she asked as she picked up the bag.

"Be my guest," Brian said with a shrug of his shoulder.

Sarah picked up the ziplock and carefully opened the top, tilting the bag downward to slide the contents into her hand. Careful as to not let it fall onto the floor, Sarah pulled the card from the bag and flipped it over to read the details. There was a name printed in small, bold black letters: *Luke Mancini*.

Chapter 23

Morning arrived sooner than Hailey was hoping as a sliver of sunshine cast through the front window. She had been so tired the night before that she had completely forgotten to put up her window cover. A warm lump weighed down on her feet. She could see that thankfully, Sadie had no desire to get up yet either.

Hailey pulled her phone from the basket and saw she had two missed calls. One from her mom and one from her dad; no doubt each call was made as they both sat at the kitchen table waiting for her to answer. Still groggy, Hailey debated whether or not she had enough mental strength to carry on a conversation with her parents. Positioning another pillow beneath her head, she decided to bite the bullet and call them back to get it out of the way for the day.

The line rang once, twice, then a third time, before her mother's voicemail spilled through the microphone. Slightly relieved, Hailey left a brief message that they would hopefully be satisfied with and not feel the need to call back. "Hey Mom, and also Dad, since I know you will have me on speakerphone—I just wanted to call you guys back and let you know that I am safe and sound at a new spot with Luke. Nothing new to really report. May go on a hike later, so don't worry about calling me back today. Love you both, talk soon."

After ending the call content with her message, Hailey began going through her morning routine, scrolling through Instagram and checking the latest news. It had been three days since she left the Vanlife meetup, but she still couldn't shake Jordan's comment from her head. *What could he have possibly meant? There's no way he knows Luke better than I do. I have been traveling with him for weeks, and Jordan's only known him for a day. Then again, maybe guys talk about different things than when they are around girls. Especially girls they want to murder. No. That's insane. He's not a murderer. Is he?*

A loud crack came from outside, snapping Hailey out of her thoughts. Hailey felt a flicker of fear as Sadie began to bark and hopped into the front passenger seat to look out the window. Startled by the noise and Sadie's frantic barking, Hailey slid out of bed and pulled on a sweatshirt and shoes, unsure of what was going on outside of the van. Leaning over the front seat just enough to peer out the window, she saw Luke strike another log with his ax. It appeared he was planning on having a fire later. Seeing this, she supposed that it was time to get up and start the day. She pulled back from the window and poured fresh kibbles into Sadie's bowl—a sure way to distract her from barking. Hailey then placed the kettle on the stove, so she could have her morning fix of fresh coffee.

It had been two days since she had heard from Sarah. Hailey had tried calling her a couple of times but continued to get her voicemail. She figured Sarah must be busy after arriving at the office in Oregon and would get back to her when she had a chance. At least that was all she could hope for her to do. Just in case, Hailey decided to shoot her one more text before heading out to greet Luke.

"Looks like a good morning workout," she called out to him as she stepped out of her van.

He held the ax by his side as he looked up at her and squinted into the morning sun. "I figured it wouldn't hurt to get some wood ready now so we don't have to worry about it later."

"Sounds like a good idea to me. Anything I can do to help?"

"You want to take over here?"

"With the ax?" she asked, surprised.

"Have you ever used one before?"

"Can't say that I have."

"Come give it a shot." Luke pulled his lips into that same crooked smile and Hailey felt the butterflies take flight.

Hailey walked over nervously and he placed the ax in her hands.

"Here," he said, grabbing a smaller log and placing it upright on the stump. "We will start with something a little easier."

Grasping the ax in both hands, she swung the handle behind her as if in preparation to make one giant swing. "Whoa, whoa, hold on there, Lizzie Borden," Luke said with a chuckle. "We're not trying to bludgeon the log."

Hailey felt her cheeks flush as she brought her arms down, and thought about his comment. If someone was openly willing to joke about a murderer, he couldn't actually be one himself, right?

She really needed to shake Jordan's comment from her head.

"Let's start with baby steps. First, we'll just get the ax head to start to split the wood," he said while helping her position her body in front of the stump so the ax head lined up with the log. "Now give it a firm tap so the blade goes into the wood." She complied and followed his instructions as he spoke. "Perfect. Now you're going to lift both the log and the ax together and bring them back down together on top of the stump." He paused, waiting for her to attempt his directions.

Hailey glanced at Sadie, who was sitting nearby on her blanket, watching just as intently as Luke. With all her strength, she lifted the ax imparted into the log and brought them down hard together against the stump. The wood cried out with a snap as the ax split the log. "It worked!" Hailey said, surprised as she admired her work.

"Pretty soon you won't even need me anymore," Luke teased as he pulled the wood fully apart in his hands and tossed it onto the pile.

They had arrived in Six Rivers National Forest late the previous evening in their effort to make it to Oregon within the next day or two. There was still a lot left in California that Hailey wanted to see, but she decided to push those adventures to a later date to get to Crater Lake sooner rather than later.

It didn't make sense that the killer had decided to commit the most recent crime in a completely different state. If he really did have a secondary location that he was taking his victims to after he kidnapped them, why change that with this last victim?

"What are you thinking about?" Luke questioned, catching her off guard.

"I just think it's weird that the most recent victim was found in Oregon."

"I mean, serial killers aren't necessarily bound to state lines," he offered. "Have you found out any more information about her or the crime?"

"Not really. I tried calling Sarah, but she hasn't gotten back to me yet." Hailey looked down at her phone to double check that she hadn't missed any calls. "My guess is that he had his sights set on this specific girl and had to travel all the way to Oregon if he wanted to execute his plan."

"That's certainly what it seems like to me," Luke agreed. "Did you see the article about her online?"

Hailey whipped her head up. "What? There is an article out?" She began scrolling through her news apps frantically. "How could I have missed it? What site did you see it on?"

"First, take a breath, calm down," he said trying to soothe her, which was probably the worst thing he could have said.

"How can I be calm? I am trying to be a reporter who checks the news every morning and I missed the most important article connected to what I'm researching right now," Hailey seethed.

"I think it was called the Herald News, or something along those lines."

Hailey aggressively tapped the screen as she searched for the article. Frustration began to rise with every word she typed. She couldn't understand how she had spent the morning looking specifically for information about the latest case and had not come across anything, yet somehow Luke had managed to find an article with no problem.

"Here it is!" Hailey exclaimed aloud.

In the second paragraph, she noticed the name of the victim had been released: Madison Pererra. Beside the paragraph was a picture of a young, pretty brunette girl who appeared to be no older than twenty-five, which was soon confirmed in the next sentence: *"The twenty-two year old recent graduate from OSU was discovered by two hikers in the early hours of the morning just outside of Crater Lake National Park."*

Without moving any further down the article, Hailey opened a new tab and searched the name, *Madison Pererra*. The first two search results were exactly what she was looking for; a link to her Instagram page and a link to her blog. Hailey decided she would look through the blog first and save the Instagram stalking for later. Hailey was impressed by the website and soon discovered that Madison had joined the vanlife the day after she had graduated from OSU, only a mere two months before Hailey had joined the same adventure.

There were several tabs at the top of the page where the reader could learn more about how Madison had renovated her van, where she had stayed, what parks she had visited, and where to follow her on social media. Seemed innocent enough. That is, until the star of the show wound up murdered in the woods.

"Find anything noteworthy?" Luke asked, pulling Hailey out of her research trance.

"I got a name and found her website, so that's at least a lot more than I had before. It at least gives me more to discuss with Sarah when she eventually gets back to me," Hailey replied with angst.

"Maybe we can take a hike around today?" Luke suggested. "Since you are awaiting a call anyway. Maybe some fresh air would be good."

Hailey looked over to Sadie, then up to Luke. "I suppose that's not a bad idea."

They packed their Camelbaks with water and snacks and headed out to a trail that would take up most of their day. About two hours and five miles in from the trailhead, a dark cloud rolled over the sun, and cold droplets began to plummet from the sky. They had made the rookie mistake of not checking the weather before they left. The drops began increasing in size and volume with every minute, and before they knew it, they were running for cover under a nearby tree as the sprinkle had turned into a torrential downpour.

"Looks like we might be stuck here for a while," Luke said, as he pulled up the weather radar on his phone.

"Well at least we have snacks, water, and nowhere to be," Hailey replied with a shrug of her shoulders.

The day was warm when they began their hike, but the chill from the rain was beginning to set in. Hailey pulled out her sweatshirt from her backpack as Luke found a dry log for them to sit on beneath the tree.

"So, did you find what you were looking for in that article about the girl from Washington?" He pulled an apple from his pack as he spoke.

"I didn't know she was from Washington," Hailey replied, tilting her head at him as she spoke.

"It was in the article." He bit off a piece of apple and fed it to Sadie. "Certainly fits the profile of the other girls, don't you think?" he asked.

"It appears so. Her website looks really good, too. I bet she has a lot of followers," Hailey commented.

"And probably fairly easy to locate if she was posting about every-where she was staying."

"That's true," Hailey agreed.

"Are you rethinking your choice to join the vanlife? I mean, learning about these murders and following along with these cases of girls who are close to your age and traveling alone just like you can't be easy," he questioned, finally looking up in her direction.

"A little bit. But at the same time, I don't feel like I am anywhere near the realm of being an influencer, so I wouldn't be this guy's type anyway. At least if that's who he really is targeting. And investigating crime is what I think I'm meant to do." Hailey thought about it for a moment, then stared out into the rain as she continued. "I guess growing up and listening to all the scary stories my dad used to tell me and my brother about the cases he was working on sort of piqued my interest in a career of investigating things and reporting on them."

Luke smiled. "Sounds like you're right then, to be chasing this goal."

More than an hour had passed before the rain let up. Neither of them had thought about bringing a flashlight with them so they decided it was time to head back. They were quiet most of the way down the trail. After all, the trail was muddy and slippery and the last thing either of them wanted was a sprained ankle.

"Want to get changed into some warmer clothes then have a campfire?" Luke asked as they made it back to their campsite.

"Sure, that sounds good to me. I've been freezing after that rain soaked my clothes!"

Despite the intensity of the storm, the evening was calm and provided the perfect night for a campfire. They each retreated back to their van to dry off before preparing the fire. While Hailey was slipping into her warm clothes, she caught herself analyzing the investigative link map that she had started to create in the space above her bed. How was it that they had only managed to have one person of interest so far? Then again, the detectives probably had their own hunches about individuals the girls had come in contact with along their journey. There had to be something she was missing, some place of overlap that would explain why these girls were chosen by the assailant.

Hailey took a deep breath and shook her head. As much as she wanted to find out who was behind the murders, she knew there was only so much information she could gather for now. She slipped into her dry shoes and stepped out to meet Luke, who was beginning to get the fire pit ready.

"I can't imagine the rain is going to make starting a fire very easy tonight," Hailey said as she walked over to him.

"It will definitely be more challenging, but not impossible."

Luke gathered up a couple of pieces of wood from the bottom of the pile in hopes that they would be more dry than those on top. As he created a teepee shape with the logs and smaller sticks, Hailey watched him with curious eyes and wondered what other survival skills he had. A flicker of Jeremy intruded her thoughts; he would have never been able to figure out how to light a fire with damp wood, let alone go camping in the woods for more than one night.

"Where did you learn all these wildlife skills? Or did you teach yourself by trial and error?" Hailey asked as she sat in her chair beside the fire pit.

"I think being a red-blooded male, part of it came naturally. Between enjoying setting things on fire as a young kid and going camping, it wasn't too hard to put the two together to create campfires." Luke chuckled.

"My ex never would have been able to do any of this," Hailey blurted out and instantly regretted mentioning him.

Luke kept his gaze on the smoking sticks. "Well, it's a good thing you're not here with him then." A slight smile crossed his lips as he continued blowing on the smoke.

Hailey reflected his grin and stood up from her chair. "I'm going to have a glass of wine. Can I get you anything?"

"What kind of wine do you have?"

"I think I got a Malbec, the kind that comes in the Black Box, so I have plenty to share."

"What's a black box?" he asked, looking up at her confused.

"You don't know what Black Box wine is?"

"Should I?"

"I suppose more women probably invest in them than men, but it's perfect for the vanlife. I'll show you."

Hailey walked to her van and returned with two plastic wine glasses and a Black Box of wine. The fire was thriving as Luke sat back in his chair in a relaxed manner. She set the box down on the stump between their chairs and poured them each a glass.

"Cheers," she said, raising her glass.

"Cheers," he replied, clinging his glass against hers.

"I have to admit, this is pretty good," Luke commented, taking another sip.

"I told you. There is no bottle to deal with and the best part is there are four bottles of wine in this thing."

"Really? Wow, that sounds like a good deal then!"

They continued drinking and talking as the fire grew brighter under the darkening sky. Hailey was surprised at how quickly she found herself falling for Luke and how easy the conversation flowed between them. Maybe it was the wine talking, but with every sip she took, the more ridiculous Jordan's comment sounded and the more attractive Luke became.

"Will you judge me if I go pee in the woods while you're sitting out here?" Hailey asked as she swallowed her last sip of wine.

"No judgment here. You have to save all the space you can living in these tiny homes," Luke replied.

"Can you make sure Sadie doesn't follow me? I'd prefer to do this without an audience," she said with a grin.

"No problem."

Hailey set down her glass and peered around their campground to find what would appear to be the thickest patch of trees.

Luke held up his headlamp. "Here, you might want to use this."

"That's a good idea. I should really get one of these," she replied as she took it from his hands and fastened it around her head. After turning on the headlamp, Hailey began walking through the trees until Luke was just a small, orange figure beside the flicker of the fire. As she squatted in the darkness, she turned off the light and kept her ears on high alert for any sounds of movement nearby. Since joining the vanlife, she quickly learned that going to the bathroom in the woods became a normal task, although it was still an undesirable and arguably one of the most daunting things to do when it was beyond dark outside.

When she was finished, she stood up and flipped the headlamp back on to guide her back through the brush. Even with the headlamp, it was still hard to see the space in front of her and the ground clearly. She held her eyes wide open as if that would help her see through the darkness as she made her way through the trees and unsteady landscape. Unsure of the exact path she had originally taken, Hailey tried to walk as straight as she could back towards the fire.

Suddenly, a loud snap rang out beneath her feet, reverberating off the surrounding trees. "What the..." Hailey directed the lamp downward to see what she had stepped on. Unsure of what was beneath her shoe, she bent down and picked up something hard, smooth, and white from the ground. "Oh my God!" Hailey quickly tossed it out of her hand as she looked down to discover that she was standing in a pile of bones.

Chapter 24

Before Hailey had gathered enough air into her lungs to call out to Luke, she saw the flash of his bright white spotlight jolt across the forest as he and Sadie began sprinting towards her.

"Hailey! Are you okay?" Luke called out as he ran.

Sadie beat him to Hailey's side, bringing her a sense of ease.

"I'm fine," Hailey replied as Luke approached. "I just stepped into a pile of bones and it scared the crap out of me."

Luke pointed his light over the area that Hailey was pointing to and located the pile of bones. "Yep," he confirmed. "It's a ribcage, alright."

"We need to call someone. We have to report this."

"You want to report a deer's ribcage?" Luke questioned in a perplexed tone.

"Wait," Hailey stammered, looking back down at the bones. "That's from a deer?"

Luke chuckled. "There are a lot of deer out here, you know. It's pretty common to come across deer or elk bones out in these places."

"Oh my God, I feel like such an idiot," Hailey replied, slapping her palm against her forehead.

"Have you never seen animal bones out in the woods before?" he asked, clearly already knowing the answer.

"No. To be honest, this whole journey is my first real camping experience."

"Really? I guess I didn't realize that," Luke said, as they started walking back towards the fire.

"I mean, my family lived in the middle of Chicago growing up, and once I moved out to California, it was never something my friends and I ever really thought about doing," Hailey replied with a shrug. "You know, weekends were spent studying or going to the occasional party in college."

"I guess that makes sense," Luke nodded.

As they made their way back to the fire, Luke refilled each of their cups. "I think you deserve this after your terrifying encounter," he teased as he filled her cup.

Hailey rolled her eyes as she brought the glass to her lips. "You're not going to let me forget this, are you?"

"Not a chance," he said with a wink as his lips pulled into a half-smile.

Hailey caught herself subconsciously biting her lower lip as the memory of their kiss replayed in her mind. Did he think about it as often as she did? Or was it nothing but a middle school kiss? Insignificant and unimpressionable?

The thing she liked the most about Luke was that she didn't feel the need to impress him. He understood what it felt like to wake up one day and want to completely change his life path to something his friends and family would never truly understand. He understood that leaving his home, his city life, and moving into a van full-time on the road was a major risk—a risk that somehow felt right.

"So how long are you planning to live this life?" she asked, looking up at the sky.

"This life on the road?"

"Yeah. Like did you have a two-year plan or something going into this, or are you just seeing where the wind takes you?"

He settled into his chair and tilted his head back, mirroring her gaze up at the stars. "I told myself I needed to at least make it a year."

"Well, that year mark is coming up," she commented looking over at him.

"I know, I can't believe it. And I can honestly say I don't think I am anywhere near ready to end my journey." He scoffed. "My dad didn't even think I'd last a month."

Hailey could hear the tension laced in his words. "Why not?" she asked.

"He was always a big shot. Student body president, top of his class, graduated with honors, and started up his own insurance company that's still booming. So as you can imagine, he didn't take the news well that his son wanted to leave the finance world to live in a car. He didn't think I had it in me to make a life for myself without him breathing over my shoulder at every moment. I thought maybe, just maybe, after he recovered from being sick that he would view life differently and encourage me to 'experience it to the fullest,' but I suppose that was just wishful thinking."

"Does he know about the website business and coding that you have taught yourself and created all on your own?"

"Yeah, but he still doesn't think that's a real career and that it's only a matter of time before I come crawling back to him for help to get reestablished and get my job back. But that's parents, right?" he said, trying to brush the anger off.

Hailey didn't want to admit that she was dealt a pretty good hand in life when it came to the category of parents, so she merely nodded in response.

"Damn, well aren't I a major buzzkill." He chuckled, taking a gulp from his cup.

Hailey smiled. "Not at all."

"So what about you? Are you wingin' it or are you going to throw in the towel in six months?"

Hailey leaned forward and looked at him sideways. "Are you the one now implying that I'm not cut out for vanlife?" she teased.

"Ha! Fair enough." He smirked. "I just think a lot of people jump into this life and don't always realize how challenging it is until they're actually out here living it."

"I suppose that could be true. I mean, I will admit there have been some challenges, like finding good cell service and finding places to sleep each night, things that I didn't think would be that hard. But I have really enjoyed my adventure so far, not to mention, I found myself immersed in an investigation about a serial killer that I never even remotely thought I would find myself being caught up in."

Luke sat silent for a moment then nodded his head. "Yeah, that's a twist I didn't think I'd find myself caught up in either."

The flames faded into glowing red and orange embers at the bottom of the fire pit like lava in the pit of a volcano. The heat was still burning against her shins as the faint glow gave off just enough light for Hailey to see Luke's face painted in a deep red color. The box of wine now lay almost empty on its side and Hailey could feel the warmth from the alcohol settle beneath her skin.

"You ready to head in?" he asked, prodding the coals with a stick.

"Yeah, I think so."

As they stood up, they both leaned in to pick up the empty box of wine. Before she even had time to think about it, her lips were on his, and the warmth of his finger tips glided across her neck. Her legs turned to Jell-O beneath his touch as a tingling sensation swelled in her core.

Chapter 25

Her head was pounding as she cracked open her eyes just enough to see Sadie curled up on a tattered rug in the middle of the dark hardwood flooring. As her body began to slowly wake up, she became aware of the fact that she wasn't wearing any clothes and could feel the warmth from Luke's skin pressed up against her back. Reaching her hand over to the counter, she flipped over her phone to see what time it was. It was nine-thirteen in the morning and she had a missed call from Sarah. The ache in her head intensified with every movement she made, but she knew she needed to get up to call Sarah back. Hailey looked over her shoulder and a slight smile touched her lips as she looked at Luke, who appeared to still be deep asleep. Careful not to wake him, Hailey gently pulled back the covers and glided out from beneath the sheet. She gingerly slipped on her pants and sweatshirt so she could step outside to make the call. As she slid into her shoes, one of them slipped from under her foot and slammed into the cabinet, sending a bin of random items crashing to the floor.

"Shit," she cursed under her breath as Sadie jolted awake. Hailey whipped her head up, assuming her clumsiness had also woken up Luke, but he didn't even flinch and remained fast asleep intertwined with the blanket. As she gathered the items from the floor and returned them to the bin, the last item she scooped up was what appeared to be a pocket knife. As she held it in her hand, she noticed the blade was sharpened just on one side. She trailed her fingers down the blade of the knife. When she approached the end of the blade where it met the handle, she noticed a dark maroon color splattered into the hinge of the knife. She pulled it towards her to take a closer look as her phone began pulsating in her hand. Startling her back to the reason she got out of bed to begin with, Hailey tossed the knife into the bin and put it back on the shelf. Assuming the front doors would be quieter to open and close, she wedged her way between the front seats and slid out of the passenger door, allowing enough space for Sadie to jump out with her. As discreet as she could be, she closed the door and began to walk towards her own van.

"I'm so sorry it's taken me so long to get back to you. Things got pretty crazy up here," Sarah confessed.

"No worries, I'm just happy to finally hear from you."

"Where are you now?" Sarah asked.

"We are currently in Six Rivers National Forest, hoping to move up to Oregon in the next day or so."

"So you're still traveling with Luke I take it?"

"Yes I am," she answered, pausing slightly, "and we may have officially crossed the friendship line last night." Hailey could feel tiny butterflies begin to flutter their wings as she spilled the news.

"Oh boy," Sarah exhaled. Certainly not the reaction Hailey was expecting or hoping for.

"What? Was that a mistake? I'm a slut, aren't I? Because I broke up with someone whom I had been with for years, and then I slept with the first guy I met?" Hailey began sputtering.

"No, no, no, trust me, you know I, more than anyone, would never judge you for sleeping with someone. Hell, I encouraged you to do it when you were with Jeremy just to see that there were better options out there for you!"

Hailey laughed. "You knew I was never going to cheat on Jeremy, but I did know how much you disliked him. And I suppose in the end you weren't wrong."

"You know I always have your best interest in mind."

"So, then what's with the disappointing 'oh' reaction?"

Sarah took a breath. "Okay, look. Don't freak out or anything, but I think you need to get out of there. Get away from Luke."

"Why? Sarah, what's going on?"

Sarah let out another sigh before she began. "As you know, I met with the lead medical examiner in Oregon and obviously he needed to take me to the lab to examine the body and go over everything he found. Well, while we were in the lab, I was looking at all the items that had been removed from the body and bagged for testing." She paused, knowing the next sentence was going to sting. "One of the things that was found in the victim's clothes and was bagged as evidence was a business card with Luke's name on it."

"What?" Hailey suddenly felt like she had been punched in the gut. "Are you sure? Are you sure it was his name?"

"Positive."

"I'm going to need more of an explanation as to how you're positive." Hailey turned around, looking back at Luke's van to be sure there wasn't any movement.

"Well, that's why it took me a little longer to get back to you. It's been non-stop since I got to Oregon. I haven't even been able to take any real breaks. Some new information came up and the team and I have been working around the clock to try and break this case wide open. And I wanted to do some internet research myself to be sure it was really his name before breaking the news to you," Sarah explained.

"I can't believe this." Hailey felt the butterflies turn into anger. "He hasn't said anything to me about meeting her or even knowing her at all for that matter."

"Well, does he know that her body was just found? Like is he aware of her name and everything?" Sarah asked.

"Yes! He is the one who found the article about her before I did! We even talked about her."

"Maybe we're overthinking this. It could have been a simple, quick meeting in passing, he gave her his card, and that was that," Sarah tried, attempting to ease the situation.

"Maybe," Hailey huffed. "Or maybe he had a relationship with her. Or maybe he's not the innocent website creator I thought he was." She could hear Jordan's voice in her head. *Be careful about the company you keep.* What did Jordan know about Luke that she didn't?

"Look, I didn't just call to tell you to run for the hills."

Hailey cut in. "But that's what you want me to do? Because that won't look suspicious at all after I just slept with the guy!"

"I just want you to be extra cautious. Maybe come up with a reason why you can't continue together. I don't know."

Hailey let out a sigh. "Well, I better come up with something quick then. So why else did you call?"

"The new details we got on the case involve evidence that the girls definitely all traveled through the same area at some point."

"How do you know?"

"We found traces of the large-flowered woolly meadowfoam on each of the victim's clothing." Sarah stated.

"Am I supposed to know what that is?"

"At first, we had no idea either, until we did some research. Turns out it is a type of flower that only grows in Jackson County, Oregon. It's actually on the endangered list, and luckily for us, back in 2010, the U.S. Fish and Wildlife service granted just under 6,000 acres of critical habitat to the plant. The thing is, even if each of the victims traveled through Jackson County, Oregon, it doesn't quite make sense that the bodies that were found in California would still have traces of this plant on them. Possible? Yes. Likely? No, considering these girls don't appear to be the type of campers who wear dirty clothes for days."

"Hmm, that is interesting."

"So we are thinking that this could be a huge clue to where this secondary location is that he is taking his victims to. You know, the place where he seems to be taking most of these Polaroids. If these girls were unconscious and he dragged them through the brush, it wouldn't be a surprise that there would be traces of this plant in their clothes."

"That's true. I'm sure his last concern was being aware there was an endangered flower in the area he decided to drag their bodies through."

"They also narrowed down that the last place the most recent victim was seen was at a convenience store in Medford, Oregon."

"That's got to be something big, too!" Hailey exclaimed.

"But here's the best part," Sarah continued, "Medford is right in the middle of Jackson County."

"That has to be the place where he is taking them! But then why was she found all the way near Crater Lake?" Hailey asked herself as much as Sarah.

"Well, it appears she was traveling there before she was in Medford. So they are thinking for some reason, he chose that specific place to take her back to and use as the dump site. I know that my unit and the unit from the station here in Oregon are already out searching the privately owned areas of Jackson County, as well as questioning people that work at the market. It's a little more complicated when they have to get warrants for those who won't allow them to search the premises without one. Hopefully they find something soon; everyone fears he already has his next victim," Sarah stated.

"What was the name of that flower again? Wooly something?"

"Limnanthes floccosa. Or better known as the large-flowered woolly meadowfoam," Sarah clarified, looking back at her notes.

"And she was last seen in Medford?" Hailey asked as she wrote down the details.

"That's correct. But Hailey, don't you dare go looking in the woods. Who knows where this secondary location is or where he is. You're trying to be a reporter, not a homicide detective," Sarah ordered in a stern tone. "Plus, I think you need to focus on your situation with Luke first."

There was silence on the line as Hailey tried to think of reasons as to why Luke's card would have been found on Madison. "Did you mention when the time of death was for Madison?"

"Let's see, the other M.E. here said that it was between the hours of seven and eight in the evening on Friday."

"Wasn't that the afternoon I was with you?" Hailey asked.

"Oh yeah, that's right. I believe it was." Sarah confirmed. "Why? Does that matter?"

Hailey stood stalk still as she began to connect the dots. Was Luke really out visiting a friend for hours in Santa Rosa the day she was with Sarah? Or was he somewhere else?

"I really need to figure out how he knew Madison," Hailey said, ignoring Sarah's question.

"Hailey, I know I can't stop you from doing anything, but please, whatever you do, just be smart and be safe."

"You remember who my father is, right?" Hailey asked rhetorically.

"I am well aware. But that doesn't make you invincible."

"I know, but what else am I supposed to do? I can't just Irish good-bye Luke in the middle of the woods. I have to at least give him the benefit of the doubt here."

"Yes, I know." Hailey could tell Sarah was rolling her eyes on the other end of the line.

"So let's go back to the cause of death details." Hailey decided if she was going to determine if Luke had something to hide, she needed all the details first. "Did you learn anything more about the weapons that were used, or any clue of why he's killing the way that he is?"

"Well the wounds that were made on two of the victim's bodies appear to be from a single-edged knife," Sarah said.

"How can you tell?"

"When looking at the lacerations, one of the ends is pointed, while the other is curved, meaning that there was a blade only on one side. It also looks like the weapon wasn't very long, either. The wounds aren't too deep."

"Do you think it could be some sort of pocket knife?" Hailey asked.

"There is a good chance of that, especially if this is someone who lives in the woods or out of their car. Although, I can't say that with complete confidence at this point."

"You said two of the victims, what about the third?"

"Well, most of Madison's wounds were made from the same weapon, but the laceration that actually killed her appears to be made from something that has more of a jagged edge."

"But not a serrated knife?"

"I'm thinking more of a piece of glass, something like that," Sarah inferred.

Hailey stepped into her van and began writing the information down in her notebook. She was definitely going to need to add some new sticky notes to her link map at the end of their conversation.

"Maybe I should go back over the articles I found on Madison and look her up on social media to see if there are any more overlapping details on all the victims," Hailey interjected.

"That's not a bad idea. I know we have our people doing that here too, but they haven't come up with much of anything yet. Although, I do have to say that your social media expertise may be more useful than the knowledge of social media these detectives have."

"They have got to be trained in social media, right?"

"Mmm, not as well as you would think. As of now, I am the youngest individual working on these cases, other than two of the other forensics officers, but digging into social media for clues isn't exactly part of their job description," Sarah replied.

With Sarah still on the line, Hailey decided to pull up the news articles again and scan through the information. There was always a chance that going through the same information again with new knowledge on the cases could bring something to light that she had glazed over before.

"Hey, did you happen to mention where Madison was from?" Hailey asked.

"Um, I don't think so. But I know that she went to school in Oregon, if I remember correctly."

"Yeah, that's here in the article, but I don't see anything about where she was actually from in here anywhere."

"Maybe you saw it somewhere else?" Sarah suggested.

Hailey pulled up Google again and decided to directly search Madison by name this time, rather than search for the articles she had previously read. This time around, more articles popped up with more detailed information about her, including her hometown of Seattle, Washington. As she continued searching through the information, she realized that all the articles that mentioned Madison being from Washington were new.

"All of these articles are dated after Luke had mentioned she was from Washington."

"Oh, so you learned that information from Luke?" Sarah asked.

"Yeah, but the weird part is that he told me he read it in the article."

"Ah, I see what you're saying. So he straight up lied to you about knowing her. This is not looking good for Luke."

"Not at all," Hailey agreed, shaking her head.

A thud came from Luke's van and Hailey knew her time with Sarah was up. "Luke's up, I got to go."

"Remember, talk to him rationally. Don't just go in accusing and jumping to conclusions. The last thing you want is for him to lose his temper on you."

"I will do my best," Hailey replied.

"Call me later! I want to know you're safe and what Luke says."

"I will." Hailey ended the call and stuck the phone into her pocket.

She took a deep breath and was suddenly very aware of the fact that she was wearing Luke's sweatshirt and hadn't brushed her hair or teeth or even looked in the mirror for that matter. Never mind that she had slept with him the night before and now suspected he had something to do with Madison's murder. Just when she thought her college years would be the keeper of awkward mornings, she was about to experience her most awkward one yet.

The door creeped open with a sluggish pull as Hailey exhaled deeply. There Luke stood in the doorway in just his boxer briefs, with tousled hair and tired eyes. Hailey wondered how someone with looks like his and a solid composure could ever be caught up in murder. Then again, Ted Bundy managed to deny and escape his rightful fate for decades before he finally confessed to murdering over thirty women.

"I don't know about you, but I could definitely use some coffee." His voice was hoarse as he spoke.

"Definitely," Hailey confirmed with a tight smile. If she was going to interrogate him about his relationship with Madison, she might as well let him be fully awake first.

Chapter 26

Hailey had never really given much thought into how she would approach a potential suspect in a murder case. Family members and friends of the victims? No problem, that was her specialty. But sitting down, one on one, with a potential killer? That was new territory. Considering the odds of that happening were slim to none, or so she thought, until she joined the vanlife.

Steven had seemed like a sure shot. All the dots connected: he found and harassed young vanlife girls through Instagram, he attended a meetup where he could easily come in contact with his victims, and he admitted to hating influencers. Yet, something about him was disorganized. He was too weak and cowardly to actually commit murder. There was no way he would have been able to easily relocate each of the victim's bodies on his own. Hailey looked at Luke, with his strong arms and charming demeanor. Could he be capable of murder? No. She refused to believe she had been traveling with a killer all this time, let alone had slept with one. Acid began to rise in her throat at the thought. If there was one thing she knew for sure about Luke, it was that he lied about his relationship with Madison and that was something she was determined to get to the bottom of.

Luke had decided that while they had their morning coffee, they should plan out their route up to Crater Lake. Unsure of how she was going to address her suspicions of him, without accusing him of murder, she simply complied. He stood with one hand on his hip as he studied the map while holding his cup of coffee in the other.

"So, I was reading over that article again, about Madison Perrera," Hailey began as she placed her coffee mug onto the card table.

"Oh yeah?" He bent over placing his mug on the top corner of the map as he leaned his hands onto the table. "Find any new information?" he asked, tracing the route with his pencil.

"Well," she began with hesitation, "I remembered you mentioning she was from Washington." Hailey glanced up at him for a reaction, but his eyes remained on the map.

"Uh huh," he responded, unfazed by her comment.

"Well, I actually couldn't find that information anywhere in the article."

Hailey narrowed her eyes, searching his body for any signs of a reaction.

"I must have seen it somewhere else then. What do you think about taking this road?" he asked, pointing to a red line that ran through two green patches on the map. His feathers weren't even ruffled. She wasn't off to a great start. Was he trying to change the subject, or was he genuinely focused on the map because he had nothing to hide? Either way, she wasn't going to give up that easy. There was more to the story of Luke and Madison.

They sat in silence for a moment, but the thoughts in her head were growing louder with every passing second. She considered Sarah's advice: don't jump to any conclusions. But Hailey soon realized she was never good at taking advice from others.

"I talked to Sarah this morning," she stated with a tilt of her head.

Luke's eyes remained trained on the map. Hailey took a breath before she continued. "And she told me she found your business card on Madison."

The pencil tip snapped beneath his fingers. A nerve had been hit. Hailey stood still, waiting for a response as he pushed away from the table. As the silence lingered between them, Hailey could feel the heat begin to rise in her cheeks as questions whirred through her mind.

"Why didn't you tell me you had met her?" she blurted out, tired of waiting.

"I didn't think it was important," he responded with a shrug as he examined the tip of his now broken pencil.

"You didn't think that mentioning you had met the woman that was just found murdered in the woods was important?" she asked with steady eyes. "Not to mention the fact that I am openly following the case and you knew that."

Luke finally looked up to meet Hailey's dark eyes. As bad as she wanted to berate him with more questions, she bit her tongue and waited for his response.

"I didn't want you to think I had anything to do with her being murdered," he confessed. "I thought that if I told you that I had worked with her, then you would automatically put me on the suspect list."

"So you thought the next best option was to lie to me about it then?" Luke opened his mouth to respond, but Hailey wasn't done with her rant. "And you worked with her?"

"Yes, I designed a website for her."

Hailey took a step back. "Wow. So even when I was talking to you about her website and how well put together it was, it didn't even cross your mind that maybe you should mention to me you were the one who designed it?" Hailey felt a sting of betrayal. "Instead, you let me go on and on about it like an idiot."

"By that point, I thought it was too late to say anything."

"In other words, you just wanted to continue lying to me about your relationship with her."

"I wasn't lying to you, I just didn't think it was pertinent information." He looked at her with sullen eyes. "Does it really affect anything about your investigation?"

"I just think it's a little weird that you happen to have a connection to two of the girls that have been murdered, and on top of that, you tried to hide it from me!"

"Once again, I wasn't trying to hide it from you."

Hailey took a breath trying to calm her emotions. She wasn't going to get anywhere good if she let her personal feelings take charge of the debate.

"When did you leave on Friday to see your friend?" she asked.

He furrowed his brow in confusion at this slight change in subject. "What?"

"What time did you leave to see your friend?" she repeated.

"I don't know. Like right after you left, maybe around eleven-thirty-ish."

"And you didn't get back to your van until three?"

"Yeah, somewhere around there. What does that have to do with anything?"

"Where did you meet your friend again?"

Luke exhaled and rubbed his hand across his forehead as if he was debating his answer. "Chico."

"Chico?"

"Yeah, I met my friend in Chico." His face was growing wearier with every question.

Hailey bit the inside of her cheek as she thought about his answer. Did he remember that he told her he was seeing a friend in Santa Rosa? Did he get the location wrong then, or was he lying about it the whole time?

"I thought you said your friend lived in Santa Rosa."

"I did. Well, he used to, but he moved to Chico. I was just so used to saying Santa Rosa. It must have slipped and I didn't even realize. What does that have to do with anything?"

"It's just weird."

"What is?"

"That it has suddenly come to light that you knew the victim, and you didn't mention it at all when we were openly talking about her, then her body just happens to be found when you're off visiting your friend in Santa Rosa, or Chico, or wherever."

"Whoa. Hold on a minute." Luke took a step back and held up a hand as he appeared to be replaying what she just said in his head. "You think I had something to do with her murder? Are you seriously accusing me of hurting those girls?" Luke now had a look of shock painted across his face.

The sound of birds chirping and wind rustling through the trees filled the space between them as they each silently stood their ground in defense. Luke scoffed, shook his head, and broke away from the stand off, walking back towards his van. Hailey debated going after him but decided it was a good time to recap on everything that had just been said. From her conversation with Sarah, to the one she just started with Luke, it was time to align the facts that lay before her.

He seemed to be genuinely shocked when she mentioned his involvement with her murder, but then again, maybe he was just a good actor. It wouldn't be the first time she was fooled by a man with a good poker face. But how could she have traveled with him this long and not seen any of the red flags? Did she let her growing feelings for him cloud her judgment of his true character?

Luke returned and in his hand was the pocket knife Hailey had just observed in his van minutes earlier. Hailey froze with terror. Why had she walked into this conversation without anything for protection? Even grabbing a canister of bear spray would have been better than nothing.

Luke picked up his broken pencil from the table. Hailey watched as he began to carve the pencil with the knife to sharpen the tip.

"I've never seen someone do that before," Hailey commented in a soft tone, slightly relieved that was his intended purpose with the knife.

Luke kept his eyes focused on the knife and the pencil as he methodically scraped off thin shavings of wood. "I don't have a pencil sharpener and this works just as well."

As she stood watching him, Hailey felt her stomach turn as she remembered that just a few moments ago, she had seen a reddish-brown splatter on the crease of the knife he currently held in his hand. Sarah's voice entered her subconscious. *The weapon used in each of the murders could potentially be a pocket knife.* Hailey chewed on her lower lip to control her nerves as she crafted her next question. "What else do you use that knife for?"

He sighed. "Cutting boxes, ropes, fruit and vegetables. Basically, whatever I need a knife for, really."

"Do you think someone could use a knife like that to kill someone?"

Luke stopped shaving the pencil and looked up at her as she stared at him with questioning eyes. "Are you wondering if I have killed someone with this knife?"

"No. I said *someone,* not *you,*" Hailey emphasized, even though at this point she clearly had placed him in the 'under suspicion' category. "I just—"

"Think I'm some nutjob who is meeting girls, making them websites, and murdering them," he said half joking, with a twinge of seriousness. He was blatantly annoyed at the fact that she had accused him of being involved with the murders at all, but could she blame him?

"That's not what I was going to say." Hailey wasn't sure how to rescue the conversation at this point. "Look, when I was talking with Sarah this morning, she mentioned that maybe this guy could have been using something like a pocket knife or a similar weapon to kill his victims."

"I see," he replied, continuing back on his pencil. "I guess it's possible, if you're strong enough."

"You know something else Sarah said?" She could tell by the way he exhaled that he just couldn't wait to hear what else she had to say, seeing how well the last comments went. "She said that there were traces of a specific plant that was found on each of the victims."

Luke gazed up at her with a puzzled look. "Oh yeah?" It was apparent that wasn't what he was expecting her to say. "What type of plant?"

Hailey couldn't tell if he was asking seriously or just happy the topic had moved away from him for the time being.

"The woolly meadowfoam," she replied.

"Never heard of it," he stated.

"Apparently, it's endangered and can only be found in Jackson County, Oregon."

"Interesting." He blew on the tip of the pencil, blowing the access shaving off.

"She also mentioned that the last victim was last seen at a supermarket in Medford." Hailey looked up before she continued. "Isn't that along our route?"

Luke dropped his head and exhaled. "Don't tell me you're thinking about going out and searching through the trees around Medford for this crazy serial killer." As he said it, he knew that was exactly what she was plotting to do.

"I mean, we'd be right there, right?"

"Does that mean you believe me when I say I didn't kill her?" he asked, looking at her with serious eyes.

"It's too soon to tell," she replied with a hint of sarcasm. She wasn't lying. It was too soon to tell who the actual murderer was, given the amount of evidence and details she had at this point.

"Why don't you call the cops then, huh? Turn me in if you think I am the one who harmed them!" His intensity shocked Hailey. Okay, so maybe it was time to rethink Luke as a suspect if he was encouraging her to call the police and turn him in. Or maybe that was just another ploy of his.

"I'm not going to call the cops. But when you lied to me about knowing her and about where you went, and then a body shows up, wouldn't you agree that's a little suspicious?"

"To an average person, no. To someone obsessed with a murder case that she really shouldn't be involved with in the first place, then yes, I suppose it's suspicious."

Hailey wasn't fond of his response, but she couldn't imagine she would be cool and collected if the roles were reversed and he was accusing her of murder.

"If you're so innocent, then why would Jordan make a comment to me about being careful around you?" she blurted out.

"What?" Luke stopped what he was doing and looked up at her. "When did he say something to you about me?"

"That last night we were all hanging out. When he pulled me into a hug to say goodbye, he told me to be careful with who I hang out with or something like that. Like I wasn't safe around you or something."

"Oh, for God's sake." Luke rolled his eyes. "You know why he said that? Because he wouldn't shut up about you earlier. He kept saying to me how attractive he thought you were. He probably was hoping his little comment would drive you away from me. And you know what? Looks like it worked."

Hailey dropped her eyes to the ground, feeling slightly embarrassed that she had let Jordan's comment get under her skin as much as it had, but it was also a little shady for Jordan to say something like that in hopes he might move in on her, if that was indeed his intent. She decided to redirect the conversation. "Nevermind. So our route..." she began as she looked towards Luke. "I was just thinking that it wouldn't hurt to look. We could think of it as a search and rescue situation and we're volunteering our time to help."

"Except this isn't a legitimate search and rescue operation; it's just a hunch that you're going off of from your friend. Nevermind the fact that you have zero protection from law enforcement or any real weapons to defend yourself if you do end up in a dangerous situation," he snapped.

Hailey looked at him, clearly displeased with his response. "I don't see the harm if we are driving through and take a little detour to check out the area."

"So what, you're going to go explore the woods and hunt down all the flowers and see if they lead you to something? Like you're living in some goddamn fairytale?"

"Look, I know it sounds ridiculous to you, but this is my job as an investigative reporter." He was now standing straight up, facing her. "You don't have a real job. This is just something you're chasing down for your own amusement. Even if you did find something, you think they are going to believe you?" As the words left his mouth, Luke instantly knew it was the wrong thing to say.

"Wow," Hailey scoffed. "So you think I'm wasting my time? That all this work I've been doing isn't real work and it's all been a pointless effort?"

Luke stepped towards her, but like two negatively charged magnets, she repelled away from him. "I'm sorry. That was out of line, I just think—"

"Think that we should go our separate ways?" Hailey ended the sentence for him this time.

"That's not what I was going to say," he countered. "I just don't think it's safe for you to go into the woods and mindlessly wander around looking for a serial killer. And think about it, what are the odds you're going to find anything at all?"

Hailey stood, staring at him with enmity in her eyes. Whether he was going with her or not, she was going up to Medford and into the woods to see what she could find. She didn't follow these cases this far to just quit. "You don't get it, and you know what? I don't think you ever will. So maybe we should go our separate ways. We didn't start this journey together, who says we have to carry on together? You go your way, and I'll go mine." Hailey was allowing her emotions to make the decisions at this point. She wasn't going to just give up on these cases, or let anyone stand in her way. Especially someone who was still on her suspect radar.

"Fine," Luke exhaled, knowing he wasn't going to win the argument. "I've already been to Crater Lake anyway. So if you want to go searching in the woods for flowers and serial killers, then best of luck to you." The bitterness in his tone stung as it left his lips. It was hard to say who was more hurt at this point.

He picked up his pencil and pocket knife from the table and shoved them into his pocket. "Here," he said, folding up the map and slapping it on the table, "you can keep this, since I won't be needing it anymore."

He turned and patted Sadie on the head as he passed by on the way back to his van. Hailey debated stopping him, but she wasn't about to give up her pride or allow him to make her feel stupid for chasing her passion. She wasn't going to stop chasing the case, considering all the information she had at this point. For all she knew, he didn't want her chasing it because he really was the killer. He didn't supply her with enough strong evidence during their argument to throw out that theory just yet.

He slammed his door shut and Hailey wondered if she would ever hear from or see him again. Had she been too tough on him? Was she crazy for accusing him of murder? She wouldn't put it past herself to over-analyze the details building him up as a villain in her head to protect her own emotions towards him that were beginning to surface. Then again, he did have a pocket knife with a suspicious splatter on it that looked a lot like blood and he did lie to her about knowing the most recent victim.

His engine hummed to life and Hailey watched as his van disappeared down the forest road, repeating his license plate over and over again in her head, just in case.

Chapter 27

For the first time since Hailey started her journey, she felt a wave of loneliness wash over her. She had spent many mornings drinking her coffee alone, but somehow it felt different this time.

She was ruminating over her fight with Luke. She regretted how she approached him, how she accused him, but mostly how she lost her calm when she needed to keep a cool head. Perhaps he only had her best interest and safety in mind. Or did he? He also let his temper get the best of him and tore her down, making her feel like what she was doing was a silly waste of time. She refused to let another man make her feel like her work was a just some dumb fantasy. Then again, she did sort of accuse him of murder, so how did she expect him to react? *But what if it was true, and his lies were all covering up the fact that...*

Hailey took a deep breath and shook her head. She needed to get the thoughts of loneliness that turned into anger out of her head and regain her focus. Hailey picked up her map and clambered onto her bed. Now with her new suspicions of Luke, he would no doubt land himself a spot on her investigative map. She pulled out a pen and with a steady hand wrote: *Luke Mancini* on the sticky note that she had previously labeled with *Person of Interest B.*

Hailey opened her laptop and her journal, setting them side by side beneath the map as she prepared to organize and analyze the details she had about each of the cases thus far.

Using the hotspot from her phone, she opened up her laptop and did a Google search for the large-flowered woolly meadowfoam plant. Hailey was surprised to see that it just looked like a regular flower to her. She had imagined something more unique and easy to pick out amongst all the other plants, but it appeared that was just wishful thinking. The more images she shuffled through on Google, the more it made sense that if the killer was dragging these women through the forest, they would end up with traces of this low-to-the-ground plant on their clothing.

Hailey located the densely populated areas of the plant around Medford that were on public land. Hailey marked each spot on her map with a green circle of where the plant could be found, according to the state records. It was a long shot that she would find anything in the area, or even locate the correct plant, but she knew she would regret it if she didn't give it a shot.

It was almost ten a.m., and Hailey knew if she was going to make any real progress in her search, she needed to get moving. She packed up her van, preparing for the long five hour drive she had ahead of her. Luckily, it would give her enough time to come up with a good reason to tell her parents as to why she was now continuing on her journey alone.

She retrieved and folded up her card table that Luke had been using outside. Hailey made one final lap around the area to be sure she wasn't leaving anything behind before jumping into the driver's seat. Before she took off down the bumpy forest road, she caught a glimpse at herself in the rearview mirror. Dark circles pooled beneath her eyes that were splintered with streaks of red, displaying her lack of sleep and dehydration. Maybe it was a good thing she and Luke would no longer be traveling together. The more time they seemed to spend together, the more distracted from the cases she seemed to become—which would support her theory that he didn't want her digging deeper into the cases because he had something to hide.

As she drove, Hailey began to think about how she could piece together an article about the cases. If she truly wanted to break into the investigative reporting world, she was going to need a portfolio of work, and what would be better to show than an article on the murders of three vanlife girls while she, herself, was living the vanlife? If Hailey was able to get a report out before any other reporters got their hands on the details of the cases, it would be a golden ticket for her to jump into her dream career; especially with all the behind-the-scenes details she had been receiving from Sarah, although Hailey realized that she was really going to need to figure out how to word everything just right so as to not get Sarah into trouble for leaking private information.

It wasn't long before the low fuel light turned on and Hailey realized she was running dangerously low on gas. Checking her map app for a fuel station, she decided to make a pit stop in Happy Camp to refill her tank and let Sadie out to stretch her legs. After she ushered Sadie back into the van and walked around to the pump, she noticed a handwritten note taped to the pump stating in all caps, 'PLEASE SEE ATTENDANT INSIDE TO PAY.'

Hailey exhaled with annoyance as she cracked a window for Sadie and locked the doors before heading into the small convenience store. After paying the clerk inside, she walked back out to her van and noticed that another van had pulled up on the other side of the same pump she was using. The van was white with speckled spots of rust and scratched paint on the sides. Maybe it was the fact that she was now traveling alone, or that she knew a serial killer was on the loose, but as she approached the pump, an unsettling feeling churned in her gut. It wasn't a large gas station by any means, but she was slightly annoyed that out of all the open pumps, they had decided to use the same one. Attempting to brush her annoyance and unease aside, Hailey popped her gas cap open and removed the nozzle from the pump. She patiently waited, occasionally talking to Sadie through the window as the tank filled. It wasn't long before she heard the nozzle click, indicating that her tank was full. She had overestimated the amount of money it was going to take to fill the tank and had to return inside to receive her change. Before walking away, she peered in the window to see that Sadie had curled up and fallen asleep in the passenger seat.

After double checking that she returned the nozzle to the pump, she looked up, unintentionally making eye contact with the man leaning against the beaten up van beside her. She gave him a tight smile, but he darted his dark, dead eyes away, causing her unease to resurface. Hailey had learned early on in her journey that this was a frequent feeling when traveling alone as a woman and tried to push the feeling of his eyes on her back out of her mind as she walked away towards the store.

Once inside, she decided to get pretzels and a couple of cold water bottles for her and Sadie's journey to Medford. As she checked out, the stout, unkempt clerk began gabbing about the weather, asking her where she was from and questioning her about where she was going. When she responded to his questions with brief answers, it seemed like he kept pressing her for more information about herself, adding to her unsettling feeling. Due to his clunky conversation skills, she thought that maybe the sign requiring customers to go inside to pay was created so he had an opportunity to interact with other humans. Not wanting to continue the conversation any further, Hailey kindly told the clerk she needed to hit the road and then bid him goodbye.

She returned to her van and noticed the other vehicle was quickly pulling away. She thought it was odd that she had never seen him walk into the store when all the pumps appeared to have the same poorly taped sign attached to the front, indicating people needed to go inside to pay for their gas. Maybe he was a local and knew how the clerk was and was aware that the pumps did actually work outside. Hailey looked around, but there was no sign of anyone or any other cars in sight, other than the one that sat in the parking spot in front of the store, which she assumed belonged to the attendant inside. She opened her door, slid into her seat and drove away, taking a mental note to start only using gas stations that were in more populated areas.

Less than two hours later, Hailey was rolling into the Medford area and noticed that the gauge on her gas tank was already dipping below the quarter of a tank line. "That can't be right," she said, looking at the gauge then at Sadie, who had woken from her slumber and was happily panting with her head out the window. Needing to restock on groceries, she pulled into a Safeway that also happened to have a fuel station just across the parking lot. *Might as well kill two birds with one stone.*

Deciding to get groceries first, Hailey parked beneath a tree in the lot to provide Sadie with some shade as she slipped inside for the essentials. Knowing she needed to be quick and efficient during her shopping, Hailey didn't take long inside. After she thanked the cashier and slipped the last bag onto her arm, she began to head out towards the sliding doors. Just before she triggered the motion sensor, the wall near the exit caught her eye. Almost the entire wall had been covered with a bulletin that displayed all of the photographs of individuals who had gone missing in or around the area. Her eyes scanned across the photographs, seeing people of all races and ages that made up each row. Then, towards the end, she had to take a step closer to confirm that her eyes weren't deceiving her. There, stapled to the wall like all the other pictures, was an image of Madison Perrera.

Hailey stood looking at the image as Luke popped into her mind. Where had they met? Did they meet here in Oregon? Was their relationship purely professional like he said? Either way, it was before Hailey had met Luke, so the relationship between them shouldn't matter. But the fact he denied, or tried to hide, knowing her was still curdling in her gut, and that was something she most certainly wasn't ready to forgive him for.

"Do you know someone?" a voice chimed from behind her.

Hailey turned around to see a short blonde woman standing just behind her, holding a bag full of groceries in one hand and a hairnet in the other. "Uh no, I thought this girl looked familiar, but maybe it was just from the news articles I saw," Hailey replied informally.

"Ah, yes." The woman nodded her head as she looked at the image of Madison. "You know, I remember the day that girl came in here."

"Really? She came into this store?" Hailey turned to face the woman, who now had her full attention.

"Yes. I work here, at the deli counter." She gestured towards the back of the store. "I sliced some turkey for her." The woman paused as a slight smile crept across her lips. "Well actually, my son did."

"Oh?" Hailey said in a tone indicating she wanted the women to elaborate.

"My son is young and single, so I let him help the pretty girls that come to the counter," she said with a grin.

Hailey smiled. "And I'm sure he doesn't mind that."

"Not one bit," the woman chuckled. "There aren't a whole lot of options in this town for a nice looking young man, and he's had one heck of a time finding a girlfriend. I'm not getting any younger while I wait for him to give me grandkids."

Hailey wondered if her son really was nice looking, or if it was just a mother's opinion. "Was there anyone else around her when she was being helped?" Hailey asked.

"Just one other man that I helped at the counter, but I can't quite remember." The woman looked up as if she was recalling the day in her memory.

Hailey nodded, considering the possibilities of Madison traveling with someone else. Or the possibility that this very market was the place she had met her killer. She was half-tempted to show her a picture of Luke, but decided against it.

"Well, I better get going," Hailey said, looking down at her groceries. "I've got a dog waiting for me in the car."

"Ah yes, I don't mean to keep you, dear." The woman smiled. "Be careful out there. You never know who you can trust."

Hailey thought it was an odd goodbye, but she didn't expect to get much more out of the woman either way. She smiled and nodded to her. "That is very true. Have a good afternoon."

Hailey took one last look at the photograph before exiting through the sliding doors. As she walked through the crowded row of cars back to her van, she looked around the lot with a nervous feeling in her gut. There was something ominous about being in a place where a girl just like her had last been seen—to be walking in the very place where Madison's life potentially took a turn for the worse.

After packing away all her groceries and taking Sadie out for some fresh air, Hailey drove across the lot to the gas station to refill her somehow already empty tank. As she pulled up to the pump, she realized no one was exiting their car. It appeared all the pumps had attendants. Hailey was surprised to see this and had no idea there were still states that had gas station attendants. Pleased that she wasn't going to have to exit her van again, she glided up to the pump and rolled down her window.

A woman with dark hair and freckles sprinkled across her nose and cheeks approached her door. "How much would you like me to fill it today, miss?" Hailey wondered if asking that same question to every car throughout the day ever got old.

"All the way, please. And can you please be sure it's filled? For some reason, the last place I was at didn't seem to fill all the way up when I thought the pump clicked off."

The woman nodded and took Hailey's card. When she came back to hand her the card back, she asked, "Where did you fill up last?"

"Happy Camp, California."

"Oh," the woman replied as she downcast her eyes. "You have to be careful there. I've heard of people getting their gas siphoned in some of the smaller cities in that area."

"Seriously?" Hailey said with dismay. "No wonder I ran out so fast."

"I'll get ya nice and filled up today, but now ya know. Be careful when going through those smaller towns. There's some shady characters out there. Sometimes the clerks are in on it, too."

"Thanks for the tip," Hailey said, mad at herself for not trusting her gut about the guy across from her at the pump. She looked back at Sadie who lay sprawled out on the floor. She wondered if Sadie had even noticed someone tapping into the van when she was in the convenience store or if she had completely slept through the whole incident. Either way, there was no way to fix it now.

Hailey thanked the attendant and headed on her way towards the forest where she had located the largest population of woolly meadowfoam plants. She was beginning to question if she was out of her mind. Was she really expecting to find some sort of evidence tucked within the trees? A piece of one of the victim's clothes, or potentially some kind of trace evidence that could provide a clue as to who the killer was? The more she thought about it as she drove, the louder Sarah and Luke's voices became in her head. Maybe they were right; heading into the woods alone in search of a type of plant, one she had never seen before other than on Google, was foolish. But it was the only lead she had to go off of at this moment and she wasn't going to back down.

It was four-thirty in the afternoon and Hailey knew that she only had a couple of hours of daylight left. She was also very aware that even if she didn't find anything suspicious in the woods, she was still in the location where a girl went missing and she did not want her picture to be the next one stapled to a bulletin board.

After addressing her map, she decided to take a forest road that split off from the main drag that should lead her into one of the green circles she had drawn on her map, at least as far as she could tell from the photographs she had found on Google.

"Alright, here goes nothing," she muttered to herself as she turned the van onto the gravel road.

It was clear the road wasn't frequently traveled. Sharp rocks and giant potholes made for a wild ride as Hailey dodged her way through the obstacles. She continued up the road for a couple of miles until she found an open spot off the side of the road to pull over and park the van. As soon as she parked, Sadie was eager to get out and explore the new location. Hailey turned off the ignition and climbed to the back to open up the side door. Even though she knew her search couldn't last too long as evening inched closer, she gathered up her day pack and made sure to grab enough snacks and water for the both of them.

Hailey admired the beauty of her surroundings, despite the ominous reason she was there to explore the wooded area. She watched as Sadie was enjoying all the smells of the forest and wondered how something so sinister could happen in such a beautiful place.

Every couple of minutes, Hailey would take a short break to check her compass and reference the map to be sure she was on the right path. She also wanted to make sure she knew her way back to the van, considering this time there would be no fire and no help from Luke to guide her. Hailey was on her own.

The evening began to blanket the forest just as Hailey made it back to her van with nothing to show for her search. Like any good reporter, she wasn't going to give up that easily. Tomorrow she would start early in the morning and continue her search deeper into the trees. Despite her initial feelings of unease to boondock in the area, Hailey clambered back up into her van and decided that she was too worn out to search for somewhere else to camp for the night. Since she was planning on searching the area again in the morning, it made the most sense to stay put and take the risk of staying in the forest, alone.

Chapter 28

The only sound that filled the silence of the night was Sadie's rhythmic breathing as she lay curled up at the edge of the bed. Hailey stared up at the ceiling, wondering if she was going to get any sleep at all. Her mind was racing. Racing with thoughts about the cases, thoughts of serial killers, and thoughts of Luke. Did she miss him? Or did she miss the presence of another human being?

There was something to be said about knowing there was another person camping nearby. Whether it was someone she knew or not, there was a sense of comfort knowing that she wasn't completely alone in the middle of the dark woods. Was it because she was used to the hustle and bustle of people at all hours of the night after living in large cities? Or was it a human instinct, the safety of the herd, that was the drive for not wanting to be alone? Hailey sat up in bed and decided that if her mind wasn't going to turn off, she might as well put it to good use.

Trying her best not to wake Sadie, she slinked out of the covers to retrieve her laptop from her computer bag that sat in the tight space behind her driver's seat. She pulled back the curtain from the door to peer out into the darkness. As far as she could tell, there was nothing but trees and stumps standing in the distance. Her body relaxed ever so slightly knowing that there seemed to be nothing but nature sitting outside her window.

Before jumping into her investigative mode, Hailey decided to start off easy by scrolling through Instagram on her computer. The page loaded and the first image that filled the screen was a post from Brianna. It was the warning post that Hailey had asked her to create just a few days prior. Brianna had executed the post even better than Hailey had imagined. Over nine thousand people had liked the post and just shy of seven thousand comments had been posted below it. Pleased at the success of the post and feeling a glimmer of hope that women in the vanlife community would be on high alert and more careful during their travels, Hailey transitioned over to Google and began pursuing her reason for opening her computer to begin with—to learn more about each of the victims. She spent the next couple of hours researching, on the painfully slow internet connection, as much as she could about each of the victims, transferring any pertinent information she discovered onto her link map. Hailey soon found herself in some deep rabbit holes. Reading their blogs, stalking their Instagrams, and even going as far as researching information about their families and friends. The more in-depth details she learned about their personal lives, the closer to each of them she felt, and the more determined she became to find the heinous person who took it upon himself to bring their worlds to an end.

It was nine a.m. when Hailey stirred out of her slumber with her hand laying across her computer. At the sight of movement, Sadie stood up from the rug on the floor and jumped up, placing her front paws onto the edge of the bed. "Sorry, pup, do you need to go outside?" Hailey asked as she scratched Sadie behind the ear with one hand and rubbed the sleep out of her eyes with the other.

Now that she was alone, she felt less concerned about her morning attire and only managed to slip on some flip-flops before opening her door to let Sadie out. Hailey stepped out into the morning air and stretched her legs as Sadie pranced around the perimeter, marking her temporary territory. Hailey pulled out her phone and called Sadie so she could get a picture of her in front of her van. After some coaxing of Sadie into the right place for just long enough, she captured a decent picture and uploaded it to her Instagram story and added the hashtag #doglife and tagged her location as "FR 837," as if anyone would know where that was, which was her way of being symbolically tongue in cheek about her current location being in the middle of nowhere.

Before Hailey stepped back inside to start up the kettle for her morning coffee, Sadie came trotting around from the other side of the van, gleefully crunching on something between her teeth.

"What's that you have?" Hailey looked at her with a look of concern. "Drop it," she ordered, and Sadie complied.

Hailey knelt down and picked up one of the broken beige shells that fell out of Sadie's mouth. "Yikes, Sadie, pistachio shells are not good for you!" Hailey threw the broken shell as far as she could back into the brush and directed Sadie back into the van for some breakfast.

Happy to begin her new daily routine of packing her Camelbak full of water and food for her and Sadie before they set out on another search day, Hailey wondered how long she would continue her search before throwing in the towel. With all the time Hailey had spent awake the night before, she had discovered what looked like another route that only showed up in the satellite view in Google Maps. It appeared that the road split from the current road where she was camping, but she would only be able to confirm that once she arrived at the coordinates. Since Hailey and Sadie had searched the area closest to the van the evening before, Hailey decided they would drive up to the other road to start their investigation for the day.

Once Hailey spotted a slight gap between the trees, she knew that she was approaching the road. Just before turning into the brush, she stopped and assessed the ground before her. It appeared the road maintenance was even worse than the one she had taken to get there. It was washed out with hefty rocks and loose rubble, more than what her van could handle. She would have to leave the van behind while she and Sadie continued up the road on foot.

The sun was warm against her bare arms, but luckily the branches hovering above them provided a decent amount of shade. Hailey wasn't expecting Oregon to be so warm this time of year and was thankful she had decided to pack an extra water. Between the heat and the elevation gain, every twenty minutes or so Hailey would stop to give each of them a break. As Sadie would roll around in the cool dirt, Hailey would check the distance they had traveled. So far, there were no signs of any buildings, houses, or people in the area. Nor was there any indication that anyone had been in the area in a long time—no footprints, no trampled brush or broken branches, or pieces of clothing that could have been left behind.

Looking back down the road as she took a sip from her Camelbak, she found it hard to believe any passenger car would be able to traverse to this point on such a treacherous road without blowing a tire or bottoming out. However, a lifted four wheeler making it over the large rocks was still a possibility, so Hailey decided to continue up the road.

An hour and a half of hiking passed and Hailey was beginning to grow tired. In need of a longer break than just a couple of minutes, she spotted a large tree that had fallen by the side of the road that was the perfect size to sit on and take a lunch break. As she sat on the log, she pulled out an apple for her and a bone for Sadie as they relaxed in the shade. Hailey also pulled out Sadie's portable water bowl and set it on the ground before retrieving a cool water bottle from her bag. When she began to pour the water into the bowl, her eyes caught a glimpse of pistachio shells that laid in a scattered pile near the edge of the log. "That's odd," she said aloud, peering at the scattered shells.

From the pile of broken shells, her eyes trailed across the dirt towards the forest behind her. As she examined the ground more closely, she noticed that the foliage was shorter in a consistent line leading into the thicket of the forest, indicating that there had once been a path that led into the woods from where she was sitting. Hailey stood up from what she thought was a fallen tree and soon realized that there was no evidence to show that the broken tree once stood anywhere nearby. There were no stumps, no holes, and the end of the log was perfectly smooth. It hadn't been moved to that spot by nature; someone had cut the large tree down. Someone had moved it there on purpose. She picked up Sadie's bowl and placed it back into her bag. There was a reason someone had tried to cover up that trail, and she was determined to figure out why.

"Come on, Sadie," she said urgently as she began walking down the old, overgrown path.

At the end of the road where Hailey had parked her car, she realized that she had lost cell service and began to question how far into the woods she should go before turning back. Not wanting to turn around completely empty handed, she pressed on, sending a plea into the universe that she would at least stumble upon something to show for her imprudent choice to head into the woods alone in search for a serial killer.

Just as she was beginning to think she was becoming more lost than making any sort of progress, a small structure came into view through the tangle of branches. Hailey dipped through the overgrowth into an opening where a one-story building stood with faded yellow paint peeling from the dilapidated walls. Moss and vines began to creep up the sides of the house in an attempt to retake the man-made intruder on their land. The tattered window frames matched the misshapen roof, where the remaining shingles sat in staggered rows that had been blown out of alignment over the years.

Hailey remained at a distance, taking in the scene. Coming across an abandoned house while walking alone in the woods, even in the middle of the day, turned out to be more frightening than she had imagined. She had been so focused on observing the abandoned house that she hadn't noticed Sadie had gone out of view.

"Sadie, come!" Hailey called out. She waited, ears alert and eyes darting across the land, until Sadie came trotting around from the back of the house, showing no signs of concern. She thought to herself that dogs must not have shared the sense of danger when it came to sketchy man-made structures as people did.

Taking a lap around the property from a distance, Hailey saw no signs of human life and decided she felt comfortable and brave enough to take a closer look at the building. By the lack of maintenance and the abundance of greenery that had taken over, she guessed that no one had lived on the property for years, maybe decades. As she approached one of the broken windows to take a look inside, she noticed more pistachio shells strewn across the dirt, creating a path around to the back of the building. Hailey followed the trail of shells until it stopped, just before the cracked concrete slab at the back door.

Hailey examined the screen door dangling at the hinges before pulling it open gingerly in fear that it would fall right off. It didn't. Then she placed her other hand on the brass doorknob that rattled to the touch. She took one last look over her shoulder to be sure no one was witnessing her entrance into the house.

"Here goes nothing," she muttered to Sadie who was patiently waiting beside her as she turned the knob and pushed open the door. The door objected with one long haunting groan as it skidded across the floor. Hailey opened it just enough to fit her body through the space, creating a 'V' shape of light spilling across the mangled, wood plank flooring. Before gliding her body through the gap, Hailey called out into the house, "Hello?" She paused, waiting for a response. "Is anyone there?" She hoped there would be no reply. After a long moment of silence, Hailey cautiously stepped onto the decaying wood floors, unsure of whether the next step would send her foot plummeting through the floorboards.

Sadie showed more bravery and bolted into the open space, excited to explore the premises. They wandered into what was once a kitchen, where broken cabinet doors still tried to cling to their hinges and empty spaces that used to house a fridge and an oven were now the home to dust bunnies and spiders. Hailey curiously opened the cupboard doors that had remained closed and unbroken. As she suspected, most of them were empty and full of more dust bunnies, dead bugs, and mouse droppings. As she pulled open the last rectangular cupboard, she was shocked to see that two cans of baked beans sat on the shelf. "Well, that's weird," she mumbled to herself. As she peered into the cabinet, she noticed that neither of the cans had any specks of dust across the tops and the wrappers still remained perfectly intact.

Just as she picked up one of the cans to examine it further, Sadie let out a single bark, startling Hailey. She dropped the can onto the counter, where it proceeded to roll off onto the floor with a strong thud.

"Jesus, Sadie, you scared me," she exhaled, turning around, expecting to see Sadie behind her, but the room remained empty.

"Sadie?" Sadie let out another bark as if she knew Hailey was unable to see her. The sound appeared to be coming from below the kitchen. Slightly perplexed, Hailey knelt down to retrieve the can of beans from the floor and was surprised to see a small hole in the flooring just beside the can.

"No way," she whispered as she crouched closer to the wood plank. She hovered her face over the dirty, splintered wood and peered through the hole. Looking back up at her with a tilted head and perked ears was Sadie.

"How did you get down there?" Hailey asked through the small hole. Sadie promptly darted out of view as Hailey stood back up, placing the can of beans on the counter. She began walking towards the other end of the house when the pitter patter of paws walking up stairs came from a small square opening in the floor just across the room in a corner beneath the busted window.

Hailey approached the opening and sure enough, there was a rickety staircase leading down to a basement. As if the abandoned house wasn't creepy enough, an abandoned basement certainly took it to the next level of spooky. She descended the stairs, taking caution with each unstable step, until she stood on loose gravel.

Hailey looked around the dim lit space. Her eyes darted from the unkempt dirt floors to the concrete walls. As she took another step she could just barely make out a rusted water pipe that protruded from one of the walls. It didn't take long for her to connect the dots and come to the terrifying realization that she was standing in the room Sarah had described from the Polaroids. As her pulse began to quicken at the thought of standing in the very room where the serial killer had been taking his victims, the screen door on the main floor let out a slow, loud squeak.

Chapter 29

Hailey froze and listened. Was it the wind, or had her trespassing just been discovered? She froze on the stairs and listened for footsteps, knowing it would be impossible to enter without making a sound. The basement walls were made of decaying concrete masonry block and a musty smell of stale air and cobwebs filled her nostrils. No sound of footsteps came. *Good, must have just been the wind.* She walked over to the wall and ran her fingers across the cool surface. The chill from the wall radiated through her body even as she pulled her hand back to her side. The further she walked away from the light of the stairs and deeper into the shadowed space, the wider her eyes grew as they tried to take in as much light as possible.

Hailey cried out as her knee hit the corner of what felt like a small table. She reached her arms out into the darkness to locate the object. It was a wood chair. After regaining her composure, she looked in front of her and could just barely make out a rectangular silhouette sitting just a few feet away from where the chair was sitting. Naturally, she assumed the shape was that of a wooden table that went along with the chair, but what she couldn't figure out was what the object was sitting on top of the table.

Hailey pulled her phone from her pocket to use the flashlight app and wondered why it hadn't occurred to her to use it sooner. She tapped on the flashlight icon and held her phone straight out before her. Her eyes readjusted to the faint light, allowing her to see that her assumption was correct; a wooden chair and table sat together in the middle of the room. The object on the table came into view as she stepped closer and realized it was a lantern. She tried the switch and to her surprise, light illuminated from the core. As the room filled with a yellow glow, Hailey felt her stomach drop as the wall before her came into view.

"Oh my God." Hailey's body went numb. Her phone fell from her hand, kicking up a small plume of dust as it crashed against the ground. The wall across from her had a dozen Polaroid pictures pinned to it with rusty nails pushed into the crumbling mortar. Her fear became confirmed as she stepped closer to the wall and the images became more clear. Each square photograph held an image of a woman, with her hands and feet bound, laying either on the floor or propped up against the wall next to the protruding rusted water pipe. Each appeared to have been beaten and had swollen eyes and bruised lips. Others lay limp and lifeless, with pale dehydrated skin. It pained her to see the fear in the eyes of each individual as they lay on the floor, wondering if they were going to make it out of there alive. Hailey looked closer at the faces and could make out that all the pictures were of Hannah, Allison, and Madison. Hailey could feel bile begin to rise in her throat as she examined the photographs. She squeezed her eyes tight as she took a deep breath. The last thing she wanted to do was leave evidence she had been in the killer's torture chamber in the form of a pile of vomit.

"You can do this," she whispered words of encouragement to herself, knowing that she needed to keep it together if she had any plans of making it out of that basement with evidence. Hailey stood motionless for a moment as she processed the wall before her. She needed to document what she was seeing and contact Sarah, but she also had to get out of there as soon as possible because now she was certain she was standing in the serial killer's holding cell, which meant he could return at any moment.

Scooping up her phone, she rubbed the screen and the camera lens off with the cuff of her shirt. She wanted to be sure she was capturing the clearest photographs possible before leaving the premises, knowing that if he found out the police were on to him, he could take everything down before they even located the dilapidated house.

Hailey pulled out her notebook and began jotting down all the details she had seen in the house since she entered, knowing the first thing the police would do is question her about her presence in the house and how she managed to stumbled upon it in the woods. She knew she needed to have as many details as possible to support her story, not only to protect herself, since she was the person who found the location, but to be sure she had all the details necessary to bring these victims justice.

Her attention redirected to the sound of tires rolling on gravel growing louder from above, igniting panic in her gut. She fumbled to get her journal back into her bag as her hands began to shake uncontrollably with fear. "Sadie, we got to go," she whispered as she flipped the lantern off and headed for the stairs. Sadie led the way up and went straight to the back door that still stood slightly ajar. When they made it to the main floor, Hailey quickly glanced out the window to see someone still sitting in a beat up truck that had rolled onto what used to be the front lawn. She ducked out of view from the window as she raced to the back door, trying to land on her toes and make the least amount of noise as possible across the rickety flooring. Once they slipped out the back door, she gently pulled the door closed behind her, hoping it wouldn't creak too loud, giving their presence away.

The sound of a car door slamming echoed through the trees. Hailey felt sweat begin to bead above her upper lip as her heartbeat quickened with every crunching step he took. She plastered herself against the back wall, with Sadie at her feet, as she silently pleaded for him to use the front door. As soon as she heard the front door screech open, she looked down at Sadie, and they took off running down the overgrown trail.

Chapter 30

Sweat was beginning to stream down Hailey's temples as gravity pulled her down the path of loose rock and uneven surfaces. The last thing Hailey needed in a time like this was a sprained ankle.

As Hailey descended the trail she came to the realization that whoever was in that truck, knew she was somewhere in the area because there was no way they would have driven up that road and not seen her van parked near the bottom with no one inside of it. Hailey looked over her shoulder and listened for any signs that a vehicle was driving down the road. Luckily, nothing but birds and a light breeze filled the air.

As her van came into view, Hailey could feel her thighs starting to burn. She was definitely going to feel the soreness in her legs for the next couple of days. Not wanting to waste any more time in the area, Hailey snapped a quick photograph with her phone of where her van was parked to document the location, time, and date that she had discovered the abandoned house. She yanked open the driver's side door and they both hopped inside, eager to flee the area. Before she was even settled into her seat, Hailey dialed Sarah.

"Come on, pick up, pick up, pick up," she pleaded before the line began to ring. When the line remained silent, Hailey looked at the screen to be sure she had selected 'Call' and was crushed to see a message stating that the cellular connection was lost.

"Of course, still no service." She turned the key in the ignition and with a lead foot headed back out towards the main road.

Hoping to find service as she drove, she kept her phone in her hand as she attempted to pull on her seatbelt. Her fingers fumbled between the two objects causing her to drop her phone straight down into the tiny crevasse between her seat and the door. "Dammit," she huffed as she tried to wiggle one hand down into the tiny gap and stay on the road with the other. Once she maneuvered her phone out of the valley, she placed it into her cup holder with the screen clicked on so she would be able to see when she was back in range of service.

Hailey debated her options in her mind as she drove. If she called the police, would they question why she was up there in the first place? Could she get in trouble for trespassing? The house looked abandoned and on public land, but was it really? There was a possibility that he owned the property and if that was the case, then she was trespassing and the police would need a warrant to search the premises. By then, he would surely have removed all the evidence from the basement, leaving them with nothing but an empty concrete room.

On the other hand, she did have all the photographs on her phone. But that raises another concern: Would they be admissible in court? After all, she shouldn't even be involved in the case. Would they think her pictures were merely photoshopped? It would be a stretch, especially considering the Polaroid photos themselves weren't made public, but he could argue that she photoshopped the whole thing. Hailey was getting dizzy from all the questions. If there was one thing she knew for sure, it was that she needed to talk to Sarah ASAP.

As Hailey sped past the spot she had boondocked at the night before, remembering she had service. She immediately scooped up her phone and dialed Sarah again. No answer. At least this time, she was able to leave a pressing message. "Sarah, it's urgent. Call me as soon as you can! I know you're still in Oregon so I'm on my way to you!"

Hailey ended the call, then promptly opened up a new text message to send to Sarah. Surely if she saw a missed call, a voice message, and a text message from Hailey, she would know something was up.

Hailey opened up Google Maps and entered: *Medical Examiner's Office in Douglas County, Oregon.* She knew she couldn't just show up at the office demanding to speak to Sarah, but she did know Sarah would most likely be staying somewhere in the area, close to the office. It was at least a good place to start.

It was a quarter past four and Hailey was exhausted. By the looks of Sadie curled up in the passenger seat, it was clear they were both worn out from their morning adventure. Hailey was almost to the main highway when she rounded the last curve of the road and had to slam on her breaks.

"Shit!" Sadie went flying forward onto the floor as Hailey felt her flimsy seatbelt instantly tighten hard across her chest.

Once the van came to a screeching halt and Hailey confirmed Sadie was okay, she looked up quizzically at the gold car that sat horizontally in the middle of the dirt road.

"Are you okay?" Hailey called out as she stepped out of her van and began walking towards the other vehicle, but there was no response. As she made her way to the driver's side door, she peered in through the open window and noticed that the car was empty.

She turned around, scanning the area and listening for any sounds of footsteps or rustling in the bushes to indicate where the driver may be, in case someone had pulled over for a bathroom break off the main road. Even if that were the case, she would hope they would have at least had the decency or intelligence to pull over to the side of the narrow dirt road. But as she stood in the middle of the road, there was nothing but silence.

Confused and still shaken up, Hailey headed back to her van in a slight jog. Just as her hand touched the door she heard footsteps emerging from the brush. Fear flooded through her limbs as she yanked her door open and jumped inside as fast as she could.

Once she pulled her door closed she saw a woman emerge from behind the thicket and onto the road. Hailey felt the fear in her stomach subside, but her confusion was still running high. Confident enough that the woman wasn't a serial killer, she unlocked her door and stepped back out onto the dirt road.

"Are you alright, ma'am?" she called out to the woman who was looking down at her phone.

"Oh!" The woman appeared startled by Hailey's presence. "My, I didn't even hear you pull up, dear."

"Are you okay?" Hailey asked as she came around the front of her van.

"Yes, I..." the woman began, looking up at Hailey. "My goodness, aren't you the young lady I chatted with at the supermarket?"

Hailey lifted her eyebrows, mirroring the woman's surprise as she came to the same realization when she saw the woman's face. "Yes. I think you're right. We chatted near the exit about the girl who had gone missing." Hailey could feel the acid bubble in her stomach as the images of the basement whirred in her mind.

"I suppose a proper introduction is due this time," the woman said with a kind smile.

"I'm Hailey," she held out her hand.

"Dorothy," the woman replied as she met Hailey's hand with a gentle squeeze.

"If you don't mind me asking, what are you doing out here?" Hailey asked.

"I got a call from my daughter and wanted to pull off the highway to take it. You know, I'm not as good at multitasking as I used to be. So I pulled off the road to talk to her, then when I was finished I thought maybe there would be a better way to turn around and get back on the highway if I went down this road. Then out of nowhere, a deer jumped out in front of me and I swerved in a panic, turning completely sideways, causing my wheel to lock. Then once I had discovered what I'd done, I grabbed my phone to call for help, but just my luck, there isn't any service here with the carrier I have. So, I thought maybe if I got out and walked around, maybe I would find a signal."

"Well, I'm so sorry to hear that happened to you. I'm sure that must have been scary," Hailey replied.

"It did give me quite the fright. I'm not as quick as I used to be, you know."

"Maybe I can help with your locked wheel," Hailey offered. "Do you mind if I take a look?" she asked as she gestured towards Dorothy's car.

"Oh, that's very kind of you, my dear. But you don't have to do that," Dorothy replied.

Hailey had no idea if she would be able to help or not, but she also knew that she wasn't going to be able to drive around the woman's car either. Also, she would feel beyond guilty if she left the older woman to fend for herself in the middle of the woods where she was now sure a serial killer was bringing his victims to just up the road.

"Really, it's no problem," Hailey said as they approached the car. "You said the wheel is locked?"

"That's right. I tried to move it, but it appears to be stuck in place."

"Let's take a look. Do you mind if I use your key?" Hailey asked.

"Oh no problem, here you go."

Dorothy handed Hailey her key as she slumped into the driver's seat. As Hailey slipped the key into the ignition, she recalled a time her mother had managed to lock the steering wheel during one of their family vacations. It was pouring rain and she had turned the wheel too hard, attempting to avoid a giant pothole full of water, causing it to lock into place. Her mother panicked and began pulling the wheel as hard as she could while her father sounded like a broken record telling her to calm down—two words that never settled well with her mother. She could hear her father's soothing voice as he told her mother to gently place the key in the ignition and turn it to the 'on' position while wiggling the wheel back and forth with varying pressure until she could feel it begin to release. Hailey smiled at the memory that was a frustrating moment at the time but turned into a family joke that they still laughed about at family dinners.

"Just a little more," Hailey jostled the wheel from side to side until she felt the lock release. "There!" she said, impressed with herself. "I think I fixed it."

"Did you? Oh, thank you, Hailey. I don't know how I'll ever repay you!"

"No worries at all. I'm happy I could help." Hailey stepped out of the car and handed Dorothy her keys.

"I guess it's a good thing I ran into you again," Dorothy responded with a smile.

"What are the odds?" Hailey replied, returning her grin.

"Aw, is that the sweet dog you were referring to in the market?" Dorothy asked looking over Hailey's shoulder towards her van.

"Oh yes! That's Sadie."

"She must be a good girl. She hasn't barked at all."

"Yeah, I think I got pretty lucky. I rescued her from a shelter," Hailey stated.

"Could I meet her? I love dogs!" Dorothy asked with a pleading gaze.

Hailey was getting annoyed, as she really wanted to get moving, but how could she say no to the sweet old woman?

"Um, sure," Hailey realized her tone was less than welcoming. "I mean, of course, she loves people," she said with a smile as she turned and walked over to the van to let Sadie out.

Sadie leaped out of the van, overjoyed with the pats and love from the stranger. As Hailey watched both Sadie and Dorothy enjoying their first meeting, she wondered if Sadie would be this friendly with everyone. Would she greet a complete stranger with the same excitement and friendliness if they were rude to Hailey? Or if someone tried to break into the van?

Hailey looked down at her watch nervously; forty-five minutes had gone by. She was already cutting it close, but she was positive she wouldn't make it to Douglas County before sundown at this point. Dorothy caught a glimpse of her gazing at her watch. "I'm sorry, I don't mean to keep you any longer."

"Oh, it's no problem. I was hoping to make it to my destination before sunset, but it's no big deal if I don't." Hailey was hoping the woman didn't see through her lie. With every moment that passed, Hailey grew more anxious and impatient.

"I need to be heading home, too. Don't want my husband to think I got lost again," she said as she rolled her eyes before turning around to walk to her car.

"Get home safe. Hopefully no more deer will get in your way," Hailey said with a smile.

"Thank you, dear, drive safe. It was a pleasure meeting you again."

"You too, Dorothy, take care."

Hailey waved as Dorothy settled back into her car and slowly reversed to turn back towards the highway. As she smiled and waved through her window, Hailey wondered what the odds really were that she would run into the same woman in the woods that she had talked to at the supermarket. Then again it was a smaller city, so maybe the odds of a coincidence such as this were greater.

As she stepped back into her van and fastened her seatbelt, Hailey's father's voice crept into her mind: *There is no such thing as a coincidence.*

Chapter 31

Hailey glanced up at the rear view mirror to see if anyone was following her, while concurrently reassuring her mother through her speakerphone, "Don't worry, Mom, I'm fine. I know where I'm going, and I still have Sadie with me. Plus, I had every intention of doing this trip on my own from the start." Hailey knew her mother wasn't going to like the fact that she was now traveling alone, but she also knew she couldn't lie to her about it either.

"So he just decided to go a different way? I thought you two had planned to travel all the way to Seattle together?" her mother pressed.

If she only knew the real reason she and Luke were no longer traveling together, she would, no doubt, want her to end her trip immediately and would send her father out to get her. Hailey had debated telling her parents the truth, but she ultimately decided that trying to explain to them that she was on a mission to find a serial killer and Luke was on the suspect list, would not only send her mother into sheer panic, but she would have to promptly end her investigation and would lose her parent's faith that she could make safe choices. And there was no chance in hell she was ready to do that after what she had just discovered.

"Yes, well, plans change," Hailey stated.

"Just be sure to continue checking in and letting us know where you are, okay?" her dad chimed in. He always knew how to subdue the tension between Hailey and her mother. "And be careful traveling at night.

You know I prefer you to travel in the daylight," he added.

"I know. I got a little thrown off schedule today, but from here on out I will do my best to travel in the daytime."

"Let us know when you get to your destination tonight, so we know you made it safely."

"I will, don't worry. I..." her voice trailed off as another call began to come through. "I got to go, Sarah is calling. I'll let you know when I'm at my destination. Love you."

"Love you too," her parents replied in unison as she ended the call with them and answered Sarah's.

"You do not know how happy I am that you called," Hailey answered, relieved.

"What's going on? I got your messages. You're driving to me?" Sarah asked with concern laced in her tone.

"Sarah, I found it. I walked inside and you should see it. It's awful. I took pictures of the scene. I thought I was going to throw up. I think I went into shock for a minute, but I knew I had to document what I saw. I knew I had to contact you," Hailey began to sputter.

"Whoa, whoa, Hailey, slow down. What are you talking about? Found what?"

"The serial killer's second location, where he's been holding his victims. I found it."

"Holy shit. Are you serious? How? Where?"

"I know you told me not to, but I went searching through the woods near Medford for any signs of, I don't know, just something, you know?"

"Uh huh."

"Well, *something* was certainly what I found. But I didn't have service at the location, so I wasn't able to call you until now." Hailey was out of breath.

"Okay, here's what we're going to do," Sarah began, "I'm going to contact my team and let them know where this place is. You marked down the location I take it?"

"Yes, of course."

"Good. You come straight to me and I'll set you up with one of the lead detectives on the case. They will document all the information that you have, but you need to remember, there is a lot of information I shared with you that they cannot know I leaked."

"Don't worry, I know. I'll make sure I have my story straight before I get there."

"Perfect." Sarah paused. "I just can't believe this. I can't believe you found it. Now we just have to hope the guy is there or that it at least tells us where he is. I won't deny that I am mad at you for going out there, but I'm glad you're safe."

"Yeah, me too, it was a close call for a minute there." Hailey paused, before adding, "someone showed up outside when I was in there."

"What do you mean someone showed up?" Sarah asked panicked.

"There was a car that pulled up in the front, that's why I rushed out of there. I don't know if it was the killer or not, all I knew is that I had to get out of there!"

"Jesus Hailey, are you serious?"

"Yeah, I debated if I should mention that to you before or after I arrived at your place."

"I'll send you the address when we hang up and you come straight to me, got it? He could be following you for all we know."

"Yes, yes. I got it." Hailey smiled and rolled her eyes. Sarah was always the mom of their friend group in college and it was clearly still a quality that she had managed to carry with her into her adult world.

"Alright, I'll go talk with the team now and send you the address. Let me know when you're close, so I can meet you up front."

"Sounds good. I'll probably make it there in a couple hours or so, I'm guessing."

"I will keep my phone by me. Drive safe. The roads here get pretty dark at night. I'll see you soon."

The call ended, and Hailey's adrenaline was kickstarted once again.

She had never really come down from the initial rush she had at the abandoned house, but talking to Sarah made the situation seem more real. She couldn't believe she was standing in the very location that he had been taking all his victims. Her body involuntarily quivered at the thought.

Her cell phone vibrated in her lap, implying that Sarah had sent over the address. Hailey flipped it over and clicked on the screen to read the message to confirm the address had come through. To her surprise, it wasn't a message from Sarah, but a message from Rachel. Intrigued, Hailey popped open the message and darted her eyes back and forth between the road and each word as she drove down the highway.

Brianna Moore has gone missing!!!! This sounds nuts, but I think she has been kidnapped.

In a matter of seconds, Hailey's adrenaline turned into shock. Her stomach dropped and her chest flooded with anxiety. She needed to pull over.

Luckily, there was a sign indicating that there was an exit just up the road. She didn't care where it went, she just knew she needed to get off the highway, recollect herself, and reread Rachel's message.

As Hailey continued down the highway, several notches above the speed limit, she took deep breaths as she approached the exit. "This can't be happening," Hailey muttered beneath her breath, in awe.

The van coasted to a halt at the stop sign that sat at the end of the exit. Knowing she couldn't just stop in the middle of the road, she turned right and continued down the little two lane road in hopes to find a spot she could pull over. Out of the corner of her eye, she began to see a vehicle inch closer in her side view mirror. She too was in a rush, but the last thing she needed was someone riding her ass adding fuel to the flame of her already burning anxiety.

Hailey pulled off to the shoulder, allowing the vehicle to pass. After it sped past her window, she looked up and down the two lane road and didn't see any other cars. It wasn't an ideal place to stop, but with the road being empty, she didn't think it would pose too much of an issue. She put her van in park.

Just as she reopened Rachel's message, another text came through from her with an article attached. Hailey opened the article and her fear was confirmed:

"Vanlife influencer Brianna Moore has been reported missing from her van parked in Ashland, Oregon earlier this morning when she was supposed to meet some friends for breakfast and never showed."

Hailey jumped out of her seat and hurdled over Sadie to the back of the van to her link map that hung above her bed. Her eyes frantically searched the maps for Ashland. When she spotted the location, she pulled her hand over her mouth. It was less than fifteen miles from Medford. When the man pulled up to the abandoned house, was it because he already had another victim in his car? Was Brianna bound in his trunk? Hailey could feel the bile begin to rise into her throat. In one swift motion, she heaved her body over the sink and held her weight beneath her arms as she grasped the edge of the cold metal. Once she regained her equilibrium, she looked up through the front windshield to see that the sun had almost completely set.

She knew she needed to get back on the road; she needed to get to Sarah. Sadie bounded into the passenger seat as if she had read Hailey's unspoken thoughts. After grabbing a cool water to help settle her angst, Hailey slid back into the driver's seat. Her head was twisting with so many thoughts she almost forgot to enter in the address that Sarah had sent. The signal was weak, but the one bar of service was at least strong enough to load her maps. She had faced so many instances along her journey where she didn't have service, so as a precautionary measure, Hailey decided to write down the directions. Also, if she received a call from Sarah or Rachel, she would want to be able to answer without the risk of losing her directions. Once she had enough information written down about where she needed to go, Hailey pulled back out onto the dark, two-lane highway.

The night was quiet as she drove down the newly paved road, but her thoughts were running rampant and loud with every passing minute. As if to appear from nowhere, a barricade emerged from the darkness. Bright orange and white stripes reflected from the sign ahead as Hailey pulled closer to the roadblock. "Seriously?" she huffed in frustration as the orange and black detour sign came into view.

Hailey glanced into her side mirrors. No lights appeared in the distance, she was completely alone on the road. The van rolled to a stop just a few feet before the giant orange sign. The longer she sat idly on the empty road, the more the unease grew in her gut. She began to question if she had taken a wrong turn somewhere further back on the side road or had missed one of her directions that she had written down. It wouldn't be the first time she had thoughts whizzing in her head while driving, causing her to miss a turn. Pushing her nerves aside, rationalizing with herself that she was overthinking the situation and knowing that she needed to get to Sarah, Hailey followed the detour sign and headed up the dark forest road.

The van rattled and shook from side to side as she slowly maneuvered the wheels over the uneven road. The darkness swallowed the van as the trees grew thicker and the moon dissolved behind the branches. The hours of driving and the intensity of the events of the day were beginning to weigh down on her. She had planned to head straight to Sarah, but at the rate the detour was going, she wasn't confident she was going to make it there anytime soon.

Riding along in the passenger seat, Sadie began to whine and moan as she peered out the window with perked ears. "Do you need to go out?" Hailey asked, patting her companion on the head. As much as she didn't want to stop in the middle of the unknown road, she knew putting comfort aside to be a good pet parent came along with traveling with a dog. There was a slight opening of trees, leaving a space just big enough for her to pull her van off the road, not that she expected anyone else to be driving up it anytime soon.

She slowly curved to a stop and turned off the van. As the hum of the engine faded, she realized how comforting the sound was when sitting in the middle of the unknown dark woods alone. Hailey switched on her lights and watched the yellow glow spill over the dirt and overflow into the trees. As she opened her door and stepped out, Sadie leapt across the center console and catapulted herself from the driver's seat, leaving a cloud of dust in her wake as she hit the dry dirt. "Jeez, Sadie, you must have really had to go. You almost knocked me over."

Hailey watched as Sadie wandered over to the bushes and sniffed the premises as she normally did when they arrived at a new location. The silence of the forest seemed quieter than normal, even colder than normal. She decided to slide open her side door to retrieve her Maglite so she could survey her surroundings and keep an eye on Sadie. Her dark colors made for great camouflage in the night of the forest.

She pointed her light out at the trees and bushes, which appeared taller and thicker—more eerie and haunting than the wooded area she had just traveled. The light fell on top of Sadie and Hailey held it steady as she watched her patrol through the brush. "Come on, Sadie, let's get going," Hailey called out, but Sadie continued on scent with her nose to the ground. "Sadie, come!" Her patience and warmth was wearing thin. Sadie lifted her head with alert ears, but she wasn't looking at Hailey. Her head was directed out into the woods.

Hailey felt a rush of adrenaline sweep through her body. Her thoughts started to race through all the possibilities of what Sadie could be looking at. A bear? An elk? A skunk? Just the rustling of wind in the distance? She took a deep breath in a failed attempt at trying to calm her nerves. Suddenly, Sadie went bolting into the darkness, barking as she weaved between the trees.

Hailey took off in a sprint after Sadie, but lost her to the darkness before she even had a chance. She stopped to catch her breath and didn't realize how far she had gotten from her van. Aside from her flashlight, she was surrounded by complete darkness. The wind blew through the trees, rattling the leaves. Squinting in the direction of her light, she thought she saw a dark figure in her periphery, but then it was gone before she could get the light on it. *Was it a branch moving in the wind or a person?* Another movement pulled her attention to her left, but that was just a little aspen tree's leaves rustling in the wind. She quickly darted the light back to where she thought there was a figure, hoping her eyes were playing tricks on her, but then, from behind a large tree, emerged a figure in all black. The figure began running towards her and her stomach dropped as her eyes widened with fear. She was no longer alone.

Chapter 32

Hailey gripped her Maglite and took off in the direction she had come from, hoping it would lead her to the van. As the fear elevated in her gut, she struggled to keep the light steady in front of her as she ran. Underbrush crunched beneath her feet as she frantically pushed her way through the maze of branches. A protruding root from a tree snagged her foot, plunging her body hard against the forest floor. The flashlight went soaring out of her hand and landed several feet in front of her, out of reach. She could hear swift footsteps gaining on her through the trees and knew she had no time to waste.

As she stretched her arm out to grab a hold of the light, a heavy force came down on top of her legs. Hailey turned onto her back and tried to squirm free from the weight as she frantically kicked her feet to try to break free. A sharp pain shot through her leg as a blade sliced through the edge of her thigh. Hailey let out a whimper as his weight shifted from her legs to her hips, straddling her. Before she had time to let out another plea for help, hands clasped around her neck. Hailey gasped for air as his fingers compressed against her trachea. She desperately tried to pry his hands off her and pleaded, "Please, stop."

"You did this to yourself," the voice said, as his hands gripped tighter. She released her hands from his and searched the ground, finding a stone and, with all the strength she could muster, clocked him across the jaw with it. The attacker let out a wail of pain and fell to his side hard against the ground, clutching his jaw.

Hailey inhaled a large gasp of air as she clawed the dirt towards the flashlight that still remained lit lying on the ground. As she clasped her hands around the cold metal, she scrambled to her feet, despite the stinging pain and warm blood that was dripping down her thigh and took off running again.

As she raced through the trees, Hailey realized that her rapid panting and the glow from her light only made her an easier target. If she was going to escape alive, she needed to come up with a plan.

Hailey came to a stop, switched off her flashlight, and consciously slowed her breathing. She had to be silent. If he wanted to play this game in the dark, then she wasn't going to make it easy for him. Her sense of hearing was on high alert as her eyes readjusted to the darkness. The only sound she heard was the wisp from the treetops blowing in the wind. The veins in her neck were thumping rapidly as her heart was racing with fear. Her thoughts were darting back and forth as she tried to decipher what her next move would be.

She should have listened to Luke when he said she needed a weapon—a way to protect herself other than relying on a dog that could easily run away at any moment. She thought he was just being bitter in the heat of their argument, but now, here she was, in the middle of the dark woods with a Maglite as her only weapon and no idea where her dog had run off to.

"I know you're out there, Hailey," a deep even voice crooned in the distance. "You can run, but I know these woods like the back of my hand."

The hairs stood up on the nape of her neck at the sound of her name being hissed from the darkness of the woods. It was hard to determine where the voice was originating from. Twenty, maybe thirty feet away? She couldn't be sure.

"You're not going to get away with this," she called back, trying to hide the shaking in her voice. "People know where I am, they will come looking for me."

"That's funny, that's what the other girls said too." A deep chuckle echoed through the trees. "And look how that turned out for them."

She could hear his footsteps creeping closer and she clutched the flashlight tighter in her hand. Slowly, she bent down and rifled around in the dirt until her hands found a stick. With one swift motion, she hurled it as far as she could and heard it snap against a tree in the distance. The footsteps stopped. She heard the twist of his feet pivoting across the dead pine needles as he headed towards the sound. Her ploy worked, but she didn't have long. As fast as her legs could carry her, she began sprinting through the brush back towards her van. Her keys had fallen out of her pocket when she plunged to the ground, but if she could at least make it back into the van and lock herself inside long enough to call for help, she might have a fighting chance.

Her legs were beginning to turn to jelly and her throat started to burn with every deep, dry breath she heaved in, but she knew she couldn't stop. The van came into view and it was just the sight she needed to see to give her a glimmer of hope that she was going to make it out alive.

After she broke through the canopy of trees, the moonlight lit her path, casting her frantic shadow before her. She was just feet away from the van when she realized her shadow wasn't alone. Gripping the flashlight tightly, she whipped her arm around and swung at the faceless figure.

"Jesus!" The man quickly ducked, but wasn't fast enough as the edge of the metal rim clipped his brow. "Hailey! Hailey! It's me!"

She held the flashlight in both hands ready to strike again before she realized it was Luke standing before her.

"Luke? What they hell are you doing out here?" Her hands were trembling as she loosened her grip on the flashlight.

"I was coming to find you." He brought his finger tips to his brow, touching the tender spot, confirming he was bleeding. "I didn't know I was going to be attacked for doing so," he said bluntly.

"We have to get out of here," she said, ignoring the fact that she just hit him over the head. "He's coming for me!"

"Who? What's going on?" he said, regaining his composure.

"I'll explain in the van, but we have to go now."

Without another word, he followed her in a rush towards her van. Her side door was still open. "Come on, hurry," she said, waving him in. Luke was only a couple feet behind her when a loud gunshot rang out in their ears and a sudden burst of fiery pain ignited in his leg, collapsing him to the ground.

"Luke!" Hailey's voice cracked with panic as she jumped out of the van and squatted by his side. They glanced down to see a circular crimson stain slowly growing in diameter across his jeans.

"Shit." Hailey pulled her flannel off her arms and tied it as tightly as she could above his knee to make a tourniquet. All those days her dad had spent teaching her and her brother how to create bandages out of everyday materials had finally paid off. "Do you think you can get up?"

"I think so." She could hear the pain in his voice as she put his arm over her shoulders as they attempted to get him back into the standing position using his good leg.

Just as they started limping back towards the van, a voice came from behind them. "I see you've brought a little friend with you." Luke and Hailey turned around to see a man stepping out from the darkness of the trees before them. The moon reflected off the pistol as he gripped it tightly in his hand and they were finally able to see who the attacker was.

"Peter?" Hailey exhaled in shock as his features came into view.

"Killing two people wasn't exactly in my plans tonight, but I suppose plans change," Peter said as he slowly inched closer.

"Why are you doing this?" Hailey pleaded, bringing his steps to a stop.

"You were getting too close. With all your questions and digging around in places you shouldn't be. I thought maybe I could still slip under the radar, but then I saw your van at the end of the road. I knew you were going to expose me, turn me in, and that just isn't something I can let you do."

"But why did you kill all those girls? They never did anything!"

"All those girls," he began, "they are toxic. Each and every one of them. They are nothing but self-centered whores who don't care about anyone except for themselves and their Instagram pages. They don't care who they hurt or who they have to step on to get to the top."

"Wait, you said they *are* toxic." Hailey took in a deep breath before she continued. "Does that mean you kidnapped another girl? Are you holding someone in that basement right now?"

"See, there you go again, asking questions and shoving your nose into other people's business." He shook his head as if he was disappointed in her.

Hailey and Luke readjusted their stance, and Hailey could tell by his groan that he wasn't going to last much longer in a standing position.

"Is it your business to ruin these girl's lives?" Hailey retorted and Luke shot her a look, but she kept her eyes on Peter. In the silvery glow of the moonlight, she could see a slimy grin pull at his lips.

"That star, Brianna Moore. It was almost too easy, really," he snickered. "She posts where she is and when she's there. Her whole life is on Instagram. You know, I think she wanted me to find her. And that's why I'm letting her suffer now."

Suffer now? That meant she was still alive. For how long, Hailey had no idea, but at least she knew there was still hope for her to be rescued.

"She's a pretty big influencer," Hailey acknowledged, in hopes that a stroke to his ego would work in her favor. "You found all of your victims on social media, didn't you?"

"It's a stalker's paradise, you know. All these young girls traveling alone in the woods and secluded places. All I had to do was search the hashtag for vanlife and there they were. The page was filled with dozens and dozens of social media whores."

"So what? You're saying that you killed each of these girls because they were beautiful, narcissistic influencers?" Hailey questioned.

"That's right!" he blurted out before Hailey even finished. "I'm doing the world a favor by eliminating these self-centered brats from the internet. No matter what you do, no matter what you say, they don't hear you over their followers. They would rather listen to a complete stranger than someone who really knows them, someone who cares for them." Hailey could tell she was getting into the heart of his anger, but she was confused about what exactly he was talking about, so she continued to listen to his rant. "I gave her everything. But it wasn't enough. Oh no, it wasn't enough. She needed their approval, she wanted that fake love from complete strangers. She would dress up for them, direct message them, tell them she loved them." He started pacing back and forth. "I wasn't enough for her anymore. My words of reassurance just passed right through her. She wanted to be an influencer like all those skanky rich girls."

Hailey was beginning to put the pieces of the puzzle together. "Them being the influencers?" Hailey asked calmly, confirming she was on the right track.

"Yes. All of them." He threw his hands in the air with anger. "She started getting random followers and she was eating up the attention, but they didn't even know her. Not like I did. They didn't love her like I did. But she couldn't see that. She wasn't living in reality anymore. She let social media run her life."

"Who is she?" Hailey asked steadily.

"Sophie, of course. My stepsister!" he said, as if they should know who he was referring to. "I gave her everything. I cared for her. She was beautiful, so beautiful, but she would spend countless hours everyday looking at Instagram, comparing herself to all the other girls. All the girls who had money. Influencers. Her mind became permeated with false expectations of how she should look, how she should be living her '#bestlife.' " He raised his hands and made air quotes when he said the hashtag. Hailey could hear the tremble on his lips as he started to get emotional, and for a moment, she almost felt sorry for him. Then she remembered the three women he murdered, and the empathy quickly faded.

"And you know what the worst part was?" he asked as he looked at Hailey.

She shook her head in response to him, then glanced at Luke, noticing almost his whole pant leg was now stained with blood.

"She became so depressed. So depressed that she would never live up to being like them, never be as loved or as popular as them no matter what she did, that the despair began to eat away at her. She ended up so deep in depression that one day she made the choice to take her own life." He spat out the word 'life' with so much fury that Hailey could see droplets of saliva spring from his mouth.

Hailey exhaled, genuinely sorry about the news that his stepsister had committed suicide. She searched her mind for the right words to say, but all she could come up with was, "I'm sorry. That's truly tragic to hear."

He looked at her and they stood in silence for a moment as she concocted her next statement. "That must have hurt you pretty bad." She paused. "And I'm sure that made you pretty angry."

"Hell yeah it did! They took her from me. She was my little sister. I loved her and it was my job to protect her, to keep her safe!"

"And you felt like you let her down by not protecting her from the impact of influencers?" Hailey asked.

"I was so naive. I hadn't realized how much she was being torn down by social media. I didn't know how to protect her from the images she would see on there. The images of lies. Of false fame that these influencers have created. It's not realistic, but she couldn't see that. She was too young to understand."

"And you think that by killing or eliminating all these influencers, you are going to be able to save other young women from falling victim to these false idealistic ways of life?" Hailey inferred.

"Exactly. And I am not going to let you get in my way." He slowly directed the pistol at her forehead. Hailey could see tears glistening down his cheeks in the faint light. She tried to remain visibly calm even though fear was screaming inside her core.

"I'm sorry," Hailey tried, "I know what it feels like to lose someone close to you." She consoled him, trying to relate to him and delay his plan.

She could see his body flinch as he considered her words. "I lost my brother when I was younger and the pain of losing him is still with me everyday." He lowered the gun ever so slightly and Hailey thought that maybe she was beginning to reach him.

"No," he said, readjusting his grip on the weapon while swinging left and aiming it right at Luke then back to Hailey, as if he was having an internal battle deciding who should be taken down first. "I am not going to let you make me feel sorry for you. I can't let you turn me in. I can't let them return Brianna to her narcissistic ways and ruin young girls' lives." A menacing look crossed his face. "I couldn't wait to hear her scream. She's the biggest influencer yet, and they will have to listen to me once they find her body. They will have to put an end to all the *influencers.*" Hailey cringed at the joy he displayed for his unspeakable actions.

"Put an end to the influencers?" she asked, genuinely wondering how he planned to take out all of the influencers on Instagram, considering there were thousands.

"That's right. Just think about it. They will have to put an end to social media. They will see that influencers destroy lives."

"But why vanlife influencers? I mean, there are tons of other categories for influencers on social media, but you selected all girls who were traveling in vans."

"Because they are easy targets. They live alone in a vehicle in the middle of the woods. They travel to places where no one is around for miles. I mean, look at you. All I had to do was put up a simple barricade and you drove straight into my trap." His lips curled as he aimed the gun towards Luke. "Except then your little boyfriend showed up. That was a new twist that the other girls didn't have." His eyes were dark. "You know, at first, I thought maybe you were different. But it didn't take me long to find you on social media too, 'haileyroaming.' " Hailey cringed at the sound of her screen name coming from his mouth. "By the looks of your posts, you're trying to be just like those girls. The only difference is, I met each one of them before I kidnapped them. Can you believe it? I met every single one of those girls and they couldn't even remember my name when they saw me again."

Hailey dissected the sentence for a moment. "You met before?" This could be a key detail.

He continued as if Hailey hadn't spoken. "I gave them the benefit of the doubt. I gave them the chance to prove they weren't just in it for the followers, that they were in this vanlife for the right reason. But each one of them turned out to be worse than the last." He waved the pistol aimlessly in his hand as he spoke.

"Where did you meet them?" Hailey asked, keeping her eyes on his gun.

"It was too easy," he scoffed. "They walked right into the store, and all of them made their way right to my deli counter. I made a little chit-chat with them. Asked them where they were headed. Made suggestions of where to get an amazing 'selfie,' " he snickered, making air quotes again, "and I simply took my truck out, set up the roadblock, and that little detour would lead them straight to me. And guess what? Just like you, they didn't even hesitate. They just followed the detour sign, straight into my trap."

Hailey felt foolish. How could she have been so naive to fall into his trap? But also, how did he know that she was hot on his trail? He seemed to be giving everything away, so she simply asked, "How did you know it was me who found the abandoned house and the basement?"

"You actually found the place?" Luke chimed in with a combination of shock and agony laced in his words.

"Hey! You shut up!" Peter barked. "I'm done with the discussion here. It doesn't matter how I knew. All that matters is which one of you

I'm going to kill first."

Luke inched his hand over to Hailey's and intertwined his fingers with hers. She squeezed his hand in response and prayed it wouldn't be the last time she would feel his touch.

Peter held up the gun, directing it straight at Hailey. As he slowly put his finger on the trigger, they could hear the click of the hammer before he whispered, "It's a shame, my mother said you were so kind." A menacing smile crossed his lips as a gunshot echoed into the forest.

Chapter 33

Luke and Hailey instinctively covered their heads with their arms and dropped their bodies to the ground in an attempt to dive out of the way of the bullet. As soon as they each realized they hadn't been hit, at least not again in Luke's case, they looked up to see Sadie had her jaw locked around Peter's arm. He let out a wail of pain as her teeth sunk into the flesh of his arm. Her pounce was so forceful and caught him off guard and had managed to knock him to the ground, digging her teeth in even harder.

"Sadie!" Hailey called out, just as surprised as she was grateful to see her bound out from the abyss of the bushes. As Hailey regained her focus and balance, she noticed that Luke had already managed to get himself to his feet and was limping towards Peter and Sadie.

It took Hailey a moment to process that when Sadie had startled Peter and bit into his arm, tearing him to the ground, the gun had flung out from his grip and plummeted somewhere unknown into the brush.

As Hailey got to her feet, she watched as Peter, in one swift motion, shoved Sadie off of him and jabbed his foot firmly into her side, releasing his arm from her grip and causing her to send a blood curdling yelp into the night. Hailey gasped at the noise and began to rush towards Sadie.

Hailey winced with each staggered step she took with her injured leg. As Hailey raced towards Sadie, who lay whimpering in the dirt, Luke lunged towards the bushes where the gun had fallen. Just as Luke's fingertips touched the barrel, Peter regained his strength and took hold of Luke's leg, pulling him down against the hard earth just before he could get a grip on the weapon.

Luke and Peter began rolling across the dirt in a battle of dominance. Hailey made it to Sadie's side and could see the uneven, jagged indentation beneath her fur coat indicating she had broken ribs from Peter's stern kick. Hailey caressed Sadie's head in a nonverbal attempt to tell her that everything was going to be okay.

"Hailey!" Luke called out as Peter was gaining an advantage in the wrestling match. "Get the gun!"

Hailey immediately scrambled to the brush and began to frantically search the ground for the gun. Like searching for a black cat in a coal cellar, it camouflaged into the darkness of the landscape. She blindly shuffled her hands across the dirt with eyes wide, trying to decipher which dark objects were rocks and which could be the pistol. Finally, Hailey felt something in a bush that definitely felt man made. She gripped her hands around the object, unsure what she was about to unveil from the shrubbery.

"I got, I got..." Hailey began to vocalize her exhilaration until she connected the dots— it was a large pocket knife she held in her hand. Maybe when the brawl broke out, or when Peter was running after Hailey in the woods, the knife fell from his pocket and landed in the bushes.

"Shoot it!" Luke shouted from within the scuffle.

"I...I can't," Hailey stammered. "I didn't find the gun. I found a knife."

Just as Luke turned his head in confusion at her response, Peter was given just the edge he needed to swing back his arm and knock his fist under Luke's chin, sending him plummeting to the ground.

"Luke!" Hailey screamed out as his head made contact with the dirt.

Peter wiped the blood from his nose with the back of his wrist as he peeled himself off of Luke's body. A wicked smile curled at his lips as his eyes, which appeared like pools of black tar, stared straight at Hailey.

Hailey was wishing she had pulled the gun from the bushes, but she at least felt like she had a slight edge over Peter with the blade that was now open in her hand.

"Well, look who wants to do some stabbing now?" Peter mocked.

"Is this the blade you used on those women?" Hailey asked, ignoring his mockery.

Peter merely tightened his merciless smile. "Actually, this is the knife I used." He reached down to his lower calf to pull up his pant leg and pulled a knife from an ankle sheath.

"You don't have to do this," Hailey begged. "I understand why you're angry. I would be, too. But you don't have to do this, Peter, I can help you. I can help them see why you did what you did."

"There's no going back now!"

Peter lurched towards Hailey and she braced for impact, but as she did, a shot rang out. Peter fell to the ground and Hailey fell into disbelief when she saw Luke propped up on his elbow with the pistol in his hand, still aimed at the place Peter had been standing.

"Are you okay?" Luke asked.

"I think so," Hailey exhaled as she began to process what had just happened.

She ran to Luke's side as he put the gun down and brought his hand to his side, letting out a long groan. His face was pale and beads of sweat clustered at his hairline. Hailey knew he needed help, and fast. He had lost a lot of blood, and she could only imagine how much time he would have left given the circumstances.

"We're going to get you help, okay?" she said as she laid her hand on his chest.

Luke closed his eyes as he was finally able to give into the burning pain that was still throbbing in his leg and now in his head. As Hailey began to search for her phone, the sounds of cars driving violently over the dirt road began to rumble through the trees. Hailey looked up to see the flash of red and blue lights bouncing off of the trees and the echo of police sirens ricocheting through the forest.

"How did they..." she began.

"Looks like they got my call," Luke mumbled, his voice a hoarse whisper.

Chapter 34

Hailey sat on the edge of the small hospital bed looking out the window when a familiar voice filled the room.

"Oh my God, Hailey," Sarah rushed across the room and threw her arms around Hailey's shoulders. "I am so glad that you are okay. I was worried sick."

Hailey returned the embrace and felt a blend of comfort and guilt flood through her body. She was thankful to see a familiar face, but had no doubt that Sarah was angry at Hailey's choice to chase down the serial killer alone, albeit Peter had lured Hailey into the isolated spot in the woods.

"I'm fine, don't worry," Hailey reassured her with a remorseful half-smile.

"If you were fine, then we wouldn't be here, now would we?" she replied. They each stared at each other in silence for a moment as Hailey assessed the bandage wrapped around her thigh.

"How's Luke? Do you know where he is?" Hailey asked, as she leapt off the bed with a cringe as her feet hit the floor. "They won't let me see him and haven't told me anything about him since I got here!"

"Take it easy, you don't want your stitches to pop open. Come, sit back down." Sarah patted the sheets with her hand as she sat on the edge of the bed where Hailey had sprung from. "I spoke with the nurse before I came in here. He's still in the ICU. They took him straight into surgery when you all arrived at the hospital. He lost a lot of blood, but he's recovering. They don't want you two together until the police have taken a statement from each of you about what happened out in those woods."

"And Peter? Is he dead?"

"No." Sarah shook her head. "He also went into surgery. I haven't gotten any word yet about his condition though. Seems like Luke has a decent shot." Sarah lifted her eyebrows, impressed. "He got him right in the lower right side of his back, just missed his spinal cord."

"Good, because I still have a lot of questions for him," Hailey commented sternly.

"Hailey, you know you can't talk to him. He is going to be in police custody as soon as he wakes up."

"But he did it, Sarah! He admitted everything to me!" Hailey suddenly realized she had started to raise her voice and took a deep breath to subside her rising anxiety. Sarah walked over and put her hand on Hailey's shoulder.

"We know." She looked into Hailey's eyes. "We found a blue apron in the back of his pickup that matched the blue fibers found on each of the bodies."

Hailey nodded, taking in the information as Sarah continued, "Detectives also found Brianna Moore bound and gagged in the abandoned house."

"What? Was she alive?" Hailey asked with wide eyes.

"Thanks to you and Luke, yes, she is. Certainly traumatized and a little battered, but she'll be alright."

"Maybe physically."

"The department will get her set up with a psychologist and trauma expert. It makes sense now why each murder seemed sort of all over the place."

Hailey looked at Sarah perplexed. "What do you mean?"

"Peter wasn't some skilled serial killer. I mean, skilled enough that he unfortunately managed to kidnap as many victims as he did before being caught, but his murders were disorganized and messy. His immaturity showed in the way he disposed of the bodies, too."

Hailey nodded. Her eyes trailed to the window again and she blankly stared out into the sky. "But how did he know I was on to him?" she asked more to herself than to Sarah, her voice a mere whisper.

"We found a pen in his basement with your name on it," Sarah replied softly.

"In the basement?" Hailey's eyes began darting back and forth as she searched her mind for the answer of why her pen would have been there.

"You must have accidentally left it there when you found the place?" Sarah offered.

"I was writing in my notebook. I was taking notes on everything that I was seeing, everything from the moment I walked into that awful place to when he returned to the house out of nowhere. I was startled and scared, and I must have dropped it and didn't even notice." Tears began to pool in the bottom of her eyes. "I couldn't figure out how he knew to target me, how he knew I was there, and how he found me."

"But thanks to you and your notebook, detectives were able to find the house faster and get help to Brianna sooner than they would have," Sarah consoled her.

Hailey shook her head as she recalled the events. "Sadie!"

"Don't worry. I took Sadie to the vet when I arrived on the scene. I was able to verify that it was your dog and take her. She's got some broken ribs and a sprained leg, but she's recovering at my hotel room here."

Hailey let out a sigh and met Sarah's eyes. "Thank you, Sarah, that dog saved our lives."

"Good thing I convinced you to get one," Sarah teased. Hailey returned her smile and nodded in agreement. Sarah added, "And it's also a good thing you posted that picture of her in front of your van with your location tagged."

"Why?" Hailey was confused.

"Because apparently your boyfriend likes to keep close tabs on you and decided to pop in for a visit at just the right time." Hailey hadn't even had time to think about how Luke had pieced together where she was when Peter attacked.

"He's not my boyfriend," Hailey replied with a grin pulling at her lips. "But I guess I'm lucky that he turned out to be my biggest stalker."

They let out a laugh and then there was a pensive pause. "You know," Sarah started, "it appears that Peter was getting help from someone else, too. We found another set of fingerprints at the house that didn't match any of the victims or yours or Peters. Did he mention anything about someone else? Or did you see anyone else with him?"

Hailey thought about it for a moment as she recalled the day he pulled up to the house. She didn't remember anyone else being in the passenger seat or getting out of the vehicle with him, but she was in such a rush to get out of there, it was hard to say. She could have easily missed someone else sitting in the shadow of the vehicle. Then again, no one else arrived with him in the woods. But that also raised another question. If she left the house first and got a head start, how did he beat her to the road with enough time to put up a roadblock?

"He put up a roadblock," Hailey said with a furrowed brow. "But I don't understand how he beat me to that road, or how he even knew I had taken it."

"Yeah, we saw that. The police confirmed that there was no plan for road work on that road. Then they found some other signs and cones in his vehicle confirming he had been the one to put up the block," Sarah replied.

Sarah's phone began to ring. "I got to take this, will you be okay?" Hailey nodded and Sarah reassured her that she would be right back. Hailey watched as she walked out of the room and over to the corner of the waiting room to take her call. With Sarah being occupied, Hailey decided it was the perfect opportunity to get up from her bed to inquire about Luke. She slipped on some hospital slippers that had been placed beside her bed and made her way to the nurses station.

"Excuse me," Hailey said timidly as she stood before the desk in a hospital gown.

"Yes? Did you need something, hun?" The woman asked with soft eyes and a gentle tone.

"I have a friend in the ICU and I wanted to see how he was doing."

"What's your friend's name?"

"Luke Mancini," Hailey replied in a hushed tone, as if she was doing something secretive.

"Let me take a look here." The woman clicked some buttons on her computer while Hailey waited nervously. "Ah, here he is, Luke Mancini. Looks like he is in a stable condition and is just about to be transferred to the recovery ward."

Hailey exhaled deeply, realizing that she had been holding her breath in anticipation as she waited. "I'm so relieved to hear that." Hailey thanked the nurse and turned around to head back to her room when she saw a woman come through the sliding doors at the other end of the hallway.

Hailey stopped dead in her tracks as she watched her look frantically around the space. She spotted the nurses station and began to stride in Hailey's direction. Hailey quickly darted back down the hallway towards her room but stopped before turning in and stood behind a cart, hoping the woman wouldn't see her. As she approached the desk, her face came into view and Hailey's fear was confirmed. It was Dorothy.

The woman spoke with the nurse, but Hailey couldn't make out what was said. Whatever the exchange was, Dorothy didn't like the answer and brought her hand to her mouth as another nurse walked over to escort her down the hall to another ward, Hailey assumed. Once she was out of view, Hailey began to head back to her room, where Sarah was waiting for her.

"There you are. I was wondering where you went," she said with a worried look on her face.

"I needed some water," she lied.

"Looks like Peter's mother just showed up." Sarah shook her head. "Can you imagine finding out that your son is a serial killer? Just awful."

A rush of adrenaline shot through her as she realized that Peter really hadn't been acting solely alone. Hailey began to replay all the conversations she had with Dorothy in her head. She remembered the first time she had spoken to her at the market that she had spoken of her son and mentioned that he seemed to be having no luck with landing a woman.

"What is it?" Sarah asked, as she could tell Hailey was deep in thought.

"I'm not positive, but I think that Peter's mom might have been the one who helped him." Sarah shot her a look of disbelief and Hailey continued, "Now, hear me out. I first met Dorothy when I was at the supermarket in Medford. She saw me looking at the missing poster sign for Madison and mentioned that she remembered her coming into the store and talking to her son at the deli counter. Then I ran into her again on my way out of the forest road near the abandoned house. She was stalled in the middle of the road, blocking me from leaving. It was weird, but I didn't think too much of it in connection with killings."

"That definitely sounds like more than just an accidental happening to me," Sarah agreed. "I'll make some calls and see what I can find out."

Hailey stood in shock as she thought about the possibility that Dorothy had known about the murders. That she had known her son was kidnapping and murdering women. Hailey shivered at the thought. She never imagined that either time she spoke with Dorothy that she could even remotely be involved. The thought made her feel sick to her stomach. The thought of a mother protecting her child Hailey could understand, but in the case of murder? She just couldn't wrap her head around it.

"Oh, I should probably warn you," Sarah began hesitantly as she stood in the doorway. "I called your parents on the way to the hospital. You seemed pretty out of it. I think you were in shock."

"You called my parents? They are going to freak out! I mean, I'm sure they are already freaking out. There is no way they are going to let me keep traveling now." Hailey walked back over and sat on the bed as she began formulating what she was going to say to them.

"You don't know that," Sarah replied. "But maybe it would be a good idea to take a little break from the road after all this."

"I didn't even make it to Seattle! I can't just stop now. I still want this. I still want to be on the road."

"Well, they should be here in a couple of hours, so you have time to concoct your position and convince them you're not on a mission to get yourself killed," Sarah said as a smile played at her lips.

As she leaned back onto her pillows, Hailey tried to assemble her thoughts. No matter what her parents say, if there was one thing that she knew for sure, it was that she would make one hell of an investigative reporter, now more than ever.

Hailey reached over and grabbed her phone off the table beside her bed. When the screen illuminated she saw ten missed calls and 7 voice-mails from numbers she didn't recognize. She brought the phone to her ear and began listening to her messages.

"Hi Hailey, this is Joanna from the Los Angeles Times. I wanted to connect with you about your recent encounter with Peter Kingston and your involvement with the 'hashtag' vanlife murders."

Epilogue

It had been two months since Hailey's story had been published and picked up by several major broadcasting corporations. Not only that, but she had managed to land herself a job as a traveling investigative reporter with a company based in Chicago. Both Hailey and her parents were thrilled. Butterflies still fluttered in her stomach each time she saw her name typed neatly beneath the title of the story that could be viewed in magazines, papers, and online. Hailey had pieced together all the information, with help and permission from Sarah's team, and put together a whole story on Peter and Dorothy Kingston—how the mother and son duo had managed to kidnap four women and commit three murders in the span of just a few months, causing panic and fear in the vanlife community.

"You did it," Luke said as he walked over to Hailey, handing her a glass of lemonade.

"I don't think I've gotten used to it yet," Hailey replied modestly.

"Well, you better, because you're officially a published investigative reporter and you're going to be seeing your name a lot more often," he countered with a cheeky grin.

Hailey sat back into her chair and watched as the white-capped waves rolled smoothly up and down, revealing a new spot of drenched sand each time they receded. The rhythmic sound was soothing and made for the perfect background noise as Hailey reread the details of her own words written in the *Los Angeles Times*.

After Peter and his mother Dorothy were convicted, Peter was sentenced with first degree kidnapping, first degree murder, and life in prison without parole. His mother was convicted as an accessory after the fact for trying to help her son get away with murder and would remain in jail for twelve months. Hailey thought that was letting her off easy, considering she could have been Peter's next victim—aided directly by Dorothy.

Despite everything that had happened, Hailey felt sorry for Dorothy. After learning that Peter had been triggered to start killing due to his stepsister committing suicide, she could only imagine how heartbroken his mother must have been and would have done anything to protect the child she still had left, even if that meant helping to cover up murder.

Hailey had managed to stay in touch with Brianna after the investigation was over, not only to interview her for the story, but she still felt some guilt that she was the reason Brianna was kidnapped. During his interview with detectives, Peter revealed that when Brianna created a post warning all the women in the vanlife community about his presence, that's when he decided she would be his next victim. Since Hailey was the one who asked Brianna to make that post, she couldn't help but feel like she was to blame for putting her in such a vulnerable position, no matter how many times Brianna told her it wasn't her fault.

As she wrote her story, she connected that Peter had decided to dump each body in the location he did because it was where each of them had taken a photograph of themselves, the very photograph he saw while perusing through Instagram in search of his next victim. He wanted to take them back to the same spot that they had posted their highest 'liked' image on their account to emphasize the very reason as to why he hated them.

It took some convincing, but after her parents stayed with her for two weeks in California at Sarah's place, they eventually agreed to let Hailey continue traveling in her van.

Luke was able to walk and was mostly healed after a couple weeks of bedrest and a month of physical therapy to get the strength back in the leg where the bullet had been lodged. After the incident, Hailey was sure that Luke was going to run as far away from Hailey as he could; after all, she was the reason he took a bullet in the leg, and she had also accused him of potentially being the serial killer, but fortunately he didn't hold it against her. Now, it was nothing but a lifelong bond that they discussed over cocktails on the beach on the Oregon Coast as they made their way towards Seattle.